"One of the year's better vampire novels, what with realistic characters, including ghosts and vampires who have plausible problems; an intriguing, if standard, plot; historical literacy; and a style of writing that encourages turning pages. Both fantasy and romance fans should enjoy Hendee's commendable effort." —*Booklist*

"Filled with action, a bit of politics, and plenty of character-building interactions, this is a strong addition to the series.... Those looking for an alternative to Patricia Briggs or Ilona Andrews won't be disappointed with Hendee's newest series." —*Monsters and Critics*

"An enjoyable and creative (not just of new vampires) cocktail cleverly blending urban fantasy mixed with strong horror elements ... a thriller of a vampire tale." —*Midwest Book Review*

"Barb Hendee ... knows her vampires." —*BSCreview*

Blood Memories

"A satisfying story line coupled with engaging characters, fast action, and a hint of things to come, make this a winner." —*Monsters and Critics*

"A good vampire story for the Halloween holiday, the story is fast-paced and intriguing." —*News and Sentinel* (Parkersburg, WV)

"Well written ... a fascinating tale with wonderful characters and delicious villains who solicit the readers into loathing them. The story line is character-driven, although there is plenty of action throughout.... The vampire subgenre will enjoy this work as an exhilarating tale of death visiting the undead." —*SFRevu*

By Barb Hendee

The Vampire Memories Series
Blood Memories
Hunting Memories
Memories of Envy
In Memories We Fear
Ghosts of Memories

By Barb and J. C. Hendee

The Noble Dead Saga—Series One
Dhampir
Thief of Lives
Sister of the Dead
Traitor to the Blood
Rebel Fay
Child of a Dead God

The Noble Dead Saga—Series Two
In Shade and Shadow
Through Stone and Sea
Of Truth and Beasts

The Noble Dead Saga—Series Three
Between Their Worlds

GHOSTS OF MEMORIES

A VAMPIRE MEMORIES NOVEL

BARB HENDEE

A ROC BOOK

ROC
Published by New American Library, a division of
Penguin Group (USA) Inc., 375 Hudson Street,
New York, New York 10014, USA
Penguin Group (Canada), 90 Eglinton Avenue East, Suite 700, Toronto,
Ontario M4P 2Y3, Canada (a division of Pearson Penguin Canada Inc.)
Penguin Books Ltd., 80 Strand, London WC2R 0RL, England
Penguin Ireland, 25 St. Stephen's Green, Dublin 2,
Ireland (a division of Penguin Books Ltd.)
Penguin Group (Australia), 250 Camberwell Road, Camberwell, Victoria 3124,
Australia (a division of Pearson Australia Group Pty. Ltd.)
Penguin Books India Pvt. Ltd., 11 Community Centre, Panchsheel Park,
New Delhi - 110 017, India
Penguin Group (NZ), 67 Apollo Drive, Rosedale, Auckland 0632,
New Zealand (a division of Pearson New Zealand Ltd.)
Penguin Books (South Africa) (Pty.) Ltd., 24 Sturdee Avenue,
Rosebank, Johannesburg 2196, South Africa

Penguin Books Ltd., Registered Offices:
80 Strand, London WC2R 0RL, England

First published by Roc, an imprint of New American Library,
a division of Penguin Group (USA) Inc.

First Printing, October 2012
10 9 8 7 6 5 4 3 2 1

chapter one

Y ou can't be serious," Wade Sheffield said.

He stood inside a dark churchyard with two other men, Maxim Carey and Philip Branté—both vampires—but he could not believe what they were suggesting.

"Am serious," Maxim answered in his typical broken speech. "Boo should stay."

"Boo?" Wade asked, his mouth hanging half open.

"His name. Mr. Boo."

Sitting directly in front of them was the largest pit bull Wade had ever seen. The dog was coal black with a smattering of gray on his muzzle. His face was covered in scars, and his left ear was nothing but tattered strips. He looked like an aging refugee from a war zone. Tilting his massive head, he peered up at Wade as if he were following the conversation . . . aware his fate was being discussed.

"I like him," Philip said in a thick French accent. "I think he should stay."

"You would!" Wade shot back. "What about Tiny Tuesday? He'll eat her."

This wasn't simply a matter of them adopting another pet. Pit bulls were known to be dangerous, and Maxim had already taken in a cat named Tiny Tuesday. Wade wasn't about to let some enormous stray dog anywhere near her.

But at Wade's outburst, Maxim blinked in surprise, and he began shifting his weight between his feet in agitation. "I already tell him he can stay. Won't hurt Tuesday. He tell me he won't."

Wade fell silent, uncertain how to respond. He was mortal, and his two companions were not. The three of them lived inside the old church behind them, along with two other vampires and a ghost. But Maxim was . . . special. Though most vampires were telepathic, Maxim had spent nearly two hundred years living alone in a forest, and his telepathy functioned only between himself and animals. Wade had no idea how this worked or how much had passed between Maxim and the dog.

"I don't know why you're making this fuss," Philip said to Wade. "Big dogs are good to have around. My father always kept five or six wolfhounds . . . and cats are useless."

Maxim turned and glared at Philip. In truth, the two of them rarely agreed on anything, and tonight was the first time they'd ever joined forces. Wade had not expected it to last. Maxim adored Tiny Tuesday and certainly didn't view her as "useless."

But then both of them glanced back at Mr. Boo, and Wade had a sinking feeling he was about to lose this argument.

With Maxim and Philip standing side by side, Wade couldn't help noticing their similarities and differences. Both were pale and handsome, but where Philip was masculine, Maxim was almost pretty. He was small for a man, maybe five feet seven inches, with a slender build, blue-black hair, and dark eyes. However, his hair was messy and wild, and he often wore the same torn blue jeans for days without bothering to find a clean pair. Philip was over six feet tall, with layered, styled, red-brown hair that hung to the top of his collar. He was dressed in a long Armani coat—that hid the machete strapped to his belt.

Wade sighed, realizing he'd already lost the fight. "The dog told you he wouldn't hurt Tuesday?"

Maxim nodded. "Never hurt her. But he hungry. We feed him." His language skills had improved somewhat since his arrival, but they still had quite a ways to go.

"What's going on?" someone asked from behind.

Wade turned to see Eleisha Clevon coming toward them. He watched her move easily through the thorny rosebushes. She was a contrast to both of the other vampires here in the garden. Dressed in a long, flowing skirt and a snug red T-shirt, she was so small she actually had to look up when she spoke to Maxim. Long, wheat blond hair hung in waves down her back, and she appeared eternally seventeen years old . . . which she was not.

At the sight of the dog, she frowned. "How did he get inside the gate?"

Wade sighed again. "Maxim let him in—probably drew him in. I think we have a new addition to the household."

Her eyes widened, and she opened her mouth to argue.

But Maxim turned to Philip quickly. "Him stay?"

Philip shrugged. "Why not?"

Eleisha's protest died on her lips, and Wade couldn't help a flash of annoyance at Maxim for turning to Philip for support and even more than a flash at Eleisha for having instantly accepted Philip's offhand decision. Philip was not in charge here.

Nevertheless . . . it appeared their group now included a heavily scarred old pit bull named Mr. Boo.

"Maxim needs to go hunting," Eleisha said quietly, still glancing between Philip and the dog. "Philip, can you take us?"

"Yes."

"Does that leave me with the dog?" Wade asked, growing more annoyed by the second.

"Him hungry," Maxim put in.

"Of course he is," Wade said dryly, "which means I get to dig through the kitchen and find something to feed him. But I'm not cleaning up any piles of poop,

Maxim. If you keep drawing stray animals here, you're going to learn to help take care of them."

He knew he sounded like some self-righteous father, but he couldn't help it. Tiny Tuesday was one thing, but *this* was something else.

"We'll try to be quick," Eleisha said, moving toward the gate. "I'll help you when I get back." Maxim and Philip followed her out onto the sidewalk.

Wade crossed his arms, looking down at Mr. Boo, who looked up at him in turn.

"All right, you," Wade said. "I've got some hamburger that I'll share until I can get some dog food. But I have a gun, and if you bite me or Tiny Tuesday, I'll shoot you. Do you understand?"

Mr. Boo just grunted once and followed him into the church.

"No, this way," Eleisha said, taking Maxim's hand and pulling him deeper into the shadows of an underground parking lot. He just let her lead him. Philip was nowhere in sight now, but she knew he was watching them from somewhere nearby, guarding over them while she took Maxim to feed.

However, taking Maxim hunting always made her feel like a failure. When she and Wade had founded the underground and begun their mission to locate lost vampires, bring them into a community, and teach them how to feed without killing, she'd never anticipated finding one who was so damaged that he'd lost his "gift."

Within a few nights of becoming undead, a specific element of a vampire's previous personality developed into an overwhelming aura—which could be turned on and off at will. Their gifts assisted them in luring victims off alone somewhere and in keeping their victims calm. Eleisha's gift was an aura of helplessness. Philip's was an aura of overwhelming attraction.

Nearly two hundred years ago, Maxim had been a brilliant scholar, and whenever he'd spouted off, telling people literary stories, his voice had left any listener in awe, trapped inside his spell of brilliance.

But after witnessing a horrific event, he'd been driven alone into the forests of England, and as time passed, he'd forgotten who he was. He'd forgotten how to speak. Eleisha and Wade were trying to bring him back slowly, but his gift was gone . . . and now she had to hunt for him if she had any hope of leaving the victim alive.

Somehow, this still felt wrong, like she was failing in her mission.

But he tried hard to meet her halfway. He always did what she told him, and at the moment, that was the best he could do—at least until more of his memory came back.

"Find a woman," he said suddenly, jolting her from her thoughts.

"Yes, I know."

With the exception of Wade, Maxim didn't like men. He didn't even like feeding on men. He tolerated Philip only because he had no choice.

Eleisha looked around, listening for the sound of

footsteps. For this method of hunting, an underground public parking lot was ideal. She seldom varied the routine when taking Maxim out. He'd learned to stay completely quiet and let her do the talking. While she knew this wasn't helping him learn to take care of himself, as yet, she hadn't come up with anything better.

The elevator doors opened and a well-coiffed couple walked out, arguing about the man's unexpectedly high cell phone bill. Eleisha dropped to a crouch behind a beige Lexus and pulled Maxim down beside her. The couple walked past without seeing them.

"I just don't see how you could have run up a six-hundred-and-forty-two-dollar bill in a month," the woman said, her voice cracking slightly. "Who are you calling?"

His murmured response was lost as they moved farther away, but Eleisha didn't care. She kept her eyes on the elevator. A few minutes later, the doors opened again, and a slender woman in her twenties stepped out—alone. She wore black pants, a white shirt, and an apron. Her curly reddish hair was pulled up in a high ponytail on top of her head. She looked like a waitress coming off a late shift.

"Good," Maxim said, his dark eyes glittering.

Sometimes, his penchant for young women with long red hair made Eleisha uncomfortable. But the yuppie couple had vanished by now and the lot was deserted; this was a perfect opportunity.

She stood up, grasping Maxim's hand and stepping from the shadows.

"Excuse me," she said. Then she turned on her gift.

The young woman jumped slightly and turned in alarm. But Eleisha's gift washed over her, through her, dulling her mind until she saw only a small, frightened girl coming toward her, leading a young man with downcast eyes.

"Can you help us?" Eleisha asked. "My car won't start, and I have to get my brother home. He's . . . he's special."

This was a ruse they'd played over and over—because it always worked. Maxim's perpetually lost expression often led people to believe there was something not quite right with him. But once Eleisha turned on her gift, anyone caught in the vicinity was driven into an overwhelming need to "help."

The young woman's face shifted instantly to concern as Eleisha's gift kept flowing. "Oh," she said, coming closer. "What can I do? Can I call someone for you?"

"No," Eleisha answered. "Could you just drop us at home? We don't live far, and my dad can come look at the car tomorrow." She took mental note of an old van on her left with a dented, jagged front bumper, but she let the intensity of her gift grow at the same time.

The woman blinked. "Yes . . . of course. This way." She pulled a set of keys from her purse and pressed the UNLOCK button. A shiny blue Ford Focus beeped, and she opened the passenger door, letting Maxim in up front as if allowing strangers into her car was the most natural thing in the world.

Eleisha climbed into the backseat.

"I'm Angie," the woman said. "Where do you live?"

She was just putting her key into the ignition when Eleisha telepathically reached inside her mind and said aloud, "You're tired. You need to sleep."

Angie's head dropped to one side, and her eyelids closed. Maxim's dark eyes were glittering, and he grabbed her wrist.

"Be careful," Eleisha warned.

He didn't even look at her and sank his teeth into Angie's wrist, loudly sucking in mouthfuls of blood. But Eleisha wasn't worried. She'd done this with him a number of times, and he always seemed to instinctively know when to stop. He was not a killer by nature. He was just . . . damaged.

Eleisha stayed inside Angie's mind, keeping the woman asleep—and monitoring her heartbeat—while Maxim fed, but just as she was about to tell him to stop, he pulled out on his own, albeit reluctantly, licking his mouth.

Eleisha took a jackknife from her skirt pocket and handed it to him. "Here, you do the next part."

She wanted him to do as much as he could on his own. Without a word, he took the knife, opened the blade, and carefully used its point to connect the puncture wounds, making the injury look more like a gash.

Then Eleisha shifted her thoughts inside Angie's mind, taking her back in time to the moment she'd stepped from the elevator. She'd not met or seen anyone. She'd walked alone toward her car and then tripped, falling forward in front of an old van, cutting her wrist open on the jagged, dented fender. She'd made it to her car and then passed out.

"You'll wake up in five minutes," Eleisha whispered in her ear. She climbed out of the car and Maxim followed, closing the knife and wiping his face with one hand.

Eleisha had taught several other vampires to feed like this, but in those sessions, the point had been to teach someone else how to use his or her gift to lure a victim into a car, put the person to sleep, feed carefully, disguise the wound, and then replace a memory.

But Maxim had no telepathic ability with people—only animals—and he'd lost his gift. How could Eleisha ever help him learn to help himself, to feed safely and not call attention to himself by either killing someone or leaving someone alive who'd remember him?

Her thoughts must have shown on her face, because he stepped around in front of her, cutting her off.

"What . . . wrong?" he asked.

She liked his face and his messy blue-black hair. But now his dark eyes were nervous and searching, as if he feared disappointing her. That was the worst part. He *cared* how she felt. He'd been lonely and beyond miserable without even knowing it, and he seemed to believe she'd saved him and given him his life back. He loved living at the church and sleeping in a bed and having companionship. He wanted to please her.

She forced a smile. "Nothing's wrong. You did just fine."

Philip stepped out of the shadows from behind a huge yellow SUV. He frowned slightly at the sight of Maxim blocking Eleisha's path. "All finished?" His voice was tight.

She moved quickly around Maxim. "Yes. Let's go home."

Wade took Mr. Boo through the front doors of the church into the sanctuary, which had been turned into a kind of library/sitting room with tastefully arranged couches and bookshelves. The main floor of the church comprised this large, open sanctuary—along with two back offices.

The upstairs sported six rooms that had once been engaged for Sunday school classes. Maxim was currently sleeping in one of them, and Wade and Eleisha later planned to use the others to house any more lost vampires they found.

The basement comprised a three-bedroom apartment where Wade, Eleisha, and Philip lived, as well as an industrial-sized kitchen the old congregation had once used for potluck dinners, but Wade had turned that area into a gym so he could work out at home.

He took Mr. Boo all the way downstairs to the apartment and headed into their small, private kitchen.

"Sit," he said.

Boo just grunted and stood in the archway, looking hopefully at the refrigerator. With some reticence, Wade opened it and took out a package of raw hamburger. He'd been planning on cooking it later, to use in a pot of spaghetti sauce. But he unwrapped the plastic and dumped most of it onto a plate.

"Here."

As he set the plate on the floor, Mr. Boo hurried over and began wolfing down the raw meat in rapid bites. Wade couldn't help noting that for all the dog's size, his ribs were showing. He'd probably not had an easy life.

"I'll get you some water."

He was just reaching for a bowl in the cupboard when someone gasped in the kitchen archway.

"Good Lord! What is that?"

Glancing over, Wade locked eyes with the only other woman in their household: Rose de Spenser.

"It's a dog," he answered, sighing.

"Yes, I can see that." She sounded almost as appalled as he'd felt out in the churchyard, and for some reason, he couldn't help smiling.

Rose was tall and slender, with long brown hair accented by white streaks. She appeared to be about thirty years old and almost always wore rayon dresses. She was the first vampire that they'd manage to "rescue" and bring back here, but she was a reserved person by nature, and sometimes Wade thought he might never know her very well.

Still, he liked her, and she helped balance out a household that was becoming skewed slightly toward too many men.

"New addition," he said, pointing to Mr. Boo and still smiling—with no idea why. "Maxim must have drawn him here."

"He's *staying*? Here inside the church?"

Wade shrugged. "I was outvoted."

"What did Eleisha say?"

He stopped smiling, filled the bowl with water, and set it on the floor. "She didn't say anything once Philip piped up . . . and Philip likes the idea of a big dog around the place."

They both fell silent for a moment. But Mr. Boo made loud sounds, licking every inch of the plate, and then he looked up at Wade in hope.

"Oh, for God's sake," Wade said, dumping the rest of the hamburger onto the plate. There went the meat for his dinner.

Rose still seemed at a loss for words when the air beside her shimmered and the final member of their group materialized into view.

"A dog?" he said in a heavy Scottish accent—only he sounded excited. "You brought home a dog?"

"I most certainly did not," Wade answered, turning to Seamus.

Seamus' body was transparent, as always. Though long dead, he looked like a young man, his brown hair hanging to his shoulders. He wore a blue and yellow Scottish plaid draped across his shoulder and held by a belt over the black breeches he'd died in. The knife sheath at his hip was empty.

He was Rose's nephew, and he'd been murdered the same night she was turned, but he'd come back as a spirit, forever tied to her. He comprised a key component in the success of their missions. Once Wade found reason to suspect a possible location for a lost vampire, he sent Seamus to investigate. As a ghost, Seamus could zero in on a vampire—or anything undead— once he was in the general vicinity. Unfortunately, he couldn't stay too long, as his spirit was tied to Rose, and the longer he stayed away from her, the weaker he became.

But still, the group would be lost—blind—without him.

Mr. Boo looked up and blinked. He'd shown no aversion to the vampires, but he did seem somewhat put off by the sight of Seamus. At least he didn't growl. After a moment, he lowered his head and lapped at the water.

"What about Tiny Tuesday?" Rose finally asked, clearly uncertain about this decision having been made without her input.

"He won't hurt her," Wade said, trying to sound confident. "Maxim promised."

Thinking of Tiny Tuesday, Wade knew she was probably sleeping in her kitty bed up in his office.

"Rose," he said. "I need to get to work. Can you find Mr. Boo an old blanket or something and make him a bed? Now that he's eaten, I think he'll want to sleep. I have a feeling he's been on the road awhile."

Just like many of them.

But now the dog had found a home. Suddenly Wade didn't mind the thought of one more lost soul thrown into the mix.

"Mr. Boo?" Rose asked.

"Yeah, that's his name."

Rose seemed to read Wade's face—she was good at that—and nodded with some hesitation. "Yes, you go on upstairs. I'll find him . . . something."

Grateful, he moved past her, leaving Seamus to watch the dog in fascination. Seamus had liked horses and dogs when he was alive. Perhaps those penchants never changed.

Wade walked through the living room of the apartment and headed for the stairway leading up to the two rooms behind the sanctuary. He had furnished one of them into a home office for himself, and Rose was using the other one as her bedroom. His long legs took the stairs two at a time. He'd always considered his own appearance somewhat mundane in comparison with those of his housemates. Tall and slender, he was in his early thirties, with narrow features. The only element about him that truly stood out was his white-blond hair, hanging below his collar. He'd just kept forgetting to get it cut, and now it seemed easier to wear it longer.

Emerging from the stairwell, he headed for his office. It was probably his favorite room in the church, with books and maps spread out all over the place and his computer waiting for him on the messy desk.

As he pushed the cracked door farther open, a small gray and white cat raised her head from a cushy kitty bed.

"Meow."

She had blue eyes.

"Meow, yourself," Wade answered, walking to the desk. He'd put her food, water, and cat box in here, since this was where he spent most of his time. Maxim may have "adopted" the small cat, but Wade took care of her. Over the winter, she'd had a litter of four kittens, and he'd managed to find them all homes.

Getting up, she stretched and hopped up onto his desk—as she always did when he was working. She seemed to enjoy watching his hands move across the keyboard.

"We have a new addition that you're not going to like," he said to her, pushing the mouse so that his dark screen lit up.

She didn't seem concerned and sat quietly while he focused on the screen, deciding to start his search in Europe tonight.

Their strategy was for Wade for seek out any online news stories of homicide victims drained of blood or of living people checked into hospitals with cuts or gashes that did not warrant an unexplained amount of blood loss. He'd once worked as a police psychologist, and he knew a good deal about *where* to search for such stories. Then he'd send Seamus out, and once Seamus pinpointed and confirmed the find, several members of their team would travel to the vampire's location, try to make contact, and try to bring him or her safely home to the church.

Two of their attempts had ended in success, and two had ended in complete disaster.

But now, several months had passed since Wade had

uncovered anything promising, and he was starting to feel antsy. He wanted a new mission.

He subscribed to an almost countless number of online newspapers, and he normally started with the *Evening Standard* from London. As he scanned through it, Tiny Tuesday meowed for attention, and he scratched the side of her face absently for a few moments. When he stopped, she batted at his hand.

"Let me read," he said, moving on to the *Connexion* from France. As always lately, he found nothing of note, and after exhausting every online paper in Europe (or at least those published with an English version), he moved to U.S. papers, beginning with the *Seattle Times*. He knew what to look for, and he was capable of scanning quickly, so he almost missed a headline from the Arts and Leisure section:

Mysterious Psychic Causes Stir in Puget Sound by Randall Smith

Wade didn't know why he paused on that one headline—but he did. Then he clicked on the story.

The affluent residents of The Highlands in Seattle appear to be fighting one another for a chance at a private audience with the newest guest of socialite Ms. Vera Olivier.

Christian Lefevre arrived in Seattle last week and has been quietly catering to the upper crust of Seattle

*society from inside Ms. Olivier's home—by making
contact with their dead loved ones.*

*Little is known about Lefevre, other than his high fees
and that he is constantly in demand. Apparently, he
dislikes the terms "psychic" and "medium" and refers
to himself as a "spiritualist." But an unnamed source
recently described him as "clairvoyant to an unprece-
dented degree," and he appears to conduct detailed conversations with the dead that convince even the most
reticent of his clients. While his potential for public attention seems limitless, he will not do television and has
consistently managed to avoid being photographed.*

*Scattered reports suggest that his séances are so intense
that afterward, some clients are faint, weak, and dizzy. To
date, he's mainly worked in the South—Georgia, Louisiana, and Tennessee. But his arrival in Seattle is causing
quite a stir. Who will be allowed to see him? Whose dead
loved ones will he contact here? Exactly how much does he
charge? I'll be following up on this story soon.*

Wade read the article twice. He knew something of
Randall Smith—who had a tendency to cover sensa-
tional stories and bend the truth a tad. But Wade
couldn't take his eyes off one line: "Scattered reports
suggest that his séances are so intense that afterward,
some clients are faint, weak, and dizzy."

That one line made his pulse race.

Philip led the way through the main doors back into
the sanctuary, while Eleisha and Maxim followed.

"What will we do now?" Philip asked. He was in the mood for an action movie, something with guns and explosions. Lately, Eleisha had insisted upon trying to broaden his horizons, but one could watch only so many Alfred Hitchcock and Orson Wells films without needing a break. "Maybe we can get Wade to play poker?"

Philip liked playing cards, too, but Maxim couldn't quite grasp concepts like five-card draw yet, and Eleisha didn't like leaving Maxim out—so Philip doubted she'd agree. Still, he had to ask. His favorite times were these lulls in between missions when they were all home and Eleisha lavished a good deal of her attention on him.

"Before we do anything," she said, "we'd better check on Wade and see if he needs help with the dog."

Maxim nodded. "Mr. Boo."

Oh . . . yes. Philip had forgotten about the dog. The three of them headed for the door behind the altar of the sanctuary, and Eleisha was just about to open it when Wade pushed from the other side and stuck his head through.

"I thought I heard you," he said. "Come and look at this."

All Philip's pleasure at possible entertainments fled. He recognized the look on Wade's face. Wade had *found* something.

Eleisha hurried through the door and across the hall into Wade's office. Philip followed more slowly, finding Eleisha and Wade already chattering away in front of the computer screen. As Philip entered the office, Maxim hung in the doorway. Tiny Tuesday sat perched on the desk, watching them all curiously.

"The term 'spiritualist' caught my attention," Wade was saying. "In the Victorian era, that was the term used for a medium." He paused, pointing. "But this part about his clients being left weak and dizzy . . ." He trailed off.

Eleisha kept reading. "Christian Lefevre," she said softly as her eyes moved down the screen.

As she spoke that name, Philip froze, and a dull roaring began in his ears.

"What did you say?" he asked hoarsely.

She looked up at him in surprise, followed quickly by concern. "Are you okay?"

"What was the name?" he bit off.

"Christian Lefevre."

The last name meant nothing to him . . . but the first name, Christian, was pounding in his ears, fighting to surface on the edge of his memory. He strode forward, moving in between Wade and Eleisha, and he read the entire story for himself. Nothing he read helped the struggling memory to surface, but that name meant something . . . something.

Turning, he looked at Wade and said raggedly, "Send Seamus tonight."

chapter two

At home in Cliffbracken—an aging manor near the coast of Wales—Julian Ashton was determined not to be idle while he waited for Eleisha to locate another elder.

He'd hired some "help" through an agency in Cardiff. So now three women had been working for the past month to clean the neglected place from top to bottom, and a full-time contractor had been engaged for interior repairs.

Julian promised himself that he would not feed on any of them no matter how hungry he became. Recently, the reputation for "disappearing servants" under his charge had become so well-known that few people would agree to work here anymore. But he'd managed to find a few satisfactory workers—desperate for employment—and he vowed not to give in to temptation again.

After checking on some recent repairs to the floor in the dining hall, he walked down the darkened passage to his study, his favorite room. The fire he'd built earlier burned in the hearth, making the aged chairs and couches look almost new in the soft yellow light. A pile of maps and newspapers completely covered a round table in the center of the room. He leaned down to examine several of them.

He was a large man with a bone structure that almost made him look heavy. His dark hair hung at uneven angles around a solid chin, and he pushed it back away from his face.

His nights had taken on a kind of routine while he waited for Eleisha to find a new lead. He normally woke, built a fire, went to the stables, took his horse out for a long ride, and then came back here to do research of his own. But once again, Wade and Eleisha seemed to be taking so long find someone new to track that he'd continued attempting to take matters into his own hands, just to see what he could find, and perhaps throw a hint in their path. He'd begun subscribing to even more international newspapers.

Tonight he was still deciding where to begin when the air beside him shimmered and a teenage girl appeared: his spy, Mary Jordane.

In addition to being transparent, the most striking things about her were her spiky magenta hair and shiny silver nose stud. She was thin, with a hint of bud-

ding breasts, wearing a purple T-shirt, a black mesh
overshirt, torn jeans, and Dr. Martens boots.

But at the sight of her, he tensed, on guard at the
hatred glowing from her eyes.

Once, Mary had seemed to enjoy working for him,
spying for him, bringing him tidbits of information, but
that time was gone.

In his last confrontation with Eleisha and her team,
Julian had been forced to behead his own vampire servant, Jasper—in order to cause a distraction. While Julian
had known that Mary harbored some ridiculous affection for Jasper . . . he'd had no idea that her attachment
bordered on madness. Afterward, she'd gone into open
revolt, refusing to serve Julian in anything until he'd finally made a new deal with her.

He'd been forced to promise that if she assisted him
with following Eleisha to track down one more elder,
he'd send her over to the "other side," where she might
be able to reconnect with Jasper's spirit.

In his mind, every instinct he possessed screamed
that this situation was wrong. One such as him did not
make deals with servants.

A servant either obeyed or suffered.

But in Mary's case, as she had no body, there was
nothing he could do to her . . . and he needed her. He
was blind without her.

Two centuries past, Julian's kind had been far more
numerous, and they'd existed by four laws. The most
sacred of these laws was "No vampire shall kill to feed."
They'd retained their secrecy through telepathy, feeding

on mortals, altering a memory, and then leaving the victim alive. New vampires required training from their makers to awaken and hone psychic abilities, but Julian's telepathy had never surfaced. He lived by his own laws, and so the elders began quietly turning against him. His own maker, Angelo, had tried to hide this news from him, but Julian *had known*. He'd heard the rumblings and he acted first, beheading every vampire who lived by the laws, including Angelo—who would have turned against him sooner or later.

He'd left a small crop of younger vampires, untrained vampires like Eleisha and Philip, alone. They were not telepathic, did not know the laws, and were no threat to him.

Then, with no warning, Eleisha suddenly developed fierce psychic abilities and began actively looking for any vampires who might have escaped Julian's net and remained in hiding.

She'd found several vampires who didn't overly concern him, such as Rose de Spenser, an uneducated creature who knew nothing of her own kind, or the feral Maxim, who seemed capable of communicating only with beasts. But she'd located several others whom he'd deemed necessary to intercept and behead. Now he was simply waiting for her to find more elders, to lure more of them out . . . and to lead him right to them.

Keeping his expression still, he looked Mary in the eye. "Yes?"

She was quiet for a minute, but she didn't look away.

"I think Wade may be onto something. He sent Seamus up to Seattle."

"Seattle?" That surprised him. Too much had already happened in the Seattle area. If another vampire had been hiding up there, surely Eleisha or Wade would have found out long ago. "Are you sure you heard right?"

She frowned. "Yeah, I heard it clear enough. Maxim lured in some stray dog, and Seamus was busy downstairs trying to make a new friend, so I didn't need to worry about him sensing me. I drifted halfway through Wade's office wall and listened to everything they said."

He knew she wasn't finished, so he didn't speak. Even while hating him, Mary never could resist showing off her ability to glean information.

"The target's not from Seattle. He's up visiting from the South . . . Louisiana, Georgia, places like that. He's some kind of psychic that talks to the dead, named Christian Lefevre." She paused. "That mean anything to you?"

"No."

But still . . . Julian walked over to the end table by his chair and picked up a large old volume titled *The Makers and Their Children*. Julian's own maker had written this book, and it was a detailed account of every vampire in existence as of 1825. Julian knew it by heart, and this was how he'd managed to hunt them all down so efficiently. But there was no vampire in the book named Christian Lefevre.

Still, it didn't matter. Any surviving elder might have changed his name.

"What caught Wade's attention?" he asked.

Mary shrugged. "According to the story, the guy just sounds too psychic, and he calls himself a spiritualist, which Wade says is an old word. And some of this guy's clients have been weak and dizzy after a séance." She paused again, tilting her head to one side. "Oh, and his named seemed to . . ."

"Seemed to what?"

"It freaked Philip out. I mean, he's always pale, but he just went white. You should have seen him."

Julian stiffened. The term "spiritualist" had given him a jolt, but this news about Philip was something else. The man's name had meant something to Philip?

"What do you want me to do?" Mary asked. "Go to Seattle and see what I can sense on my own?"

He pondered the possibilities. "No," he said finally. "Just go back to the church and keep an eye on Wade and Eleisha. If there's a vampire in Seattle, Seamus will find him. Once he reports, come back to me."

The hatred in her eyes glowed again. "And if this Christian is an elder and I help you kill him, you'll keep your promise, right? You'll send me to the gray plane to find Jasper."

"Of course."

Her transparent cheekbones tightened. "You'd better. Remember the promise I made if you're lying."

How he wanted to strike her, to see her bleeding on the floor. She'd sworn to give Philip and Eleisha his lo-

cation if he didn't abide by their deal. Of course he had
no intention of letting her go—not yet. But he'd cross
that bridge when he reached it. So far, he'd been able to
manipulate her into doing his bidding. He'd just have
to think of something else to keep her serving him.

"Go," he said.

The air shimmered and Mary vanished from sight.

Once she was gone, he was embarrassed by his own
sense of relief.

After Wade sent Seamus up to Seattle, Eleisha went
downstairs to see if Rose needed any help with Mr.
Boo, but it seemed that although Rose wasn't thrilled at
the prospect of a tattered pit bull, she was quite capable
of caring for one.

The dog was resting on a pile of old blankets in a
little nook on the floor between the wall and the
couch—with a bowl of water beside him. He looked
different now than he had in the churchyard, almost
like he belonged here.

Rose was sitting on the couch reading a Sherlock
Holmes novel.

"I'm sorry we just sent him inside," Eleisha said immediately. "I know we should have asked you first."

"It's all right," Rose said, and her tone suggested it
really was all right. "We certainly have enough room
here, and Seamus . . . well, he seemed so pleased."

A voice spoke behind Eleisha. "Seamus likes Mr.
Boo. Knew he would."

She turned to see Maxim, and then Philip, coming in

from the stairwell. Maxim made a beeline for Mr. Boo, but Philip turned without a word and headed down the hallway to the bedroom he shared with Eleisha.

She watched him go, feeling helpless. Something was very wrong, and he'd never been skilled at communication. She knew she'd have to draw it out of him. Rose was watching her, but Rose understood— she always understood.

"Go on," Rose said. "Maxim and I are fine here."

Maxim was already sitting cross-legged beside the dog, and Eleisha assumed they were engaged in some form of mental communication. She wished she understood that a little better. Maxim was such a blank wall to her sometimes. But right now, she was more worried about Philip.

Nodding gratefully to Rose, she turned and headed down the hallway, pushing the bedroom door open and peeking inside.

He was standing by the window, looking out into the dark churchyard. Although Eleisha had deeply loved several people in her existence, she'd never loved anyone the way she loved him.

And she'd never been *in love* before.

Tonight he wore his usual black jeans and black T-shirt. Once, he'd worn nothing but expensive designer clothes. But over the past year, he'd seemed to care less and less about designers and price tags.

She thought he was the most handsome man she'd ever seen—or anyone had ever seen, for that matter. Most of the time, she didn't care what he looked like.

His appearance was just part of his gift, something to fool mortals. But when she was with him, she didn't feel alone, and after so many years on this Earth, that counted for more than she could express.

Of course he had faults—more than most people. He was vain and self-centered, and he'd once been a savage killer. But he had an appetite for life that she lacked, and when he touched her, she forgot about everything else.

He didn't turn from the window as she stepped inside and closed the door.

"Are you all right?" she asked, knowing the words sounded lame even as they left her mouth.

He didn't seem to notice that it was a stupid question. "No . . . I don't know."

She moved closer. "Philip," she said softly. "What's wrong?"

His face was ivory in the moonlight shining through the window, but his frustration and his pain were clear. The sight made her stomach tighten. She wanted to help him.

"That name," he whispered. "It means something, but I don't know what. I can almost see it . . . I can almost remember, but then it slips away."

She blinked and touched his arm. "Do you mean something from before you were turned?"

One of the four laws stated that no vampire should ever make another vampire within a span of less than a hundred years. The physical and mental energy it required was so extreme that breaking this law could produce flawed results. Philip was the third vampire his maker had created in a span of about twenty years. As a result, he had come out . . . wrong, with no memory at all of his mortal life. His early nights as an undead had been ugly—and he'd been feral. He had few memories of that time period either.

Turning from the window, he looked down at her. "I don't know, and I need to know. Seamus will come back soon, and he'll tell Wade that he's found a vampire. I'm sure of it. Then Wade will want to start packing, and you'll want to start to packing, and I need to know who we're chasing . . . I need to remember before I take you and Wade anywhere near Seattle."

That's what he was worried about? Something was tugging at his buried memories, and he wanted to know what she and Wade would be walking into?

She hesitated before offering, "Do you want me to read your earliest memories? Try to find the right one?"

All three of them—she, Wade, and Philip—had the ability to read memories telepathically, but their skill levels were different. Philip had more control over his own when someone was reading him. But Eleisha had a natural ability to take people deep inside a memory and get them lost, to make them show her much more than they'd ever intended, including images of things they'd forgotten themselves.

Philip winced at her questions. This was delicate ground. He cared what Eleisha thought of him to an almost pathological degree. Apparently, he'd hated what he'd been like . . . looked like . . . behaved like in the early nights of his undead existence, and he kept those memories locked away inside a mental box, never to be seen.

"Maybe Wade could look?" she suggested.

"No!"

His voice was ragged again, and she touched his arm. "Philip," she whispered. "It doesn't matter what you were like back then. I know you now." She let that sink in. "If you have memories of this Christian Lefevre, that means he's an elder. Let me in. Let me look."

His expression crumpled, and she'd never seen him so openly unsettled. Normally, most of his deeper emotions stayed on the inside of his face.

She took his hand and led him to the bed, sinking down. "I swear . . . I swear that nothing I see will change how I look at you now. But if I try this, you can't fight me. You have to let all your defenses down."

His arms were shaking as he sank down beside her, reached out, and took her other hand. Carefully, she let her thoughts flow into his mind, tangling with his until she hit a wall.

"Let me in," she repeated.

The wall dropped.

HARFLEUR MANOR, FRANCE, 1819

Philip was screaming while somebody held him down. He was naked. His chest and face were covered in blood.

His entire body bucked, and he tried snapping at the hand pinning his left shoulder.

"Julian!" someone shouted. "Get his other arm."

Two incredibly strong hands came down on his right shoulder and arm as he bucked again wildly, trying to throw his captors off.

"How did he get out in the first place, Angelo?" a deep voice demanded from his right. "You said you'd keep him locked up. Look at the state of him! Can you imagine the mess he's left behind? You're going to bring some local constable down on our heads."

"Quiet!" ordered the voice from his left. "You are not helping." One hand lifted from Philip's shoulder, and it began to stroke his cheek. The movement calmed him, and he didn't try to bite it again. "It's all right, my son," the voice whispered. "You're home."

Philip was lying on a stone slab. His vision cleared, and he looked up to a see a face . . . a face he knew, haggard, with deep lines of strain marring a white forehead. Shifting his gaze, he also saw a thick-boned man with dark hair and angry dark eyes.

Angelo and Julian.

Philip tried to remember who they were. He knew that Angelo was often kind to him, but he didn't know how to respond. He sometimes understood their words, but he couldn't form words himself. He didn't know how.

He knew only that he wanted blood, more and more blood. It tasted good in his mouth. It fed him strength.

Angelo's hand continued to stroke his face. "I'm going to find you some help, my son. I swear I will help you."

The image vanished, and Eleisha felt Philip fighting her, trying to rechannel the memory to shift it away and hide something. She knew if she spoke, she'd probably just break the connection. Instead, she held on and drove deeper, forcing her way through the layers upon layers in his mind.

Without warning, she broke through.

HARFLEUR FOREST, FRANCE, 1819

Philip was on his back again, but this time, he was dressed . . . or at least wearing pants. He was in a forest, with trees and the moon above him, and someone was sitting on his chest, holding him down. He snarled and spit, trying to pitch his captor off.

He wanted more blood.

"Shhhhhhhh," a familiar voice said, and a hand stroked his cheek. "Be still now."

"Jesus Christ," another voice said from a few feet away. "This is madness, Angelo. Do you see this woman? He's torn her head off. You have to put him down."

Philip did not know the voice, and from where he lay, he turned his head. A slender young man with wavy steel gray hair was standing over a bleeding lump of what had once been a woman.

"No!" Angelo answered.

It was Angelo sitting on Philip's chest.

"This is wrong," said the young man with gray hair, moving closer. "And you know it. You've broken the third law, and this is the price. Is this why you lured me out here? To stop this slaughter? If so, we're too late. He's a danger to our secrecy, Angelo. Either you put him down or I will."

Angelo sat straight, but he didn't get off Philip's chest. "I will not, and neither will you. You owe me, Christian."

Both men fell silent, and Philip turned his head farther, looking eagerly at the lump, wondering if there was more blood left inside it.

"*I* make the demands here," Angelo said. "Or you will become a new chapter in my book . . . and I have many details to include."

"You swore you'd leave me out," Christian answered.

"And in return, you swore to do me a service when I asked. I am asking now."

More silence followed, and Philip tried to pitch Angelo off again. He wanted more blood. But Angelo held him down.

"What do you want?" Christian asked finally.

"He cannot speak, so I have no idea how much he understands. Go inside and help him to find words. You're the only one who can implant suggestions. Just help him to find speech. After that, I can help him myself."

"Inside his mind?" Christian asked, incredulous. "No. I'm not going in there. Not for you. Not for anything."

"Then you leave me no choice."

The words between them blurred in Philip's ears as he longed to get free and go back to the body before all its blood ran out onto the ground. But the argument went on and on until he suddenly had a feeling Christian had lost.

For some reason, this unsettled him, and he tried harder to buck Angelo off. He fought and snarled and then screamed as he saw Christian's face coming closer. Christian knelt down on the ground, just above his head, and Philip had no idea what was coming.

But he was afraid.

Two slender hands settled on his shoulders, and then he felt a sharp pain slicing through his head. It was blinding.

He heard a voice in his mind.

Where are you? Where is Philip Branté? I know you are here.

In terror, Philip tried to squirm away. The voice in his head wanted something, searched for something, and he did not know how to make it go away. He tried to fight, but it just kept cutting deeper and deeper into his thoughts.

The words are in you. Use your mouth. Use your voice. Speak.

Philip kept fighting, tried to hide from the voice, but after a few moments, he stopped hearing any words at all, and he just felt an impulse that was growing harder and harder to fight.

Finally, the resistance inside him built to such a frenzy that he thought he would burst. His mouth and tongue struggled to move, and he heard himself scream.

"No!"

The word felt as if it had been ripped from his throat, but then the slicing pain in his head vanished. It was gone. His body trembled and relaxed.

"Don't make me do that again!" Christian choked out.

But Angelo leaned low over Philip's face. His eyes glittered, and he said, "Philip, what is my name?"

Philip knew his name. He'd known it for some time now, but the impulse struck him again. He forced his tongue and mouth to move, and he said, "Ang . . . elo."

Above him, Angelo smiled.

Eleisha released Philip and pulled out of his memory.

He gasped and coughed and then slid off the bed onto the floor, wrapping his arms around himself. He stared at nothing.

"Philip!"

She slid off after him, trying to hold one of his hands, but his arms were crossed, and he wouldn't let go of his own shoulders.

"It's all right," she said, feeling more than guilt for what she'd just put him through. How awful it must have been to see himself like some feral animal.

But her mind was reeling. She could still see Christian's face clearly, so young and unlined, but framed by wavy, steel gray hair, and she tried to make sense of the images she'd seen through Philip's chaotic memories. Angelo had been unable to awaken spoken language in Philip, but he'd forced Christian to try, and he'd suggested that Christian's telepathic ability was stronger than his own. What had he said? *You're the only one who can implant suggestions.*

And yet Angelo had gained Christian's help only by making a threat . . . to include him in the book cataloging detailed accounts of all vampires in existence before 1825. To the best of Eleisha's knowledge, all of the elders knew that Angelo had made this account, and none of them had objected. A few had even helped him. Why had Christian been afraid to be included?

Philip's teeth began chattering, and Eleisha got up onto her knees, putting her arms around him. He didn't push her away, but he didn't respond either.

"At least we know," she whispered in his ear. "We know there was an elder named Christian . . . who wasn't listed in the book. And we know what he looks like. You've helped us, Philip."

Of course there was no way to tell yet if this "spiritualist" that Wade had read about had any connection to the vampire from Philip's past. Christian was a common enough name.

But Eleisha could not help feeling certain they were onto something.

A telepathically powerful vampire named Christian had been left out of Angelo's book. It had to mean something.

Mary Jordane watched through the bedroom window as Eleisha held Philip and rocked him back and forth. At first he didn't respond at all, but finally, one of his hands released his own shoulder and he pulled her closer.

The sight of them in such an embrace did not move Mary in the slightest.

She'd lost the only thing she'd ever loved, and she had no pity for Philip. Plus, she hated it when these vampires sat silently reading each other's memories, as it left her nothing to report to Julian.

But tonight she'd picked up a few juicy details. Right after they came out their trance—or whatever the hell they were lost in—Eleisha had said, *At least we know. We know there was an elder named Christian . . . who wasn't listed in the book. And we know what he looks like. You've helped us, Philip.*

That alone was worth reporting back to Julian, and it filled her with hope.

Her biggest fear had been that Wade and Seamus would uncover some new vampire who wasn't an elder— someone like Rose or Maxim who didn't count—thus dragging her deal with Julian out for God knew how much longer.

But this? This sounded promising.

Julian had sworn to her . . . just one more elder, and

he'd send her back to the in-between plane, where she was certain Jasper would be waiting. He wouldn't want to move on without her. But each passing day brought more fear that he might fall into despair and give up on her and go onward into the afterlife. She'd never been there, so she had no idea if she'd be able to find him. No, she had to get to the in-between plane as soon as possible.

That meant tracking down an elder and helping Julian kill it.

She had every intention of moving this hunt forward as fast as she could.

chapter three

For some reason, Seamus was having a hard time focusing in his search through the Puget Sound area of Seattle.

Well . . . maybe he did know the reason. He couldn't seem to stop thinking about Mary.

He kept seeing her on her knees in that graveyard in England, wailing in sorrow over a dead vampire. He'd once believed that if she served Julian, she must be evil . . . but he didn't believe that anymore. He also kept seeing her standing in the rain in front of the church a few nights later, looking up at the stained-glass windows, with her face so sad.

He'd wanted to help her. To protect her. But she'd vanished, and he had not seen her again.

Sailing through the night air over a Seattle golf

course, he was trying to force himself to focus when he sensed a hole in the fabric of life somewhere ahead. All thoughts of Mary fled. He had a mission tonight. It wasn't that he could exactly feel an undead's presence. It was more like he felt an absence in the vicinity, and that's what he zoned in on.

He was moving west, toward the water, and suddenly he stopped, midair, about fifty feet off the ground, and he tried to sharpen his senses . . . and realized he felt two black holes.

Two undeads?

That concerned him. Vampires didn't normally travel in pairs—except for Eleisha's group. Had he found something else?

Even in the darkness, the area all around him was beautiful, thick trees and sculpted gardens—and high fences with stout gates. This was where the affluent of Seattle often chose to live. Focusing hard, he began drifting forward again, moving faster until he reached a winding street called Cherry Loop, and he sailed through the trees to see a mansion spread out before him.

It boasted no front yard, but once someone made it through the front gates, he or she would drive about a quarter mile over elaborate stonework in shades of cream and tan, which then formed a kind of courtyard. Over the top of the house, Seamus could see the dark water of the Puget Sound, so the view must be from the back.

But he didn't hesitate long enough to get a good

look at the house. Instead, he moved around to the north side, sensing for those two black holes.

Whoever he was tracking . . . they were inside.

Zeroing in on their location, he pinpointed them on the main-level floor, so he blinked out and blinked back in on the second floor, directly above them, hoping he would materialize in a room by himself.

He did.

Looking around, he realized he'd appeared inside a guest room that was currently not in use—or did not appear to be in use. The furnishings were lavish, from the four-poster bed to the gold-gilt curtains hanging from ceiling to floor, but somehow, the décor seemed to lack good taste. For one, the room was hopelessly over-crowded with tables, brocade-covered settees, vases, huge brass lamps, and far too many paintings on the walls . . . and nothing seemed chosen to complement anything else. Seamus was certainly no expert at inte-rior design, but it seemed to him that someone had spent a great deal of money to make the room look like an extremely expensive garage sale.

However, he believed himself to have arrived in a good location for his own purposes, and he floated downward, turning his body to achieve a horizontal position so he could pass his face down through the floor.

Within seconds he could hear voices, and then his face just breached the ceiling so that he could look down and see what was happening below.

The sight caught him off guard for almost a full minute before he began to take stock of the situation.

The first thing he truly absorbed was the sight of a large round table with a candelabra at the center. But the room did not appear to be a dining area, more like an old-fashioned sitting room of some kind—with the large table placed dead center. As in the guest room, there was far too much furniture scattered around and far too many paintings on the walls . . . and Persian rugs and vases of dried flowers and candles and Chinese vases and Egyptian statues and uncountable crystal and porcelain knickknacks everywhere.

But once he'd assessed the room, he turned his attention to the six people sitting around the table.

Of course the first ones he studied were the vampires—as they indeed were vampires. He could tell easily from this close range: a man and a woman.

The man looked about twenty years old, but his hair was steel gray and hung in waves to either side of his forehead and curled around his ears down to the nape of his neck. His face was narrow, and his eyes were almost clear, with just a hint of sky blue. He wore a wine-colored shirt and a black sport jacket, which seemed an odd contrast to the thick gold ring in his right earlobe. Something about his expression and facial structure reminded Seamus of a silver fox.

But the man's companion was even more striking, and she held Seamus' attention longer.

She was lovely, small and delicate. Her hair was fine

and white-blond, similar to Wade's. She wore it nearly to her shoulders, with the bangs tucked behind her ears, and a small jeweled clip held about half of the length pulled back at the crown of her head. Long silver earrings dangled from her lobes, glinting in the candlelight. Her eyes were green and slightly slanted, and she wore a burgundy V-neck evening gown.

"Do we have enough for the circle, Christian?" a short, stocky woman in a purple caftan asked him. "I can always call in a few servants. They won't mind."

"No, Vera," the male vampire answered. "Six is a perfect number."

His accent was French.

Vera clapped her hands cheerfully. "Good enough, then. Shall we begin?"

Seamus took a better look at her. She had short hair, dyed orange-red, and a string of huge blue stones around her neck. The other members at the table comprised a middle-aged man in a suit, a slightly younger man—also in a suit—and an attractive woman about thirty years old. Both of the younger people looked distressed, but the middle-aged man looked more . . . annoyed, as if he was wasting his time and would rather be someplace else.

Christian leaned forward, looking at the three of them in turn, beginning with the middle-aged man. "Richard . . . Nathan . . . Laura, you understand how this will work?" His voice was soft and comforting, as if he wished for nothing in the world but to help them. "I will call upon your mother, and when I reach her, she will speak through Ivory." He gestured to the delicate woman beside him. "In this way, I can ask questions, and she will be able to answer."

Seamus wanted to roll his eyes. Were these people paying good money for this show?

As he took in the sight below in its entirety, the whole scene reminded him of several episodes of a terrible television show Wade had forced him to watch on DVD—called *Night Gallery*.

"Yes, yes, of course," Richard answered absently, still seeming annoyed at the prospect of being here. Perhaps he was the only one with any sense.

"Reach out and join hands," Christian said, closing his eyes. The table was so large they had to reach out to touch one another, but he joined hands with Vera on one side and Ivory on the other.

In spite of the ridiculous sham playing out below, Seamus found himself curious about what would happen next. Would chains rattle? Would the candles go out? Would eerie voices wail? He couldn't wait to see.

But none of those things happened.

With his eyes closed, Christian called softly, "Althea, I call to you from the other side. Hear me. Come to us now."

Oh, for heaven's sake, Seamus thought, wanting to roll his eyes again. Fortunately, no one looked up to see him peering down at them through the ceiling.

"Althea?" Christian said, opening his eyes. "Is that you?"

Laura gasped sharply. "Have you reached her?"

Christian smiled. "Yes, she is with us. She is standing beside you . . . a tall woman, about sixty, but her hair is still long and black. She's wearing a wool skirt with a light blue sweater set." He squinted slightly. "And a charm bracelet."

"Yes," Laura breathed. "That's her."

"What is it you wish me to ask her?" Christian said.

Nathan shifted uncomfortably in his chair. "Her will was read last week, and she left everything to Richard. All three of us would like to know why."

Christian focused on the empty air beside Laura's chair. "Althea, why did you cut your two younger children from your will? Why would you leave everything to Richard?"

Ivory's green eyes were wide open, and she stared straight ahead. "I did not," she answered. Her voice was like music, and once again, Seamus could not wait to see what happened next.

This time, Nathan gasped. "Mother, what do you mean?"

"She can hear only me," Christian said. He paused. "Althea, what do you mean?"

Suddenly Richard looked less annoyed and more . . . uncomfortable.

"The will read last week was not the one I wrote," Ivory said, still staring into open space. "Richard replaced it with a new one."

At this, Richard was on his feet, but his breaking the "circle" seemed to have no effect. "This is absurd," he said, though his face had gone pale.

"Richard is right," Laura said, speaking directly to Christian. "Mr. Bransen authenticated the will that was read, and he'd been mother's lawyer for twenty years."

"What of Mr. Bransen?" Christian asked the empty space.

Ivory answered. "He was working with Richard, and he signed off on the false will for a payment of two million dollars. You can have his accounts checked for the deposit last week."

"Stop this nonsense!" Richard roared.

But by now, Nathan was on his feet as well, and he was taller than he'd appeared sitting down. "If that's true, then where is the real will?"

"Althea," Christian said. "Where is the real will?"

"The same place it's always been," Ivory answered, still lost in her trance, "in my safety deposit box in the Seattle National Bank, box number four-six-seven. Richard has not yet been able to gain access to the box and destroy the papers there. Nathan, you must alert the authorities and have it opened yourself."

Richard's mouth fell open in shock the instant Ivory spoke the numbers for the box.

Laura simply seemed confused, shaking her head at her eldest brother. "Richard . . . ?"

Nathan looked as if he were close to taking a swing, but Richard suddenly grabbed his head, as if dizzy, and leaned against his chair.

The buzz of voices continued below as Seamus pulled his face back up until he was floating in the guest room again. Was Christian for real? Had he truly been speaking to a ghost through his partner?

Regardless of the ridiculous trappings of the scene below, it appeared that Christian had just saved two people from penury by speaking to their dead mother—and he'd exposed a criminal at the same time. Or was Ivory the real medium, and Christian was simply asking the questions?

Seamus did not know, and in truth, he wasn't sure it mattered.

What did matter was that he'd located two vampires, and he needed to get back and tell Wade.

It was a bit late to be coming home from a grocery run, but Wade didn't like leaving the church during the day, so he tended to go shopping at night.

Eleisha, Rose, Philip, and Maxim all fell dormant during daylight hours, and nothing would wake them. It just seemed . . . wrong to leave them like that. He had no idea what might happen if somebody got past the locks on the doors and went nosing about inside while he was gone. Even Philip would be helpless. Without telling anyone, Wade had stopped sleeping in his bedroom. Now he napped during the day on a couch in the sanctuary, and he slept lightly.

Maybe this leaned too far into paranoia, but he couldn't help it.

So he tended to run his errands at night, while the others were up and awake. Until recently, Philip had insisted on going with him, to stand guard, but after

Wade had blown one hole in Julian's chest and a second in his stomach on their last mission to England, Philip hadn't been quite such a mother hen anymore.

And Wade carried his gun everywhere.

Tonight he was coming home with a full grocery bag in one arm and a bag of Science Diet dog food in the other. He had no idea what Mr. Boo might prefer, but he had a feeling the dog wouldn't be too picky.

Strolling down the quiet street in front of the church, he shifted the dog food slightly to free one hand, and he'd just reached out and opened the wrought-iron gate leading into the garden when a voice sounded from behind him.

"Hey, man, any spare change?"

Letting go of the open gate, Wade turned. A down-on-his-luck type had appeared from nowhere and was standing right behind him. The man wore baggy pants and a shabby coat and was badly in need of a shower. His eyes were bloodshot, and Wade felt sorry for him. Normally, if Wade had cash, he never minded helping out the homeless, but tonight he'd used his debit card for the groceries.

"I'm sorry," he said, "I don't have any cash." Most of the food in his bag had to be boiled or chopped or fried to be of any use, so he wasn't sure about offering that either. "But I come this way a lot. Try me again."

He started to turn away, and the man said, "No," in a surprisingly hard voice.

Startled, Wade turned just in time to see something flicker across the man's bloodshot eyes. Without waiting, Wade reached out telepathically and slipped into the man's mind. A wall of rage and violence hit him so hard he almost backed up. He was normally a good judge of character, and this man had seemed so calm. Reading beyond the surface emotions, Wade saw that he was an alcoholic who hadn't had a drink in two days, and he was desperate.

"Just give me your wallet," the man said.

Still reading his mind, Wade then realized he had a knife hidden in his right hand. Of course, Wade was carrying a loaded automatic pistol under his jacket, strapped to his chest, but he'd need to drop either the dog food or the bag of groceries to pull the gun, and that would leave him wide open for a few seconds—long enough to get stabbed.

"Do it," the man ordered.

Wade didn't care about his wallet, but the rolling rage in the man's mind made him careful. He wasn't certain that just passing his wallet over would be the end of this.

"Okay," he said. "Just let me put one of these bags down."

His mind was still racing. He wasn't exactly afraid. Anyone who'd face down Julian wouldn't tremble too much over a homeless alcoholic, but the last thing he wanted to do was to shoot someone right here in front of the church. He didn't want the police anywhere near their home.

"Now!" the man said, his voice breaking this time.

"All right. Take it easy."

Wade began lowering the grocery bag, still wondering how this was going to play out, when a low rumble sounded from his left side.

He looked down.

Mr. Boo stepped out of the open gate. His jowls trembled, and his fangs were bare, and his low growling turned into a snarl as he stared up at the unknown man. Even though his ribs still showed, he no longer looked quite so thin. He looked more like ninety pounds of pissed-off bone and muscle.

The desperate man took a step back, and Boo stepped after him, snarling louder.

A second later, the man turned and bolted down the street.

Wade just stood there, looking down at the dog's tattered ear. Boo stopped growling.

"Not that I'm not grateful, but how did you get out of the church?" Wade asked. Then he peered through the darkness to see Maxim coming toward him from the front doors. "Did you let him out?"

Maxim nodded. "He ask me."

"He asked you to let him out?

Maxim nodded again. "He sense a bad thing out here, and he likes you. You feed him when he very hungry. When he sad."

That last word made Wade feel like he'd been punched in the stomach. But the dog had sensed something and then asked Maxim to let him outside . . . to offer protection.

"I get it," Wade said quickly. He hefted the bag of

dog food over his shoulder. "Come on, Boo. Let's see if you like this stuff. You can't keep eating up all the hamburger."

Once again, Mr. Boo just grunted and followed him into the church.

Eleisha was curled up against Philip on the living room couch. He'd been so unsettled by her forcing his memories to surface that she'd brought him out here and put *Hard Boiled* into the DVD player. For some reason, John Woo films always seemed to make Philip feel better.

Maxim had watched the first few scenes with them, and then he'd gotten up rather abruptly to take Mr. Boo outside. Eleisha assumed that Boo simply needed a little trip outdoors, and so she didn't ask any questions—though she hoped he would not ruin any of her rosebushes.

But in what seemed like an awfully short time, she heard voices and footsteps on the stairs, and then Wade, Boo, and Maxim all emerged into the living room, passing through toward the kitchen. Wade was carrying groceries and a big bag of dog food.

"Come on, you," he was saying to Boo. "I hope you like this."

She wondered if she should try to get him off alone and tell him what she'd seen in Philip's mind. She didn't want to tell him right in front of Philip or the others.

On the surface, this night felt normal. Rose was in the kitchen, at the table, drinking tea and reading a novel, and Eleisha could now hear her speaking softly to Wade as he carried in the groceries. Maxim was speaking to Mr. Boo in one- or two-word sentences, and Philip was watching an action movie.

Yes, everything . . . seemed normal. But she couldn't help feeling that they were all on the edge of something, and it wouldn't take much to push them forward into motions that could not be stopped.

As if on cue, the air shimmered and Seamus materialized near the kitchen archway, but he was facing Eleisha.

"I found them," he said immediately. "Two of them."

Five minutes later, they were all gathered around the table in the kitchen listening to Seamus' bizarre account of what he'd witnessed in the Seattle manor. Eleisha almost couldn't believe what she was hearing.

"You don't really think this vampire was speaking to a ghost, do you?" Rose asked. "About a faked will?"

"Why not?" Seamus answered. "You talk to a ghost all the time."

"That's different," she said, sounding slightly put out.

Wade glanced at Eleisha and held her gaze for a few seconds. "Which one did you say got dizzy?" he asked Seamus.

"Richard . . . the one trying to cheat his brother and sister."

"Then it's more likely that this Christian was just reading his mind and then telepathically sending information to his partner."

Seamus blinked his transparent eyelids. "Oh, I'd not thought of that."

Eleisha didn't blame him. Seamus wasn't telepathic, and he was such an honest soul that a scam might not occur to him. Frankly, the idea shocked Eleisha, too— but that didn't mean Wade's guess was wrong.

Philip was leaning up against the kitchen counter with his arms crossed. "Seamus, what did he look like, this Christian?"

"Tall, slender . . . with a young face, like maybe he'd been turned when he was twenty or so, but his hair was steel gray."

Neither Philip nor Eleisha even glanced at each other, but in the moment, they both knew. They were dealing with an elder, and not just an elder, but one who was powerful enough that Angelo had called on him for help.

"The girl was lovely," Seamus went on without being asked, "small like Eleisha but with lighter, straighter hair. He called her Ivory."

"And they work as a team?" Rose seemed to ponder aloud. "I wonder how that came about."

"Well, we'll have to go and talk to them," Wade said. "Tell them about the underground. Invite them to join us. I'm sure they've been on their own for a long time."

Yes, that was true, but after these "report" meetings, once Seamus had found something, an uncomfortable scene inevitably followed regarding who would go and who would stay. With Maxim in the mix, that issue had become more complicated.

As if reading Eleisha's face, Rose said quickly, "I'll stay with Maxim. We'll be fine here."

Whether or not they'd be safe was still debatable.

"Stay?" Maxim said, suddenly alarmed. "What mean?"

Was he asking what Rose meant?

Eleisha tried to answer as best she could. "Maxim, we need to go away for just a little while. But Rose will stay here with you."

His alarm grew, and his dark eyes widened. "Leisha . . . Wade go away? No! No go away!" He started shifting his weight between his feet.

Eleisha jumped up and moved to him. "It's all right. Seamus found two other vampires like you once were. They're alone, and they don't know we exist. We're just going to go and get them . . . or at least see if they want to come here."

His body stilled, and he looked into Eleisha's face. "Like me?"

That seemed to get through to him, but it made her feel guilty. He was so grateful that they'd found him and brought him here that he would not begrudge them going after someone else. However, the situation of this Christian and Ivory didn't sound anything like Maxim's.

Suddenly, watching Maxim, Wade seemed to waver. "I don't know, Eleisha. I need to come with you, but if

I'm gone, who's going to watch over them during the day?"

Well, what was the alternative? Take them both along? What would Maxim do all night in a hotel room in Seattle? And would he and Rose be any safer there in the thick of things?

"Not worry," Maxim said quietly. He pointed down to the dog. "Mr. Boo be awake. He protect Rose during day." He paused. "You go and get vampires who are alone."

While he did not look happy about the situation, he seemed to understand the importance of this mission. But Eleisha didn't think Wade would agree to letting a tattered old pit bull take his place.

To her surprise, Wade was watching the dog thoughtfully, and he nodded. "Okay. I think he can protect you."

"Good," Philip said, cutting off the discussion, but his voice was strained. "Then it's just you, me, and Eleisha. Let's get packed."

Poor Philip. Too many times now, one of these missions had led him right down a memory lane he desperately wanted to avoid, but he always kept on going.

"I'll book the plane tickets," Eleisha said.

Philip shook his head. "No, Seattle's only a three-hour drive. It'll take us longer than that to get through airport security. Just rent us a car."

She wanted to groan but stifled herself. Seattle was only a three-hour drive if Philip drove eighty miles an hour the entire way . . . and she knew he would insist on driving.

But she wanted to make this trip as easy on him as possible. "Okay," she agreed.

Wade didn't bother to stifle his groan.

Julian was alone in his study. He was agitated—and he hated feeling agitated. A part of him longed to drag one of his new housemaids off alone and feed on her. But he managed to refrain.

He'd looked through *The Makers and Their Children* three times in the past few hours, searching for any hint, any reference to the name Christian, but he'd uncovered nothing.

Now he was just pacing back and forth in front of the fireplace, as there was no telling when Mary might have something to report.

To his surprise, the air shimmered and she materialized by the table.

Although he rarely noticed her demeanor, she seemed agitated to him as well. Her transparent magenta hair glowed in the firelight.

"Seamus found two of them in Seattle," she blurted out, "running some kind of scam together."

Julian froze, taking in only a few details of her rushed words.

"Stop," he ordered. "What do you mean 'two of them'?"

Her eyes narrowed, and the hatred he'd come to

expect glinted out. "Two vampires, a man and a woman, named Christian and Ivory. They're both in Seattle."

"Are either of them telepathic?"

"Yeah . . . or I think so. Seamus was there, so I couldn't stay long or get too close. He's sensing me pretty fast these days. From what I picked up, this Christian does séances, but Wade thinks he's just reading minds, not really talking to ghosts." She paused. "So that means he's probably old, right? He's the elder Eleisha was talking about?"

Julian turned away. Yes, he knew by now they were dealing at least one elder: the man. He didn't recognize the name Ivory either, so he wasn't sure about the woman, but earlier, Mary had recounted a verbatim statement from Eleisha. *At least we know. We know there was an elder named Christian . . . who wasn't listed in the book.*

Somehow, this Christian had escaped being listed in Angelo's book.

"So are you buying a plane ticket or what?" Mary asked harshly.

Startled by her manner, he turned back and glared at her. "Excuse me?"

"I don't know what you're waiting for. You've got a target and a location. Get your sword and buy a plane ticket. Let's get this done."

For the first time since swearing to her absurd bargain, he felt uneasy. He'd thought that once she was working with him again, once some time had passed, she'd realize how fortunate she was to be on this plane, in the world of the living. Not only had that not happened, but she actually seemed to want him to accelerate the hunt.

Well . . . in truth, she was right. There was nothing left to wait for.

"Meet me in Seattle," he said coldly.

"Where?"

"The Grand Hyatt."

Without another word, she blinked out. Still feeling uneasy, he headed for his room to pack and get his sword.

chapter four

SEATTLE, WASHINGTON

As Eleisha nearly fell through the door into a suite at the Renaissance Hotel in Seattle, she was just glad for the prospect of not moving for a few minutes, and she dropped onto the closest couch.

"Good idea," Wade groaned, dropping beside her. "I have to use the bathroom, and I don't even want to get up."

Philip came in behind them, set down his suitcase, and closed the door.

"What's wrong?"

Eleisha couldn't bring herself to look at him, even though he wasn't to blame for all the difficulties she'd been through tonight. Back at the church, they'd managed to pack quickly enough, but then Wade spent nearly forty-five minutes going over several lists with Rose regarding how to properly care for Mr. Boo and Tiny Tuesday . . . down to his preferred method for cleaning the cat box and how to warm a bowl of wet cat food for ten seconds in the microwave. By the end of this, Philip was ready to jerk him out the front door.

Once Philip decided to go someplace, he had a penchant for wanting to get there as fast as possible.

Eleisha had been able to find only one car-rental facility open this late at night, and they'd had to take a taxi to reach it. By the time Philip was finally behind the wheel, he was in so much of a hurry that he'd raced straight to Interstate 5 and then gone eighty-five miles an hour all the way from Portland to Seattle while Eleisha clutched the backseat, expecting to hear police sirens at any moment. He'd refused to stop for anything, including a bathroom break for Wade.

By some miracle, they'd not been pulled over, and at least for now they were safe inside a hotel room. But dawn was not far away, and although there wasn't much they could do tonight, she couldn't help pondering their next step.

"So where do we start?" Wade asked aloud, as if reading her thoughts. He hadn't been reading her thoughts—or she would have felt him—so her face must have been an open book.

"What do you mean?" Philip asked. "We've got an address. We just go and talk to them tomorrow night. These are not like Maxim or Simone. They live in secrecy among wealthy mortals. They would not do anything to jeopardize their position."

Eleisha watched him as he finished. That was quite a speech for Philip. He'd been unusually quiet, even for him, since that ugly scene in their bedroom earlier, but he seemed to be recovering. At least she hoped so. As yet, she'd not been able to tell Wade what she'd seen in Philip's memories.

"Well . . . yes," Wade answered. "But I already checked, and Vera's phone number isn't listed. Seamus said the house was in a wealthy neighborhood *and* it was heavily gated. If we just drive up and introduce ourselves at the gate, no one's going to let us in. And even if we just climb over, we have no idea what kind of security is in place. If Christian decides he doesn't like us, he'd be well within his rights to suggest having us arrested for breaking and entering."

Philip frowned. Normally gates and locks didn't stop him from doing anything he wanted, but perhaps even he could see the sense in what Wade was saying. And this wasn't like "the old days," when Philip would just kill any arresting police officers without a second thought.

"Besides," Eleisha put in, "if we're trying to win Christian and Ivory's trust, the last thing we want to do is break into the house where they're staying. No, we'll need to arrange a proper invitation . . . or get them to come out and meet us somewhere."

"How?" Wade asked.

The air beside the couch shimmered, and Seamus materialized. But his normally vivid colors were faded, and Eleisha could see he was exhausted. "You need to get back to Rose," she said.

"I've got a phone number," he answered. "I was just at Vera's house. Of course the vampires are still up, but so is Vera. I overheard her leaving a message on someone's answering service, and she gave her home number. You could try calling and asking for Christian. If you can get him to come to the phone, maybe he'll listen to you."

Eleisha looked at Wade. "It's a worth a try," she said.

He nodded. "You do it."

Suddenly nervous, she stood up. Everything just seemed to be moving too fast. She hadn't planned on launching into making contact tonight, but if she could get him to listen, perhaps they could go and see him in person tomorrow night.

"Okay," she said, glancing at her bag with her cell phone inside. She wished she knew more about the situation. Her experience with the socially affluent was pretty limited. Before picking up the bag, she turned to Philip. "Do you know . . . I mean, what exactly are Christian and Ivory doing there? Why would someone like Vera Olivier invite them to come and stay at her mansion and let them use it as a base to hold séances?"

He unbuttoned his long coat, dropped it on a chair, and unstrapped his machete. "As an attraction to others of her class," he said. "She's probably a widow, lonely, with few attractions of her own. But now she's the toast of the town, with other rich friends banging on her door. Christian needs access to the wealthy. She provides it. He provides company and entertainment for her."

Wade was listening with an intense expression. "So . . . Christian and Ivory are basically high-paid companions?"

Philip nodded. "In a way. It sounds like they earn much of their own money, but they owe their position to Vera. They'll need to keep her happy."

"Huh," Eleisha said thoughtfully. What an odd arrangement. But at least she had a better idea of the situation now. Reaching down into her bag, she pulled out her cell. "Seamus, what's the number?"

He wasn't looking well at all, and as this soon as this phone call was over, she was sending him home.

He gave her the number, and she punched it in.

After three rings, a prim-sounding male voice answered. "Ms. Olivier's residence. How may I help you?"

Suddenly Eleisha's mind went blank. He sounded like a butler of some kind . . . and so superior!

"May I please speak to Mr. Lefevre?" she asked.

The line was quiet for just a second. "Mr. Lefevre does not accept calls."

Grasping for anything, anything at all, she blurted out, "Tell him I know Julian Ashton. He'll want to speak to me."

This was a gamble. Threatening Christian with Julian's name would hardly earn his trust, but she couldn't think of anything else to get him to come to the phone.

Another quiet second passed. "Wait one moment."

Relief flooded her stomach, but it vanished when a voice with a thick French accent came on the line and said, "Who is this?"

Again, she was at a loss. This was just all happening too fast. "I'm a friend," she said. "I'm like you. I'm here in Seattle with Philip Branté. He's standing right beside me. We need to speak with you, in person."

"With Philip . . ." The shock in his voice was profound, but then he trailed off and his voice dropped low. "Whoever you are, stay away from me. Do not call this number again or I'll have you traced and arrested. If you come near me or this house, I will have you arrested. Do *not* call here again."

Click.

He'd hung up.

She looked at her cell, then at Wade, and shook her head. "He told me not to call again. I don't know what to try next."

It wasn't as if they were a crack investigative team with a plan B ready at hand. They had a tendency to do almost everything by the seat of their pants.

But of them all, Seamus seemed the most frustrated. His eyes narrowed. "I might have an idea," he said.

They all turned to him.

"While I was there tonight," he said, "I heard that Vera's arranged for another séance tomorrow. I need to go to Portland now and be near Rose, but I'll come back tomorrow night. If Christian wants to call up a ghost, maybe we should give him a ghost. Maybe we should keep on giving him a ghost at his fancy little parties until he agrees to talk to you."

Eleisha shook her head in confusion, but Seamus just smiled.

Less than an hour later, just before dawn, Philip was covering the windows of the suite's one bedroom with spare blankets, making sure no light would come in. Out in the main room, he could hear Eleisha speaking softly to Wade.

"Be sure to order yourself something to eat," she was saying. "You're so good about feeding the animals, but sometimes you forget to feed yourself."

"I will."

"You'll be all right here on the couch?"

"I'm fine, Eleisha. Go to bed."

Her light footsteps approached, and she came inside and closed the bedroom door. Philip turned to her. She was still wearing the same long skirt and little red T-shirt, and this struck him as the only proof that just a single night had passed since she'd walked out to find them arguing over the fate of Mr. Boo.

So much had happened.

He dropped into a chair, took off his boots, and pulled his shirt over his head. Then he watched her go to the bed. She seemed so small and fragile. Her mass of dark blond hair fell in a somewhat tangled mess all the way down her back and over her shoulder. She tried pushing some of it out of her face.

No one in his memory had ever loved him, cared for him, looked at him the way she did. He wouldn't be able to stand it if that ever changed.

"I'm too tired to bother with a nightgown," she said, but she seemed to just be filling the silence.

Standing up, he moved to join her and sat down on the bed, scooting backward to lean against the pillows at the headboard. All night long, he'd felt ready to explode, and he'd kept it inside. Now he couldn't wait any longer.

"Look at me," he said.

She was sitting on the bed, taking off her sandals, and she jerked slightly in surprise, turning her head to look at him.

He'd wanted to catch her in a moment of surprise, off guard, and he locked her eyes with his, seeking, searching for any hint of revulsion over what she'd seen in his mind earlier. He couldn't stand the sight of himself like that . . . screaming, mad, covered in blood. How could he expect her to stand it? To see him the same way now?

"What?" she asked instantly, crawling closer. "What's wrong?" But then she just seemed to know. "Oh, Philip," she said. "Everything's all right."

Leaning in, she pressed her mouth against his, and he was too overwrought, too relieved, to even kiss her back. Instead, he grabbed her, using both his arms to hold her down against his chest.

Maybe it was all right. Maybe she honestly didn't

see him any differently. He found that hard to believe, but it was possible.

"Too tight," she murmured.

The sun must be rising, as her eyelids were fluttering. He lessened his hold just slightly but kept her pinned against his chest.

"Sleep now," he said.

chapter five

The following night, Julian landed in Seattle a few hours past dusk. He'd been unable to arrange a flight out of Cardiff the night before, so he'd had no choice to wait. Fortunately, traveling west, he was moving backward in time, and he'd managed to catch an early flight out of Wales, landing with nearly a whole night ahead of him in Seattle.

As a result, he was not too displeased at the one-night delay. Eleisha certainly couldn't have accomplished much yet either.

After taking a taxi to the Grand Hyatt on Pine Street, he checked into his room quickly and took his own luggage up to the fifth floor. He hadn't even bothered reserving a suite and just took the first room he was offered. He didn't care about accommodations on this trip.

Using his key card, he stepped inside and barely glanced around. The room was mundane but service-able, decorated in cliché shades of tan, brown, and burnt orange. A sliding glass door near a small desk provided a view of the city lights. He paid no attention to the view. Instead, he dropped his suitcase and the long cardboard box containing his sword onto the bed.

"Mary," he ordered, "come here now."

Since he had brought her over from the gray plane, he had the power to call her to his side whenever he wanted.

The air shimmered and she appeared abruptly, with an almost surprised expression at having been pulled so suddenly from wherever she'd been. But she recovered quickly and cocked one transparent eyebrow.

"You rang?" she asked dryly.

He'd have given almost anything to strike her right then, but he kept his voice controlled. "Do you have an exact location yet?"

"For who?"

Anger flowed through him, and he clenched his jaw, but she just kept talking.

"You mean Christian?" she asked. "No, you didn't tell me to locate him. I figured you'd want to me to stay on Philip and Eleisha. They're over at the Renaissance Hotel on Madison . . . which is kind of close if Seamus decides to come back and do a search for you."

That got his attention. "What? Where is Seamus? I thought he'd be exhausted by now."

"He is. Eleisha sent him home."

Some of his anger faded. Perhaps she'd been right to stay on top of Eleisha.

"Find Christian," he said coldly. "Now."

She shrugged. "That was my plan as soon as you got here and I filled you in." She started to dematerialize, but he stopped her. "Wait." He was hungry and couldn't hold off another night. "I may be going out. If you come back and I'm gone, just wait for me here. I shouldn't be long."

"Going out?" she asked. "Where? I thought we were going to get this job done tonight."

The urge to strike her flooded back. Who did she think she was? She was his servant.

"Find Christian," he said.

Glaring at him, she blinked out.

He stood there a moment, trying to calm himself. Feeding would help. With that thought, he broke open the long cardboard box, took out his sword, strapped it to his belt, and buttoned his long black coat over the top.

Then he left his room, took the elevator down, and headed back outside. He'd never hunted in Seattle before, but he'd memorized a layout of the city, and he didn't need a taxi. From Pine Street, it was an easy walk to the Elliott Bay waterfront. Water was always the best place to dump a body.

Earlier, he'd spotted a ferry terminal on his map of the city, so he made his way in that direction, walking down the dark streets ignoring everyone around him. None of the homeless people sitting on corners asked him for spare change.

He kept moving toward the bay, but as he approached the water, he stayed on the outskirts of the ferry terminal. He'd read that several arrivals and departures ran all the way through midnight, and he had no desire to find himself among a line of slowly moving cars. However, all such places were built organically over time, and the outskirts always contained old docks and piers and nooks and crannies and foolish people walking alone in the darkness.

That had not changed in a hundred years.

Once he'd reached a place that seemed isolated enough and yet was still close to a concrete overhang above the bay, he kept to the shadows but glanced to the right upon hearing voices.

"No!" a girl was shouting angrily. "I'm not just going back to your place again. You said we were going to *do* something tonight."

Julian focused, and through the darkness, he could just make out two people facing each other in an argument. His sight sharpened. A young man in a jean jacket had hold of a girl's arm. "Jesus, Brittney, are you going start that again? I told you I don't have any money. What is it you want to do?"

She jerked her arm away. "Nothing!" she shouted at him, walking away. "Just go home."

She was walking straight toward Julian.

The young man started after her, and then he stopped. "I'll call you tomorrow."

She didn't answer and kept walking, pounding the concrete with angry steps. There was no one else in sight, and the young man turned away, going in the other direction.

Julian slipped between two shabby buildings to wait. His routine was nearly always the same. He varied it only slightly based on the situation, but he often hunted near water—a river or the sea. Waiting there in between the buildings, he almost allowed her to walk past, and then he turned on his gift.

Fear.

Waves of fear flowed outward, surrounding her, engulfing her.

He could see her out there, and she stopped, her eyes widening.

"In here," he said.

The girl turned her head toward him. She looked about sixteen, wearing boots and a short tank-style dress. She was slightly heavy, with dark, curly hair. She wore too much makeup, which he didn't like. It tasted bad if he got any of it in his mouth, but at the moment, he was too hungry to care.

"Come in here now," he said, letting more fear seep out, until she was too terrified not to do as he ordered.

Occasionally, strong-willed people fought him at this point, but she already seemed completely lost in his gift. With her round face twisted in fear, she walked straight to him.

The second she was close enough, he grabbed her arm and jerked her farther into the darkness between the buildings. Then he slammed her up against a wall. Her mouth moved as if to scream, but she was too lost in fear to make a sound. Her expression pleased him.

He didn't hesitate and bit down hard just below her jaw, holding her tightly while she bucked and struggled. She smelled of cheap perfume and drugstore hair spray.

But the blood tasted good in his mouth, and just as he began to swallow mouthfuls of it, he turned off his gift. He always did at this point, reveling in the feel of his victim's natural terror as reality set in and she knew she was about to die.

She gasped and struggled harder, trying wildly to push him away, but he was drinking hard and fast, and soon she grew weaker and he was forced to hold her up.

It wasn't difficult.

He knew that other vampires saw the memories of their victims, pieces of the mortal's entire life, while feeding. He did not. He had no telepathic ability at all.

Her heart stopped beating, and he regretted the experience being over so quickly, but he felt sated and strong again.

Still holding her up with one hand, he pulled back to look at her. Her throat was torn and her head lolled forward. Blood ran freely down onto her dress. The waves of the bay were strong, with an undertow, so he decided he didn't need to weight the body.

After wiping his mouth to make sure no traces of blood remained, he looked out to check if the way was clear. Picking her up with one hand, he carried her rapidly to the edge of the concrete overhang. Then he dropped her body into the bay.

Without a glance downward, he turned and headed back toward his hotel. By the time he reached Second Avenue, he'd forgotten what she looked like.

Christian Lefevre stood in Vera Olivier's sitting room with a glass of red wine in his hand. His wavy, steel gray hair was tucked behind his ears, exposing the gold ring in his ear—a touch of the gypsy for effect. But he was dressed in dark slacks and a black sport coat. As always, his expression was carefully constructed to show a mix of compassion and mysterious passivity.

The normal routine was for Vera to serve any guests a lavish dinner in the main dining room and then bring them in here, where they would finally be joined by Christian and Ivory—thus building upon any expectations or anticipation.

Christian had walked into the room only a few moments before, but he'd already managed to do a surface read of the client's thoughts, and he was bored before the séance even started.

Tonight's guest was an investment banker named Jonathon Renault, who'd recently taken a business trip to London. His wife had begged him to stay home—saying she had a feeling something bad was going to happen. He'd laughed off her "feeling" and gone off on his trip, and while he was away, she'd been killed in a car accident. Now his guilt was overwhelming him, and he wanted to tell his wife how sorry he was. He wanted to be forgiven.

Just thinking about it, Christian tried to hold back a yawn. It was cliché beyond words. Some mortal charlatan pretending to look into a crystal ball could handle this one.

"Did you enjoy your dinner, Mr. Renault?" Ivory was asking politely. She looked lovely tonight, in a slinky red silk gown that was so long it hid her small feet. No matter what happened, she was always good with the clients, her expression carefully maintained. The only time it ever slipped was when she accidently looked at Christian and a hint of poison flowed out.

She hated him.

Since there was nothing to be done about that, he normally didn't give it much thought, but tonight he was having a hard time keeping his thoughts in check. The phone call from last night was still bothering him—and he knew it would keep bothering him. The shock of a girl's voice saying she knew Julian Ashton . . . and that Philip Branté was standing beside her had shaken him to his core. Those nightmares had been over a long time ago.

He wanted them to stay buried.

The more rational part of him knew she had to be lying. Philip could not have survived, and the girl could not be a vampire. To the best of Christian's knowledge, Julian had killed them all. So who was she? Probably a mortal servant of Julian's, maybe a housemaid with an eye for an opportunity. She'd learned something, heard something, and she'd probably been planning to blackmail Christian—threaten him with giving his location away to Julian.

But another voice inside him wondered how that was possible. Julian didn't know his name, didn't even know he existed, so how could some mortal servant ever have made a connection?

He didn't know.

"Christian, darling," Vera said, coming toward him with an empty martini glass in her hand. "Shall we begin?"

He smiled. "Of course."

Tonight Vera wore an orange caftan with gold inlay and six strings of pearls around her neck. Countless silver bracelets jangled on both her wrists. She was short and stocky, and from his perspective she was overpaying her hairstylist by a wide margin, but she was necessary, and he knew how to keep women like her happy.

Since Mr. Renault had come alone, Vera had engaged her cook and her butler, Simmons—who also functioned as her driver—to fill the necessary spots. The table was so large that at least six people were required to be able to join hands.

"Ivory?" he said.

She tried not to look at him as she turned and glided toward the table, red silk moving about her feet. Perhaps she knew her eyes gave too much away.

But really, this entire affair was too tedious. If the money hadn't already been transferred into his account, he might have pleaded a headache and begged off. But that wouldn't do either. He and Ivory were there for a reason—for this reason—and they were being well paid.

Mr. Renault sat down across from Christian. Strain and sorrow had caused deep creases around his eyes.

"Who is it that I am calling from the other side?" Christian asked. He normally made a point of being told almost nothing before meeting the client for the séance. That made the whole event seem even more miraculous.

"My wife, Debra."

Christian forced his expression to exude controlled compassion. "I will try for you. The spirits often speak to me. Do you know precisely what you wish to ask her?"

Mr. Renault nodded. "Yes."

Christian instantly entered his mind again, but going deeper now, seeing images of an attractive woman in her forties, with cropped auburn hair and a warm smile. All Christian had to do was get Mr. Renault to think of the words he needed to hear, and then Christian could have Ivory parrot them back. This wouldn't take long.

Vera had the servants sit, and then everyone joined hands. Even after nearly a week, this room still appalled Christian. It was just so . . . overstuffed. But he'd always known that real money and good taste did not necessarily go hand in hand. Poor Vera was lonely, and perhaps all the things taking up space made her feel less so.

He closed his eyes. "Debra Renault, I call to you from the other side. Hear me. Come to us now."

An incredibly clear image flashed through Mr. Renault's mind. Debra was dressed in jeans and a cable-knit sweater. She was near tears and seemed to be trying not to grab her husband's arm.

Unfortunately, due to his scattered state of mind—over that unsettling phone call—Christian had not prepared himself for the onslaught of emotion, and so Mr. Renault's guilt and sorrow suddenly hit him hard. He had to fight to keep his eyes closed.

What's wrong? Ivory flashed.

Nothing. Stay with me.

"Debra, is that you?" he said aloud. "Are you with us?"

But just as he finished asking the question, Vera's cook screamed. "Ahhhhhhhhhhhhhhh!"

The sound was loud and long, and then Vera gasped and Mr. Renault was shouting. "What in the hell . . . ?"

"Who disturbs the peace of the dead?" shouted a deep male voice with a heavy Scottish accent.

Christian opened his eyes.

To his complete shock, a transparent, six-foot-tall Scottish Highlander was floating four or five inches above the floor on the other side of the room—near a collection of Egyptian statues.

The cook was still screaming, and Mr. Renault was on his feet now.

"That is not Debra!"

"Who disturbs the dead?" the ghost shouted again,

and he sailed up into midair, flying over the table and swooshing toward Christian. On instinct, Christian ducked, and Ivory dashed off her chair to one side.

"You will pay!" the ghost yelled, turning in midair and swooshing back again.

Vera jumped up so quickly she knocked the candelabra over, spreading hot candle wax across the table. Even the stoic Simmons looked alarmed as he watched the Scottish ghost flying around the room.

The cook went on screaming, and Mr. Renault's face had gone quite red.

Christian had absolutely no idea what to do.

Once Mary reached the correct area near Puget Sound, she had no trouble zeroing in on two undead signatures, and within moments, she'd located the mansion.

Wow, she thought, taking in the exterior. *Fancy.*

From what she could sense out here, both vampires appeared to be located near the center of the house on the main floor, so she blinked out and rematerialized in what appeared to be a guest room directly above them.

Looking around, she couldn't help thinking, *wow,* again, only for different reasons. The outside of the house seemed so regal. This room didn't fit her expectations. It was just stuffed with tables, brocade-covered settees, vases, huge brass lamps, and paintings covering every square inch of the walls, and nothing seemed to go with anything else.

She didn't look around too long, however, and floated downward in a horizontal position so she could pass through the floor and allow just her face to be able to peek through the ceiling downward. People were sitting around a table with their hands joined, and she'd just started to take stock of everyone when a third undead presence hit her senses . . . only this one was different, less distinct and more ethereal.

Not a vampire.

A ghost. She could feel the difference.

A second later, Seamus materialized in the sitting room for everyone to see!

"Who disturbs the peace of the dead?" he shouted.

She nearly gasped aloud, but someone down below was screaming, and people were shouting, and candle wax was flying, and Seamus was sailing around the room, diving at a pretentious-looking vampire with a young face and steel gray hair.

Mary missed some of the shouting and then heard Seamus yell, "You will pay!"

What in the hell was he doing? Suddenly Mary found herself fighting not to laugh out loud. He had almost everyone in the room either furious or scattering or screaming in panic. She had nothing at all against Seamus. In spite of the fact that he worked for the other side, he'd been kind to her once when she'd badly needed a bit of kindness.

She was seized by an urge to blink down there and help him. Between the two of them, they could cause quite a scene.

But she held off. That wasn't her purpose here.

Seamus floated directly in front of the male vampire's face and said, "Do not disturb the peace of the dead again."

Then he vanished.

Mary still couldn't believe he'd just exposed himself like that. Seamus had seemed so . . . so reserved. He was clearly up to something. But what?

Down below, the scene had degraded into both vampires trying to calm everyone else down, and then Mary started wondering if Seamus had sensed her as clearly as she'd sensed him. She had a location and a visual confirmation of the vampires. Maybe she should just get out of here.

"Mary," said a deep voice from behind her.

She floated up swiftly and whirled to see him floating near the door. He had sensed her. He wasn't angry. His expression was almost sad as he gazed at her. God, he was big. She took in the sight of his shaggy brown hair and the blue and yellow plaid over his shoulder.

"Is Julian here?" he asked.

She knew she should blink out instantly, but instead she answered. "Yes."

"Don't tell him anything. Don't tell him where we are."

"I have to."

"Mary," he said again, still sad but floating toward her.

This time she vanished, and when she rematerialized in the courtyard outside, she waited just long enough to make sure he didn't follow.

He didn't.

For some reason, she was slightly disappointed that he hadn't even tried.

A half hour later, Christian finally slipped inside his room and closed the door, leaning back against the frame, trying to figure out what had just taken place and if he'd handled the damage control adequately.

Although Mr. Renault may have presented a tedious spiritual request, he was an important figure in Vera's circle, and Christian had done some very fast talking about "crossed messages" and "an unfortunate receiver" somehow intercepting Christian's call to the other side. All the while, he was reading Renault's thoughts and reveling in relief that the man was not ready to give up, but was still quite angry—and disappointed.

Christian assured him that such a thing had never happened before, and Vera rushed in to help support this claim. In the end, they rescheduled. Christian said he could not go on tonight, and Renault had agreed.

However, alone in the quiet of his room, he closed his eyes, and the shaky feeling at his core was beginning to expand. First that unsettling phone call . . . and now this? As he had no idea what had truly transpired tonight, he had no idea how to stop it from ever happening again.

A real ghost? Is that what they'd all really seen?

"Over here," said a deep voice with a Scottish accent.

Christian opened his eyes. The tall, transparent

ghost was floating beside the bed. He looked as calm as a summer breeze, and Christian wondered if the emotional outburst in the sitting room had been a ruse.

"That wasn't very nice," he said, hoping to buy a few minutes in order to take control here and get the upper hand.

"We tried being nice," the ghost answered. "Eleisha phoned you. You hung up on her."

Christian froze. The girl who'd called him last night and this ghost were connected?

"I swear on my honor she's not working for Julian," the ghost went on. "But she needs to talk to you. Tonight. You get Ivory and borrow a car from Vera's garage. Go to McMenamin's Pub on Roy Street. But you have to bring Ivory. She needs to hear what Eleisha has to say."

The ghost knew Ivory's name and was making demands of her as well? This was too much.

"Forgive me," Christian said, allowing a small bit of the anger he felt to seep into his voice. "But your honor means nothing to me, and I'm not going anywhere."

"If you don't, I'll start showing up at every séance you hold, and I'll make that little show tonight seem tame. Just try me."

Anger began shifting into real anxiety. Christian was cornered—and he never let himself get cornered. As an experiment, he reached out with his mind, trying to read the ghost's thoughts, but he found nothing, as if there were no one else in the room.

"She just wants to talk," the ghost said. "I swear."

To his own humiliation, Christian heard himself begin to bargain. "What does she want to tell us? Why can't you tell me yourself?"

The ghost waved a transparent hand in the air dismissively. "Are you going?"

Christian stood there a moment, with his back against the doorframe. He didn't see a choice—at least not yet. "Tell her we'll be there in an hour."

The ghost nodded, watched him for a few seconds as if deciding whether to believe him or not, and then vanished.

Alone again, Christian let his thoughts roll for any way out of this, but nothing came to him, and he wasn't about to just cut his losses here and run. Not now.

Stripping off his sport coat, he walked to the closet and opened it. A sheathed short sword leaned against the back wall. He grabbed it and strapped it to his belt. Then he took a long coat from a hanger and put it on, buttoning it up to his chest.

Ivory, he flashed. *Get up here.*

Upon waking that night in the hotel room bed, Eleisha realized there was really nothing they could do until they'd heard from Seamus—who'd suggested he had some sort of plan. But she wasn't worried yet. They'd only arrived in the wee hours of the previous night, and so this second night in Seattle would be their first full night of action, and she had faith in herself and her companions. They would make progress . . . somehow. After getting dressed, she fussed about with their luggage for a while and then turned on the television and asked Philip to choose a movie from the list of pay-per-view films. About two hours after that, Wade reached over and picked up the room service menu . . . and she was still wondering how she might get him off alone somewhere to tell him what she'd seen in Philip's memories. Before they launched into any kind of action here, he really needed to know, and she still couldn't bring herself to talk about it right in front of Philip. He seemed to be feeling better now, but he'd been so disturbed by the images, she feared that discussing them aloud with Wade might send Philip back inside himself again.

She'd dressed carefully tonight, in a sleeveless linen blouse with brass buttons, a new pair of jeans, and black boots. She'd also pinned part of her hair up and let some of the wisps fall loose.

"I like your hair like that," Philip said, but he always said that if she did anything with her hair.

Wade glanced up from the room service menu. "What do you suppose Seamus is going to do tonight? I'm still trying to figure out what he meant by 'giving' Christian a ghost." He paused. "You don't suppose he's going to . . ."

The air shimmered right next to him, and Seamus materialized, looking exhausted, his colors more transparent than usual.

"I've got him," he said immediately. "I interrupted a séance he was holding and embarrassed him. He and Ivory will meet you at McMenamin's Pub on Roy Street in less than an hour."

Eleisha jumped to her feet. "What?"

Seamus shook his head, as if he had no intention of repeating himself. His colors were still fading, and she could see he needed to get back to Rose. "Just meet him there," he said. "But you need to get there first and keep a close watch. Julian's already here in the city."

Wade sucked up a breath, and Philip jumped up off the couch.

"No," Wade said, shaking his head. "We just got here ourselves. There's no way he could have—"

"Did you see him?" Philip interrupted.

"No," Seamus answered. "I saw Mary, but she told me he's here."

Wade shook his head in confusion. "Who's Mary? And what do you mean she 'told you'?"

Seamus' expression twisted in frustration, almost anger. "The girl ghost. But she doesn't want to serve him. He's holding something over her head. I know he is."

The vehemence in his voice startled Eleisha, but that wasn't her main concern. She was stunned at the news of Julian's arrival. She'd known he would come after them eventually—as he always had before whenever they undertook a mission. But since they'd acted so quickly and rushed up here, she'd assumed they would have time to meet Christian and Ivory, gauge each other, and decide on the next step.

In centuries past, even vampires who didn't live together had at least known *of* each other, kept in contact, written letters . . . and so even if Christian and Ivory didn't want to return to the underground, they deserved to have contact with others of their own kind. Eleisha would never let fear of Julian put a stop to this.

But his arrival here in Seattle changed things. She hadn't even been able to get off a warning to these two vampires.

"How did he learn about our trip here so quickly?" she asked.

"Probably the same way you did," Seamus answered, sounder weaker. "He has his own ghost, Mary."

It bothered her that he was now calling Julian's ghost girl by her first name. When did that happen? And why did he sound so . . . protective?

And what in the world had he done to convince Christian to meet them in a pub?

Seamus' colors wavered, and she stepped forward. He was on the verge of exhaustion. "Go to Rose. We'll meet Christian, but when you're stronger . . . we need to talk."

Without nodding, he vanished. For all the confusion and worry he'd just caused, he *had* succeeded, and a meeting had been set up. But if Julian was here in the city, they needed to go right now.

However, Wade couldn't walk into this meeting without knowing a few things, and there was no time or opportunity to tell him aloud. They'd all made a pact not to enter each other's heads without warning, but she didn't see a choice.

Philip started walking toward his coat, and he was momentarily distracted.

Don't change your expression, she flashed into Wade's

mind. *Just listen. Philip let me read some early memories, from just after he was turned. Christian was in one of them, so he's an elder. That means he knows the laws, he's over two hundred years old, and he somehow escaped Julian.*

The barest flicker passed across Wade's face. But she couldn't read it.

Philip was busy buttoning his coat.

Why didn't you tell me? Wade flashed back.

No time. Philip was too freaked out, and I haven't seen you alone.

"Ready?" Philip asked from the door, watching them both with a slight frown.

Eleisha grabbed her bag from the table. "Ready."

Julian walked back into his hotel room to find Mary there waiting for him.

She stared at him coldly for a few seconds, almost quizzically, as if trying to figure him out. He didn't speak and just waited.

"I've got an address, near the waterfront on Cherry Loop. Two vamps. Both are at home."

"What do they look like?"

"He's got a young face, but his hair's gone totally gray . . . good-looking, nose up in the air like you."

The description meant nothing to Julian. Most of the elders were haughty, but he'd never known one with a young face and gray hair, although this simply supported Eleisha's statement that Christian was an unknown elder who'd managed to avoid being listed in Angelo's book.

"The girl's pretty," she went on, "but kinda typical ... you know, skinny, blond, low-cut dress, blah blah blah." She tilted her head to one side as if considering something.

"And?" he asked.

"I wasn't there very long, but I got the feeling the guy's definitely the one in charge."

Mary's instincts were normally good, so he filed that information away. It suggested that Christian was the oldest of the duo and he'd probably turned the woman himself. But Mary still seemed thoughtful, as if deciding on whether or not to tell him something else. He didn't like that.

"What?"

She shook her head. "That's it. You want me to meet you there?"

He couldn't help feeling that she was holding something back from him. But there wasn't much he could do about it. She gave him the full address, and he didn't bother taking off his coat or his sword while calling to arrange for a car.

chapter six

Eleisha sat in a large corner booth at McMenamin's Pub. She and Wade were on one side, and Philip was on the other. Every inch of the interior of this place seemed to be made from dark wood. Normally she liked wooden décor, but the effect here was slightly suffocating. It was also a good thing two of them couldn't eat food and that Wade wasn't hungry. They'd been sitting for nearly twenty minutes, and no one had even brought them a menu or a glass of water—not that Eleisha gave this much thought.

She was too nervous and kept glancing at the door.

"Maybe I should have waited outside," Philip said. "Kept a lookout for Julian."

Eleisha shook her head. "The streets here are too public. He'd never attack out there. Hopefully, Christian and Ivory will just drive into the parking lot or get out of a cab in front. They should be okay for now."

But no one was talking about what might happen later. What would happen if these two vampires wanted nothing to do with the church or with a community? Eleisha couldn't help a sinking, guilty feeling that she'd just led Julian straight to them. If they agreed to come home to Oregon, she and Philip could protect them both.

But what if they didn't?

In her eagerness to make contact and her desire to "help," she always seemed to assume any vampires they found would *want* to come back to Portland. She should have thought this situation through a little more carefully before just blundering into Seattle like this.

If both these vampire were elders, then they already knew how to feed without killing, and they posed no danger to society. They seemed to have carved a comfortable life for themselves, and they had each other, so they weren't alone.

What if by coming here, Eleisha had done nothing more than put their lives at risk?

She pushed the thought away. No, these two at least deserved to know that others of their kind still existed and were forming a community together. She would never give up on the underground. There was safety in numbers. They had to at least be offered the chance, and that couldn't be done through a letter or a phone call. They had to see Eleisha and Philip in person . . . to have proof that others of their kind still existed.

Glancing over, she saw Philip watching her. He looked especially handsome tonight, in a stark white shirt under his black Armani coat, which was buttoned only high enough to hide his machete. His hair had less product in it than usual, and it hung in red-brown layers past the upturned collar of his coat.

"It will be all right," he said. "Whenever you talk, people listen."

She blinked, not sure how to respond, wishing she were as confident of her own abilities as he was. Wade hadn't said much since they'd left the hotel, but she knew he must be worrying about many of the same things. Leaning back in the booth, he shifted his weight. Tonight he wore his usual faded jeans and old canvas jacket with the plastic buttons—with his gun strapped underneath. Philip hated that canvas jacket and was always trying to replace it, but Wade cared little about fashion.

"Philip," he said. "See if you can flag down a waitress and order me a beer. They pay more attention to you."

Philip appeared to accept this statement as truth, and he looked around for anyone wearing an apron.

Just then, the door opened, and two people stepped in from the night air.

Time seemed to slow as Eleisha took in the sight of them. Ivory appeared to be in her early twenties, wearing a coat over a long red dress. She was lovely, with shining white-blond hair.

But Eleisha didn't look at her for long, as Christian

spotted their booth almost instantly, and he began walking toward them with purpose. Even from across the room, Eleisha could feel the power of his personality as people around him automatically moved out of his way. He looked exactly as she'd seen him in Philip's memories, but she'd forgotten how clear his eyes were, with only the slightest hint of blue.

He stopped at the end of the booth.

His face showed little emotion, but his eyes widened just a bit at the sight of Philip, and then he turned his head to look at Eleisha, drinking in her face. She knew he'd sense her as a vampire, no heartbeat, no scent of warm blood. But he seemed fascinated by her face and hair.

Philip stood up, leaving his side of the booth open, and he motioned for Christian and Ivory to take his place. Then he slid in beside Eleisha.

Both the newcomers sat down, but Christian continued to stare at Eleisha.

"Well," he said in a French accent. "This is unexpected."

Christian had no idea what he might find upon arriving here, but *this* was certainly not it. It took him a few seconds to even recognize Philip, who now looked like he'd just stepped off the cover of *GQ*.

He'd seen Philip only once—screaming, mad, half-naked, and covered in blood.

Christian ignored the mortal in the booth as unimportant.

But the girl . . .

Small boned and pale, she was staring back at him with a kind of vulnerable hope in her hazel eyes. She wanted something from him, and she wanted to please him at the same time. Just the sight of her expression brought excitement bubbling up into his chest. Dark blond wisps of hair hung around a pretty face without a speck of makeup. And she was a vampire. He almost couldn't believe it.

Where had she come from?

She opened her mouth as if trying to speak, and he hung there in anticipation on the edge of his seat, wondering why she'd gone to such lengths to call him here.

"My name is Eleisha," she said finally. Her voice was soft and hesitant. He had the immediate impression she'd be easy to dominate. Under the right circumstances, she'd do anything he told her.

"You know Philip," she went on, as if they were friends meeting for a social engagement, "and this is Wade Sheffield." She gestured to the mortal—who was busy studying Ivory. "He knows . . . everything about us. We can speak freely."

Christian snapped his fingers, and a waitress stopped instantly. "Five glasses of red wine," he ordered.

"Yes, sir."

"I'll have a beer," Wade said.

Christian already didn't like him. For a mortal who was apparently well aware that he was sitting in a booth with four vampires, he seemed far too sure of himself. Philip looked distinctly unsettled, which was good, but how *had* he survived? Christian needed to get control here quickly. He leaned back in the booth.

"You seem to have me at a disadvantage since I don't need to introduce myself or Ivory. You already know our names," he said. "And your ghost might have cost me a good deal of money tonight."

To his further fascination, Eleisha looked chagrined. "I'm so sorry about that. He didn't tell us what he was going to do . . . just that he'd get you to speak to us." Good God. She did sound sorry. She meant it.

Christian smiled. "Well, he managed that much. We're here. What is it you wish to say?"

In truth, he didn't really care at this point.

For so many years now, more years than he could count, Ivory had been desperate to leave him, but he couldn't let her go. The routine he'd developed required the both of them. He needed both a spiritualist and a conduit for the shows to work. They were unique, and their reputation preceded them: Christian Lefevre and his beautiful conduit to the spirits.

But for his conduit, he needed a telepath, another vampire.

In the few moments that he'd sat here, he could already see that Eleisha was far more pliable and far more eager to please than Ivory could ever be. What a relief this girl would be to him. She was not sophisticated, not yet, but he'd trained Ivory once, and he could do it again. With the right makeup and a silk gown, Eleisha could step right into Ivory's place; they could go to a different state and find a new patron, and no one ever would know the difference.

"We've started looking for others . . . like ourselves," Eleisha said, "and we've purchased a large church that we call the underground, where we're living. We were hoping you might want to join us."

As she said this, he stopped thinking about himself and his immediate future, and he actually began to listen. He did need to know why she believed she was here. But she was looking at Ivory now as her soft, hesitant voice rolled on, speaking about this church they'd furnished, about their methods for finding lost vampires—which she called her "mission"—and about their hope of forming a community. She said Wade used a computer to locate possible search locations and Philip provided protection.

Christian had trained Ivory to be silent unless she was handling a client or playing the ethereal conduit, so he was surprised when she asked, "Have you found anyone else?"

Eleisha nodded. "Yes, we found Rose de Spenser in San Francisco, and Maxim Carey in London. They're both living with us at the church."

Christian stiffened. "There are two more of us?"

"Hopefully more than that," she said. "Every time we're on the verge of giving up, we seem to find someone else."

He didn't care for this news—at all. It tied her to her current existence even more. Of course he had no interest in going back to her little "community." He had no interest in Philip or Wade or in forming friendships with other vampires. For the most part, he never had, even in the old days. Eleisha was the only thing at this table that interested him. He'd been reading people long enough to know sincerity when he saw it. She was the soul of sincerity. After a little training, anyone would believe anything she said.

However, from the way she was talking, she seemed eager to get back to her old brick church as soon as possible.

He had to find some way—any way—to keep her here a little longer.

Wade was struggling to stop staring at Ivory. He'd once believed himself to be in love with Eleisha, and even before that, he'd always found her pretty to a heartbreaking degree. But this woman was different. She reminded him of a shining jewel. She'd hardly said anything, and her expression was guarded; yet she was hanging on Eleisha's every word. He caught a few stolen glances into her green eyes, and he couldn't help seeing a hint—possibly more than a hint—of sadness. He wanted to know what she was thinking, and he fought to keep from entering her mind to try to see as much as possible before she pushed him out.

What a foolish notion. They wanted her to trust them, and that trust would not be gained by invading her mind without an invitation.

Still looking at Eleisha, Ivory asked quietly, "You

said Philip's job was to protect whomever you found. Protect them from what?"

Eleisha blinked. "From Julian."

"So he comes after the vampires you find?"

Wade flinched. The conversation had suddenly taken a wrong turn. It was moving toward dangerous ground, and he had no idea how to stop it.

Eleisha nodded.

"Has he killed any of them?" Ivory asked.

"Yes," Philip answered, speaking up for the first time. Perhaps he considered this his territory. "Two. But one of them had moved outside my protection, and the other was mad. I'd have killed her myself."

Ivory fell silent at this, but something in Christian's face flickered. However, he didn't look frightened. Had Wade not known better, before the quick flash vanished, he could have sworn Christian almost appeared . . . pleased.

Then Christian's expression shifted to anger. "So you've led a killer right to us, and you expect us to trust you enough to travel to Portland after a few moments' chat? I don't think so."

This time Eleisha flinched. But the truth here had crossed Wade's mind as well. Good intentions or not, they'd led Julian right to Seattle.

"I promise we can protect you," Eleisha said. "I have . . . defenses, too. You just need to stay near us."

Christian tilted his head to one side, studying Eleisha, and Wade couldn't help having second thoughts about him already. Something about his manner was unsettling. Wade couldn't say exactly what that was . . . but something. He just seemed so calculated.

"I agree with staying near you," Christian said. "But we must all be better acquainted before there is any talk of Ivory and me going with you to this . . . community . . . and indeed before you should consider inviting us to take such a step. You know nothing about us."

"What are you suggesting?" Eleisha asked.

"The three of you should come and stay at the mansion for a while. You will be close and can offer this protection you promise, and we can come to know each other better." He paused. "Does that not seem the wisest option? The mansion is gated. Could you not protect us more easily there?"

To Wade's surprise, Philip nodded. "Yes."

But Eleisha looked flustered. "What about Vera? What will she say to three more houseguests?"

To Wade's further surprise, Christian laughed, looking Philip up and down. "Do not concern yourself. She'll be thrilled."

He stood up and pulled a cell phone from his pocket, pushing a button, putting it to his ear, and walking toward the bar. The waitress brought their drinks.

Eleisha turned to Wade with questioning eyes.

What do we do? she flashed.

Although Christian's suggestion had caught him off guard, too, they certainly could not expect these two vampires to just pack up and leave for Portland tonight. And the knowledge that Julian was already here in the city meant that they both needed protection.

I think we have to agree, he flashed back. *We can't ask them to come with us so quickly, and we can't just leave them on their own.*

After a few seconds, she nodded, and he was suddenly ashamed of his own excitement at the prospect of living in such close quarters with Ivory. He knew nothing about her, and he was far too old for a schoolboy's crush on a stranger with a beautiful face.

Julian stopped his car about thirty feet outside the manor's gates. He got out and quietly closed the door, letting his eyes run down the high fence as he pondered the best way to get inside. It bothered him that he didn't know much about either of the vampires Eleisha had located—and he liked having more information before attacking. But since he knew exactly where they were, it just seemed prudent to go ahead and kill them tonight.

His normal method for hunting members of his kind was to hide in the shadows until the target walked past and then step out and take a swing, severing the head before anyone saw him coming or knew he was there. But he had killed two vampires at once before, and he could do so again, as long as they were together when they walked past him and he moved fast enough. He'd taken out a male/female pair, Demetrio and Cristina, in Italy in 1826 by hiding behind a door on the terrace of their villa.

Since Julian had never developed telepathy, he could not be sensed or tracked by telepathy, and so none of his own kind knew he was there if they couldn't see him. He'd simply stepped from behind the door and taken off Demetrio's head in a matter of seconds. Then he'd swung backward before Cristina even had time to gasp.

It had not been difficult.

He could employ the same tactic here.

But he needed to get inside. Since his method of hunting always depended on the element of surprise, he could not simply ask to be admitted—even if he thought he had a chance of gaining entry. He stepped onward, taking stock of the fence.

The air shimmered beside him, and Mary appeared. Her transparent face seemed frustrated.

"He's not in there anymore," she said. "They're both gone. I think maybe they know you're here in the city."

He tensed. "And how is that possible?"

"Seamus saw me. He might have warned them."

Julian went cold with anger at this news. It must have been what she was holding back earlier. But to make it worse, when she saw his expression, her frustration vanished for an instant, and she almost seemed to be enjoying his rage. Her eyes glinted with amusement. His desire to punish her doubled. He would find a way to make her do his bidding like she used to.

But then he looked back at the gates. He almost couldn't believe he'd tracked down a possible elder and his child, only to lose them again so quickly. Well, they couldn't have gotten far.

Turning, he started back toward his rented car.

"Find them," he said.

Eleisha did not refuse when Christian offered to drive them all back to the manor in a black Mercedes. At the time, it had seemed sensible, as this would certainly keep all five of them together.

He'd also said he would "send someone" to their hotel for their luggage. Again, she'd agreed, but as he pulled the Mercedes up to the front gates of the manor, lowered the window, and punched in a code, Eleisha watched the gates swing inward, and she was struck by an uncomfortable feeling that she'd handed over too much power in this situation.

They had no car of their own here. They were passing through a gate for which she did not have a code, and Christian was making all the decisions. Wade sat beside her in the backseat, and she could feel his tension as well, but on her other side, Philip just kept looking out the window. Maybe he'd realized this was their only option, and that's why he'd agreed so quickly. There simply wasn't anything else they could do.

Christian drove toward the north side of the manor and hit a button on the key chain. A huge garage door opened, and as he pulled inside, Eleisha saw a row of luxury cars. He parked in an open spot.

"Home, sweet home," he said.

Philip opened the door, and Eleisha climbed out after him. Ivory had been in the passenger seat, and she pointed toward the back of the garage at a door. "That way."

Again, this all somehow felt wrong—too alien—and Eleisha regretted their hasty decision to accept hospitality here. But again, what choice did they have?

Wade fell into step beside Ivory, and they all headed inside the manor, walking up a flight of stairs and passing through another door before emerging onto the main floor.

They passed down a wide hallway . . . and then Eleisha stopped three steps inside a vast room, trying to take everything in at once. The sight was overwhelming.

She believed herself to be standing in some oversized living room—maybe.

The first thing in her sight line was a huge white fireplace, but every inch of the mantel was covered in Victorian teapots. She counted at least six couches or settees. There were stuffed chairs, tables, brass lamps, Persian rugs, Chinese vases, candleholders, and small crystal or porcelain knickknacks everywhere. A full-sized painted carousel tiger—with a saddle—stood near the fireplace, and mismatched paintings hid every inch of space on the walls.

Philip and Wade were staring as well.

Eleisha had never seen anything quite like this. There was barely room to walk.

"Christian, darling!" a cheerful voice called.

A woman swept in from an open archway, coming toward them with her arms wide—apparently having no trouble navigating the furniture. She appeared to be about sixty year old. She was short and stocky, wearing an orange caftan with gold inlay and six strings of pearls around her neck. Countless silver bracelets jangled on both her wrists. As she smiled, the entire scene struck Eleisha as something right out of an Agatha Christie novel.

Christian leaned down, and the woman kissed both his cheeks, after which she greeted Ivory warmly. Then she took a good look at Philip. "Oh, Christian, you did not exaggerate. Who *is* this divine creature?"

Philip smiled slightly and leaned over, grasping her hand and kissing the back of it. "Philip Branté," he said. "Charmed."

Eleisha had seen him in this persona before, usually when he was trying to lure off a victim, but his ability to shift so rapidly caught her off guard. She herself had no such skill and felt completely off center.

But the woman beamed up at Philip. "Vera Olivier," she said, turning quickly to Wade and Eleisha. "You are all most welcome. When Christian called to tell me that members of his own circle had arrived here in Seattle, I insisted he bring you here."

His own circle? Did she think they were some kind of spiritualists as well?

"Of course you did, darling," Christian said, stepping forward and taking charge again. "It's in your soul to be generous. Can we get them settled? Have you arranged three guest rooms?"

As these words left his mouth, Philip glanced at him

and then reached out, placing one hand on the back of Eleisha's neck. "Two guest rooms," he corrected.

A flash of surprise crossed Christian's face, followed by a frown. But both vanished as quickly as they'd appeared. "Of course. Two rooms."

Vera laughed and grasped Eleisha's hand. "Good for you, my dear," she said. "I'd have done the same thing myself twenty years ago." Looking Philip up and down, she sighed and then pulled Eleisha along through the maze of furniture. "This way."

Though Vera's countenance was cheerful, Eleisha knew the scars of loneliness well enough to spot them, and in spite of being embarrassed by the woman's behavior, she couldn't help a slight rush of affection.

But then she wondered what their guest room was going to look like.

Julian paced the floor of the hotel. He'd decided to come back here and wait for a location report from Mary. In spite of having fed, he was restless and couldn't seem to sit down. He just felt too blind in the situation.

He wanted to know more about Christian. How old was he? Where had he come from? Why wasn't he listed in Angelo's book? What was his gift? Knowledge was power, and Julian was in the dark here.

Worse, if Christian had been warned about Julian's presence, he'd be on guard, and that would affect how Julian should proceed.

What was taking Mary so long?

She'd been the one hounding him to finish this as fast as possible, and if he'd had a chance at the mansion, he might have finished it already. Now that his target had been warned and had gone into hiding, Julian needed to know a little more about what he was walking into himself, and he wasn't quite ready for her to demand he keep his promise.

No, he might have to drag this out a little longer.

The air shimmered, and Mary materialized beside the bed. She didn't look happy.

"What?" he asked, alarmed. "Do you know where they are?"

"Yeah, but you're not going to like it."

He waited.

She glanced away. She'd never done that before, or at least not with so much self-deprecation. "They're back at the mansion," she said. "But Eleisha, Philip, and Wade are all there, too, and I think they're staying."

He stared at her, absorbing her words.

"You'll never get near Christian with Eleisha and Philip in there," she said, "and even if you do, you'll never get back out."

chapter seven

Not long past dusk the following evening, Eleisha found herself gathered with the others back in the overstuffed living room.

Although she and Philip had slept out the day in their guest room, since waking, she'd learned a little more about the place. Vera employed two maids and a cook. Eleisha had also briefly met the stalwart butler, Simmons, who seemed the run the house with surprising efficiency. If he was appalled by the overabundance of furniture, paintings, and knickknacks everywhere, he didn't show it, and Eleisha had yet to find a speck of dust on anything.

But apparently, Vera had scheduled a séance to take place at eleven o'clock that night, and she expected

Christian's "guests" to participate. Eleisha was both nervous and curious.

However, they had nearly five hours to get through before the event took place, and even though Philip managed to maintain his charming persona with Vera, Eleisha could see he was getting restless. Normally, by now she'd have found some way to entertain him for the evening. He wasn't big on just sitting around and socializing.

Vera stood by the fireplace and pressed her hands together in what looked like glee. "Well, darlings, what should we do now?"

Eleisha glanced over at her in gratitude.

Vera's caftan was bright pink tonight. Christian wore dark slacks and a sport jacket, and Ivory was stunning in a black evening gown and diamond pendant. Philip had on black jeans and a snug-fitting turtleneck sweater, but he always looked well dressed in anything he wore.

However . . . Eleisha was slightly embarrassed by herself and Wade. Since Seamus had observed two consecutive séances from the previous two nights, she hadn't expected a third séance to be scheduled for tonight, and she'd not been told about tonight's until a few moments ago, so she was dressed in a long broomstick skirt and one of Philip's V-neck sweaters, which hung halfway to her knees. Wade was even worse, wearing old jeans and a T-shirt with a depiction of a Blue Öyster Cult album emblazoned on the front—

Some Enchanted Evening. His shirt wasn't tucked in, and she could see the small lump of his gun in the back of his pants. What had he been thinking? Maybe he'd just assumed they'd be on guard duty and nothing more tonight.

But Vera didn't seem to mind, and she was enjoying the rather eccentric mix of company. Eleisha stepped toward her, mulling over Philip's favorite pastimes.

"Do you play poker?" Eleisha asked.

Vera beamed. "Poker? What a lovely suggestion."

Philip perked up. "For money?"

"Of course!" Vera answered. "What other way is there?"

Even the near-silent, serene Ivory looked interested at this prospect, and Eleisha stepped back again, just listening as a short exchange of suggestions and warnings followed.

"We can use that table over there . . ."

"Do you like five-card draw . . . ?"

"Watch out for Philip," Wade said. "He cheats."

"I do not!"

Within a few moments, cards and chips were produced, and then Vera, Philip, Wade, and Ivory began sitting down around a small table. Christian was on a settee reading a book, and Eleisha now stood near the fireplace.

Wade looked over at her. "Are you playing?"

"I think I'll just watch," she answered.

He nodded while picking up the deck, and Eleisha sank into relief that she could just be alone with her thoughts for a little while and not responsible for entertaining anyone else.

She noticed an open archway on the other side of the living room, and she crossed over to see into the next room. It was just as overstuffed as the rest of the house, but this room boasted a large round table with a candelabra and a number of Egyptian statues. She recognized it from Seamus' description and realized this was where the séance would be held.

Walking in, she touched the table.

"I know it's a bit of a cliché, but trust me, this is what the clients expect."

Eleisha jumped slightly and turned to see Christian standing in the archway. He seemed to be studying her with his strange light eyes. Candlelight glinted off the ring in his ear, and she didn't know how to respond.

"Maybe it's time you and I had a real talk," he said. "I have a few questions."

For some reason she couldn't explain, she took a step backward.

Watching the girl as she touched the table, Christian couldn't believe how charming she looked in a simple loose skirt that hung to her ankles and what appeared to be a man's sweater. It was probably Philip's, and that thought rankled him. At the pub last night, he hadn't minded pretending to be helpless, acting as if he'd needed both Philip's protection and his sword. In truth, Christian had been knife fighting in the streets of Paris before he was twelve years old.

But he'd been shortsighted not to have noticed the possessive way Philip looked at Eleisha, and as a result, he'd been caught off guard when Philip so pointedly corrected him by asking for only two rooms.

Christian didn't like being caught off guard.

Worse, if the girl belonged to Philip, it complicated matters. Nothing he couldn't handle . . . but it was a complication.

However, just now, when Eleisha's eyes widened slightly and she took a step away from him, excitement began building in Christian's chest again, and he knew he'd started down a path he had to finish.

"What do you want to know?" she asked.

He moved closer and delighted in watching her struggle not to step back again.

"Everything," he answered. "Where did you come from? How did Philip survive? How did you find each other?"

At his open barrage of questions, she suddenly smiled. "What do you want to know first?"

Her expression changed to the same one she'd worn in the pub last night—of wishing to please him—and it hit him harder than her anxiety had. How long since one of his own kind, someone who *knew* what he was, had looked at him like that?

"Who made you?" he asked. He was well aware by now that she'd never agreed to be turned. Someone like her would never give consent. That meant one of his own had broken the third law.

Her smile faded. "Julian."

"Julian? No. He hates other vampires. He'd never make one."

She nodded. "He did. His father became ill from old age, senile, and Julian turned him, trying to save him. But it didn't work. His father was still sick and senile . . . and immortal. Julian wanted a caretaker for him, and he needed someone who wouldn't die."

"So he forced you?"

She glanced away, as if embarrassed to answer, and he was tempted to reach into her mind and see more of her thoughts for himself, but that might scare her off, and he didn't know how quickly she could block him.

He glanced out toward Philip, who was cheerfully calling Vera's last bet.

"I can already guess his gift," Christian said, "but you are more of a mystery. What's yours?"

She met his eyes and seemed to gain some composure. "It's my turn to ask. I answered one of your questions."

Her flash of courage surprised him. He didn't like it.

"Ask away," he said.

"What's your gift?"

He wasn't quite ready to answer that yet. His gift was unique. So instead, he changed the subject, looking pointedly at her sweater. "Explaining that may take some time, and my client will be arriving in a few hours." He paused, as if the next topic pained him. "It's important that we all look the part for this to work. I took the liberty of borrowing a dress from Ivory earlier, and I know this is awkward, but I need you to . . ." He trailed off as realization dawned on her face.

"Oh, you want me to change?"

"If you wouldn't mind. I also have some of my things laid out for Wade. Could you come up to my room?"

"Your room?"

Her voice wavered with anxiety again, and he managed an expression of offended hurt. "I don't see how we're ever going to become better acquainted if you can't even accept an offer to properly dress for the evening."

"Oh, no. I didn't mean . . . Of course I'll come up and change."

She seemed horrified at the thought of offending him, and pleasure swelled up in his chest anew. She was delightful. So easy to manipulate. He might not even have to use his gift.

"This way," he said, pointing to the archway at the back of the sitting room.

"I'd better go back and tell Philip first."

"He's busy, and we won't be long."

She hesitated but did not seem to want to offend him again. Nodding, she followed him out the back of the room toward the stairwell.

Fifteen minutes later, Eleisha was wondering how she'd let Christian talk her into changing her clothes right there in his room. But she was behind a large Asian screen, pulling Philip's sweater over her head, and she could hear Christian clinking brushes, combs, and small glass jars over at the dressing table.

Every time she tried to refuse him something, he made her feel as if she were the one in the wrong—and maybe she was. After all, she'd led Julian right to him and Ivory, and Christian had been good enough to arrange an invitation for them here so that he might come to know them better.

Wasn't this what she wanted?

"That dress unzips in the back," he called from somewhere out in the room, "but the zipper is well hidden. Let me know if you need help."

"I'm all right."

After pulling off her skirt, Eleisha lifted the gown hanging from the screen and turned it around. She could see what he meant. The zipper was indeed difficult to spot. But the gown itself intimidated her. It was silk, in a shimmering shade of off-white pearl. Slipping into it, she realized it was backless, so the zipper came up only a few inches above her tailbone. The dress was snug and slinky, with spaghetti straps that fastened at the back of her neck. In her entire existence, she'd never worn anything like it. The long, shimmering skirt fell around her feet, but the top half seemed to include very little material.

"Christian, I don't know about this. Doesn't Ivory have anything else?"

"Let me see it."

Reluctantly, she stepped out from behind the screen, and when he turned to look at her, his eyes brightened with intensity.

"It's perfect," he said.

Something about this felt wrong—all wrong—but she had no idea what. It wasn't unreasonable of him to expect her and Wade to look their parts in the séance, and in order to wrangle their invitations here, he'd had to claim they were members of his circle.

He motioned to a chair in front of the dressing table. "Come and sit here. I need to do your hair."

"You know how to style a woman's hair?"

"Of course. I used to do Ivory's all the time."

She didn't miss the "used to," and it reminded her of something else that had been nagging at her. For two vampires who worked and traveled and lived together, Christian and Ivory did not seem close. They never spoke to each other, and Eleisha couldn't help wondering why. Had something happened between them? It frustrated her that she knew so little about this situation.

But she sat down, and he began brushing her hair. She wondered what the séance would be like and considered that a safe topic.

"How does it work?" she asked. "The séance itself. Wade found a newspaper article that said your clients are sometimes weak and dizzy afterward. You don't feed on them, do you?"

He picked up a can of mousse and sprayed a dollop into one hand. "Feed on them? No." He paused. "How developed is your telepathy?"

She had no intention of letting him know that just yet, not when it was her only weapon. She hadn't even let Rose know that much for a while. "Developed enough. Strong enough that I've taught several vampires how to follow the first law."

"Really? Good. Then just stay with me when the show begins tonight. Stay inside my mind, and you'll see how it's done." He rubbed his hands together and began working the mousse into her hair. "I want you to see how it's done. But I have to read detailed images and emotions from the clients, and sometimes I have to go so deep it drains them."

That startled her. "You don't do any damage?"

"Nothing lasting."

Once he'd made her wavy hair even wavier, he pulled her long bangs back and pinned them at the crown of her head with a jeweled clip. Then he picked up a black eye-lining pencil.

"Oh, Christian, no . . . ," she said. "I don't wear that."

"Just sit still."

He put eyeliner at the corners of her eyes. He also used mascara and then a light lip gloss.

"Perfect," he said again, and the relief in his voice bothered her. Looking into the mirror, she saw a stranger looking back, but he seemed to much prefer her like this, as if he wanted to change her.

She stood up, moving away.

Warning bells were going off inside her head. What did he want? Was this just about making her look presentable for the séance?

She decided it was time to push guilt aside and start

listening to her own instincts. In the end, it would be safer for Christian and Ivory to come back to the underground—perhaps pick up their business from there. Portland had its areas of affluent society. Or if they really decided they didn't want to come back, they could just vanish for a few months, perhaps change their names, and then set up with another patron like Vera someplace else—and keep themselves out of the newspapers.

But suddenly Eleisha realized that no matter how civilized Christian appeared, she wasn't going to bring him near Rose or Maxim until she knew a good deal more.

Glancing at a clock on the dressing table, she saw they still had hours until the séance.

Maybe it was time to push a few of his buttons.

Slowly, gently, she let a hint of her gift seep out, making him see her as helpless, but she was careful, ready to shut it off if he noticed what she was doing.

"Christian," she said, pitching her voice to a tone of deference. "I've answered every question you've asked me, and you've told me almost nothing. Would you do something for me?"

He stepped toward her, seeming intrigued. "What?"

"Philip, Wade, and I have learned how to look inside each other's minds and see memories, not just thoughts and images but real memories. If you would let me see a few of your memories, it would help me to know you better, to trust you more."

"You don't trust me?"

"I don't know you."

He wavered, and she let the aura of her gift grow a little stronger, making him see her as something so far beneath himself that he need fear nothing she could do.

Of course she didn't tell him that if he agreed, once he let her inside his mind and he focused on a past memory, she could lock onto it, get him lost completely in the past, and force him down a chronological line for as long she wanted—seeing anything and everything she wanted. None of the elders had learned to do this, and they'd had no idea it was possible. This was something new that she and Wade had discovered in their early days together, and Eleisha was very, very good at it.

"Please," she said. "Just let me see a few of your early memories, of where you come from. It will help me understand you."

"Where I come from?" He seemed hesitant but still intrigued.

She sat down on the bed. "Just come sit beside me. If you think back, I'll be able to see scenes from your life."

She knew how he was imagining this, that he might show her a few carefully chosen memories and thus please him by doing something so simple . . . and she knew she'd tempted him by sitting down on the bed.

He came to join her, sitting slowly.

"I need to touch your hand," she said.

"By all means."

Reaching out, she grasped his hand.

"What do you want to see?" he asked.

"Go back to before you were turned."

"That wasn't a pretty time."

"Please show me," she said, reaching her thoughts toward his. "Let me in."

Reaching her thoughts into his, she could feel his reluctance, but then unbidden, unwanted, the image of a squalid, crowded room began to form in his mind.

She locked on hard, and the world around her vanished.

chapter eight

Christian's first real memory was hunger.

Early years of malnourishment may have affected him, because he could barely recall his mother's face or the seemingly endless mass of brothers and sisters crowded into single filthy room on a filthy street.

But when he was about eight years old, he clearly remembered the fierce pain in his stomach and the emptiness eating away at his body, and he remembered the sight of a pouch hanging from a belt. Two well-dressed men were arguing loudly in front of a flower seller's cart, and other people had begun gathering around them.

But Christian saw only the pouch hanging from the belt of a bystander. Like all boys who'd survived there to the age of eight, he carried a knife, and he pulled it out, hiding it in one hand. As he slipped through the crowd, no one noticed him. He was small.

He moved as close as he dared.

Then one man slapped the other. Some people in the crowd gasped and some cheered, and when the scuffle began, Christian slipped past as if to escape the press of bodies, and he cut off the pouch in one movement and was gone before anyone saw what he'd done.

Hiding in an alley, he counted the coins—more money than he'd ever seen.

That night, for dinner, he bought himself ham and fresh-baked bread from a tavern owner, and he paid a few small coins for the privilege of sleeping in the back storage room. It was warm and dry, and his stomach was full.

He never went home again.

But he also never forgot the lesson of that first successful attempt. Christian wasn't stupid, and he'd seen what became of pickpockets who were caught. To him, the key to this survival method was simple: Don't get caught.

This meant he would never make an attempt unless the target and everyone else around was thoroughly distracted.

Paris was a large city, and as the years passed, he came to haunt the markets where street performers most often set up on the corners, trying to earn a few coins by juggling or performing acrobatics or even putting on short plays.

Over time, Christian learned which performers could get the crowds gasping or laughing, and he used the laughter and press of bodies to cut a purse quickly and then vanish. By the age of thirteen, he was still so small that few people even noticed him.

To him, the city was divided between a small number of the rich and the great masses of the starving poor. But the clothing of the wealthy always fascinated him, especially anything worn by the men, and he imagined himself in an embroidered waistcoat or ruffled shirt or white stockings pulled up beneath the knees of his breeches. He often wished he could just touch such clothing, but his trade depended on the utmost speed.

The years blurred, one into the next.

He never looked ahead or back and simply lived each day as it came, until his body began to betray him. He started to grow. By the time he was seventeen, he'd grown too tall to slip amid a crowd unnoticed, and when he was eighteen, his hair began turning steel gray. His eyes were light and clear, with just a hint of a blue. He knew that women found him handsome—as many of the local whores flirted with him and offered to take him home for free.

But in spite of a few advantages, he had a difficult time finding this state of affairs very welcome. He stood out too much now. People noticed him.

Pickpockets should not be noticed.

He tried covering his head in various ways, but his days of invisibility were behind him, and for the first time, he began to worry about the future. Over the next three years, he learned to survive on less and less and to take fewer chances. He had no wish to end up locked away in a prison—or worse.

Then one night he was out of coins and hungry again, wondering where he would even sleep, when he spotted a woman alone walking up ahead of him. It was summer, and she wore a light blue gown, tight at the waist, with a full skirt. Her head was adorned with a powdered wig and wide-brimmed hat decorated with a plume. Such women did not normally walk the streets unescorted.

A small silk purse hung from a dainty cord on her wrist.

He followed her. She was not distracted yet, but she must have had some destination, a rendezvous perhaps, and he might be provided with the right moment to walk past and slip the purse from her wrist.

He followed her a few more blocks, until there were fewer people around them, and he considered abandoning the hunt. He knew how to work only in crowds.

But then, to his shock, she suddenly stopped and turned around to face him.

"Can I assist you?" she asked, speaking directly to him.

No one of her class had ever spoken to him, and he took a step back, ready to bolt.

"Wait," she said, coming toward him. The split front of her gown exposed an embroidered petticoat beneath, as was the current fashion.

For some reason, he didn't run. She was staring at

his face, his hair, his dirty clothes, and he stared back. She was about forty years old, with pale skin and large brown eyes. But the pale cast of her skin might be due to powder, and her cheeks were reddened with rouge. Her painted lips were thin and her nose was hooked, but dressed in such finery, she was beautiful to his eyes, and he couldn't believe she'd spoken to him.

She seemed to look through him, inside him, and he just stood there.

"Are you hungry?" she asked, but her tone implied she already knew he was. "Come home and dine with me. I am all alone, and I long for company."

His shock began to fade. He'd heard some of the prettier boys of the streets speaking of wealthy men, or sometimes older women, who invited them home to provide . . . entertainment. Christian wasn't a boy anymore. He'd definitely crossed over into qualifying as a man, and such a thing as this had never happened to him.

"I have roast chicken and strawberries and wine waiting," she said. "Will you not join me?"

At the mention of meat and wine, any reservations fled. Would it be so wrong to go home with her, flatter her a bit, and do whatever she asked in exchange for a warm bed and a fine meal? He wanted to go with her. But some instinct inside him seemed to know that more than a nod would be expected by way of response.

Although he admired her dress far more than anything else about her, he stepped closer and said, "You have beautiful eyes."

She smiled.

*   *   *

Her name was Madame Bernadette Desmarais. She told him to call her Bernadette, and she took him in a carriage to her apartments near Versailles. When he entered her home, his reservations returned, and he was afraid to sit on anything.

She smiled again and ushered him into a side room, where she opened a white wardrobe with gold inlay. "Here," she said, taking out a red silk dressing robe. "Put this on while I order dinner to be laid out. You'll be more comfortable."

She left him, and he fingered the robe. He'd never felt anything so soft. Within moments, his old clothes were lying on the floor and he was wearing the robe. A standing mirror across the room reflected his full image, and he saw himself clearly for the first time. He was startled. The whores had not been wrong.

He was handsome.

The red dressing robe set off the steel tones in his hair, and his eyes glittered.

And in this robe, he no longer resembled a pickpocket. He looked like he belonged in this room.

Perhaps he did.

Bernadette came back in, and she seemed about to say something, but the words died on her lips when she saw him. She was quiet for a moment, just taking him in, and then she said, "My God."

She'd taken off her hat but still wore the powdered wig, and he wondered what her hair looked like.

"Come and eat," she said quietly.

He was starving and followed her through the apartments to a room of burning candles and low tables—most of which were white with gold painted inlay. Two wineglasses, a full bottle, and a variety of plates waited on a table.

"Go on," she said. "It's all right."

Fighting the urge to lunge, he sat down and began eating as politely as he could. He had no idea what the protocol was, but she didn't seem to care. After pouring them both wine, she sipped at hers but did not touch the food.

"You're not eating?" he asked.

"No, it's for you."

"Thank you."

His gratitude seemed to please her even more than the flattery about her eyes, and though the chicken and wine were delicious, he did not stop taking careful note of anything that pleased her. His enjoyment of the food pleased her, and he thanked her for letting him wear the robe.

"I have never been inside anyplace like this," he said.

"And you like it?"

"Yes."

She kept watching his face by the flickering candlelight. He wondered what would be expected of him next, but he didn't care. He'd do anything she asked.

When he finished eating, she motioned him over to sit beside her on a different couch, but she also opened another bottle of wine and poured more into his glass.

He'd already had three glasses and could feel it in his head.

"Tell me about yourself," she said.

He didn't know what to say and looked into her eyes in confusion, asking without words. Whatever could he tell her that she might possibly want to hear?

"It has been difficult for you, no?" she went on. "Struggling to exist among people little better than animals. The poverty. The filth. The petty squabbles that turn into bloody fights over a cup of ale or piece of cheese." She paused. "And so you are astonished to be here now?"

Her voice was husky as she spoke, and suddenly, he knew what she wanted. She wanted to hear the sordid details of his life on the streets, and after that she wanted his gratitude. He began to talk, weaving stories in small ugly increments as she poured him more wine and listened with her eyes closed.

Occasionally, she asked a question or asked him to elaborate, but for the most part, she just kept pouring him wine and listening. Not long before dawn, she took the glass from his hand. Then a strange sensation began to wash over him, through him, dulling his senses. He felt so grateful to her. He'd do anything for her.

"Kiss me," she whispered.

Although he'd been expecting this, by now he was so drunk and his senses were so dulled that he forgot to be careful, and he made a demand. "Let me see your hair."

She looked at him in surprise and then slowly reached up and pulled the wig back. Her hair was pinned up, but he could see it was still deep chocolate brown.

"Beautiful," he whispered.

She grasped the back of his head, running her fingers through his hair, and he kissed her. He knew how to kiss a woman softly. He knew how to use his tongue. Cecilia, one of the whores where he lived, had taught him.

He expected this to progress rapidly. He understood why he was here. But after a few moments, Bernadette pulled away and drew his hand up to her mouth, turning it over, and kissing his wrist.

That was the last thing he remembered.

Late the following afternoon, he woke up in a bed. His head ached and his wrist hurt. Opening his eyes, he looked at his lavish surroundings and had no idea where he was. Upon hearing movement, he looked left and saw a man by a polished dressing table.

Christian jumped down to the floor in a crouch, instinctively going for the knife that he always kept in his boot, but his feet were bare.

The man by the table whirled and held up both hands. "It's all right, sir. I am in the employ of Madame Desmarais."

Christian blinked. No one had ever called him "sir" before. Then some of the previous night came flooding back. He remembered everything up to the point where

Bernadette had kissed his wrist . . . but nothing after that. Glancing down at his wrist, he saw it was bandaged. Had he injured himself? Such things could happen after too much wine.

The servant cleared his throat. "Madame Desmarais has given instructions that you are to remain until she awakens."

Then the man paused, as if uncomfortable, and Christian watched his face, trying to read it. It seemed that the young men from the streets whom Madame Desmarais brought home were not normally asked to stay, and this manservant appeared put off by her instructions.

But the man continued. "I've arranged for a bath and clothes."

Clothes? A spark of excitement ignited in Christian's chest.

"This way, sir," the manservant said.

For the next hour, Christian allowed himself to be bathed, groomed, and dressed. He could hardly believe the suit of clothing that had been laid out for him when saw it. There was a well-tailored gentleman's jacket of amber brown, a cream silk waistcoat, white stockings, and dark breeches. He stared at a pair of low-heeled shoes.

Once he was fully dressed, he turned to the mirror and barely recognized himself.

"I hope you have no objections to remaining here and waiting for Madame Desmarais?" the manservant asked.

Objections? If Christian had his way, he was never leaving.

"None at all," he answered.

For the first few months, Bernadette kept him mainly to herself. She did take him out in the evenings sometimes to see a tailor for him or a dressmaker for her, and sometimes to shop for perfume or handkerchiefs. She showed him parts of Paris he'd never seen.

But she also spoke of poetry, art, music, and politics, and she began teaching him to read.

He was never hungry again.

There were oddities he did not expect. For one, she never asked him to share her bed, and at first this surprised him more than anything else. But later, other things seemed even stranger.

She never ate. Not once had he ever seen her put a bite of food in her mouth. At first, he thought she was simply eating in private, that she had some feminine reluctance to eat in front of him. But after a while it began to bother him that she never once shared a meal with him.

Also, he'd never seen her in daylight, and she kept her bedroom door locked. He was given strict instructions not to try to open her bedroom door for any reason, and she was so serious about this that he realized his place in her household depended on obeying that order. Again, at first he barely noticed this eccentricity. In truth, most of the affluent members of French society lived by night and slept by day, but as the weeks passed, he began to notice that she vanished before dawn and reappeared at almost the same time every night.

He soon learned to live by her hours, and he did not ask any questions. Instead, he focused on playing his own role. He provided her with flattery and gratitude and company. He found he had a gift for keeping her happy.

In midautumn, after giving him lessons on social etiquette and diction, she began to show him off, taking him to the opera or late-night dinner parties or gatherings in the salons of her friends. She made up a story that he was the fourth son of a minor nobleman from the south and that she had taken him on as a protégé, introducing him into society. She even asked him about his surname, but he didn't know what it was, so she gave him one: Lefevre.

Of course everyone believed he was sharing her bed—which was what she wanted them to believe—but on the surface, they all treated him as Monsieur Christian Lefevre, a young aristocrat she'd taken under her wing.

He loved this. He loved the pomp of the opera. He loved the barbed verbal sparing matches at dinner parties. He loved listening to the discussions of art or politics in a salon.

He especially loved the way the women looked at him, both with hunger and as if they somehow sensed he was different. This was how he figured out why Bernadette had chosen him when she might have chosen among her own caste.

The first time they walked into a salon, a wigged man wearing face powder had fallen to his knees in front of Bernadette and kissed her hand. "My love!" he exclaimed. "Where have you been hiding? My heart would have broken had you not come before long."

Christian stared at him. The men all seemed to speak in flowery, insincere phrases, as if any and all masculinity had been bred out of them long ago. Christian was attentive and unfailingly polite, but none of these men would have demanded that Bernadette take her wig off and show them her hair. And even if they had, they would have used too many words to flatter her.

Christian's one breathy whisper of "beautiful" was something foreign to these people. They all used too many words.

He was something new to them, and he became an overnight attraction. Bernadette did not hide her pleasure. She was flooded with invitations, and Christian came to understand that in the past few years before his arrival, her invitations had been dwindling. But now she was in demand again—because of him.

Even after learning this, his gratitude to her did not fade. He loved their apartments and the fine food and the wine and the clothes and the fascination of wealthy women. He sometimes wondered how these same women might look at him if they knew that only a few months before, he'd been cutting purses to survive and had occasionally slept in alleys with rats running over his legs.

But as time drifted by, he began to forget the streets,

and he almost came to believe that he really was Monsieur Christian Lefevre, the fourth son of a minor nobleman from the south of France.

His happiness was broken only by two separate events—which both happened with some regularity. About once a week, Bernadette would slip out and leave the apartments without him. She refused to tell him where she was going, and she would sometimes be gone for hours.

This tortured him, as he feared she might be meeting someone else. He feared being replaced more than anything else, and for the next few nights, he would always work harder to please her, finding little ways to make her smile.

The other event tended to happen about once a month, and it followed the same pattern as his first night with her. She would serve him a meal, sometimes feeding him with her fingers, along with several bottles of wine, and then she'd ask him to tell her about his life before he met her. He began to loathe doing this—as he preferred to forget that life. But he would do anything she wanted, so he told her ugly, sordid stories, followed by swearing to her how grateful he was to be living here with her and how she'd saved him. After that, she would want him to kiss her mouth for a while, and he'd be enveloped by the same mind-dulling sensation of overwhelming gratitude.

Then she would kiss his wrist and he'd black out, waking up the following afternoon with no memory of what had happened after, but with a bleeding, bandaged wound on his arm. This began to trouble him more and more, as did her complete abstinence from food and daylight.

After six months, on one of these nights, he made a point of drinking less, and he somehow managed to hold on to his senses when the mind-dulling feeling of gratitude swept over him. He snatched his wrist away when she moved to kiss it. Her eyes flew to his face in surprise.

"Christian?"

"What are you doing?" he asked. His voice sounded hard to his own ears. "I don't like it."

She heard the edge in his voice, too. He might have joyfully turned himself into her handsome escort, but underneath, he was still the same young man who'd cut purses to survive.

Suddenly he found his head clearing even more, and he began demanding answers. "Why don't you eat? Why do I never share your bed? Why do you always vanish before dawn? Why am I forbidden to enter your room?"

She stood up, perhaps shaken by his questions, but he couldn't be certain. Her back was turned.

"Do you truly wish to know?" she asked.

"Yes."

"Even if the answer is difficult to believe?"

"Yes."

She turned around. "I have never known anyone like you. You are the best of all worlds." She paused. "What if I told you that I could make it so you never aged another day, that your current charm would increase threefold, that you could stay with me forever?"

He stood up, his heart pounding. The first part sounded like madness, but he'd do anything to ensure the last part.

She raised one hand to stop him from speaking. "There's a price. You too will never eat food again, and you will never again see daylight."

"I don't care," he said.

She moved closer. "Truly? You would want this?"

"I want to be with you."

She closed her eyes, but he could see the stark relief in her face. Did she fear losing him, too? Was that possible?

Stepping even closer, she ran her hands up his chest. "You have to consent," she whispered. "You have to tell me you agree."

"I consent," he whispered back instantly, and the open relief on her face now astonished him.

"Sit," she said, and she moved into his lap, kissing his mouth again, only harder this time, deeper. Suddenly the sensation of gratitude began to engulf him again, only this time, it was stronger than ever before. He was so grateful to her. The feeling seemed flow through and around him. She was the fountain of all good things, and he would do anything for her. He'd let her do anything to him.

Her mouth moved to his throat, kissing his skin, and then without warning, she bit down hard on his throat, not like a love bite, but her teeth sank deeply, ripping his skin. The pain was blinding, and his hands instinctively shot up to pitch her off, but the feeling of gratitude grew even stronger, engulfing him, and he stopped.

She was drinking his blood in gulping mouthfuls, pushing him slowly down onto the couch. His body grew weaker, until he could hear his heartbeat in his ears, slower and slower until he thought it would stop. She pulled her teeth from his throat and used them to tear open her own wrist, and then she pressed it into his mouth.

"Drink," she whispered.

That was the last thing he remembered.

When he woke up again, he was lying on the same couch, but only one candle was lit. He had a sense that some time had passed, but he didn't know how much. The candle glowed too brightly in his sight. He could see colors in the flame he'd never noticed before.

"Christian?"

Bernadette was suddenly kneeling beside him. He could hear a beetle making its way across the floor.

"What did you do to me?" he whispered.

She smiled. "Given you a new life. A life with me. Forever." He felt her hand upon his head, stroking his hair in a way she'd never done before. For some reason, he didn't like it, and he wanted her to stop. But he said nothing.

The first fifteen years passed quickly as Christian became comfortable with the term "vampire."

He had so much to learn, so much to discover about himself. Bernadette had not been wrong that his charm would increase threefold, but when his telepathy began to develop, he reveled in the power. How had he ever existed without it? To know what everyone was thinking put him at an advantage beyond his previous imagining.

Bernadette also taught him how to hunt, how to feed, how to blur a victim's memory.

She'd been slightly unsettled at first that he did not develop something she called "a gift" quite in the way of other vampires. Her gift was to exude an overwhelming feeling of gratitude in her victims. He'd felt this from her himself, so he knew how strong it was—especially when she used it in full force.

But no element of his personality swelled into an aura when he hunted. Instead, he was gifted with a mental power of emotional suggestion. He could plant an impulse inside the mind of a mortal and make the person *feel* as he wished.

"Is this so unusual?" he asked. "Can others of our kind not do this as well?"

"To a point," she answered. "We can make mental suggestions in order to do things like put a victim to sleep or of course to blur memories, so we can feed safely. Some of us can use quick mental impulses to both confuse and lure someone off alone." She hesitated. "But I've never known a vampire who could go inside a mortal's mind and plant an emotional impulse the way you can, any emotion you choose in the moment. Your ability is unique."

He liked that. He liked being unique.

She also taught him that there were a number of others of their kind and that they existed by four laws—laws that he must learn and never break. She made him recite them back to her:

> *First Law: No vampire shall kill to feed. This ensures our safety and secrecy.*
>
> *Second Law: No vampire shall make another until reaching the age of one hundred years as an undead, and no vampire shall ever make more than one companion within the span of a hundred years. The physical and mental energy required is so great that any breach of this law will produce flawed results.*
>
> *Third Law: No vampire shall make another without the consent of the mortal.*
>
> *Fourth Law: The maker must teach the new vampire all methods of proper survival and all four of the laws in order to protect the secrecy of our kind.*

With the exception of the first law, they all seemed far too removed from himself. But she was so serious about these laws that he obeyed and memorized every word. His main function in life was to please her. That never changed. If anything, it increased. He loved this new life even more than the one he'd begun when he'd first come to live with her.

Now he was the absolute toast of dinner parties or evenings in a salon, although it took him a little while to learn how to properly push food about on a plate and pretend to eat. With the possible exception of the silent servants taking the plates, no one seemed to notice that he never consumed anything.

He knew what every lady wanted to hear. He knew what every man thought of him. He could read five or six minds simultaneously, and he could pick lines of poetry he'd never even read from someone's mind or draw upon political opinions regarding topics he knew nothing about. He could discuss art he'd never seen. He became the sum total of everyone in the room, and everyone thought him brilliant. His pale skin glowed and his eyes glittered, and women adored his young face and his wavy, steel gray hair.

He owed all of this to Bernadette.

Then in 1788, his happiness was tarnished again when a dark feeling came over him one night while he was out walking in the streets. For some reason he could not explain, he suffered from a sensation that something horrific was coming . . . not to him personally, but rather to Paris itself. The mood of the people around him had changed, and he sensed hunger and hatred as never before.

So when he arrived at home that night and Bernadette suddenly announced that they were leaving the city, he looked at her in confusion, but he did not argue.

"Why?" he could not help asking. Had she felt the same dark premonition?

But she said nothing of darkness looming over the city. Instead, she told him that the circle of the "right people" there in Paris was not infinite, and although they had changed their core group of friends several times, some members of the Parisian elite were beginning to notice that she never aged.

He hated the thought of leaving their beautiful apartments, but he did understand. Christian was a survivor.

"Where will we go?" he asked.

She smiled. "It's time you met some others of our kind. I thought we'd go to Harfleur first, to visit an old friend. Then I'll take you to Italy."

Any lingering regrets over leaving the apartments fled, and excitement flooded through him. He'd never expected this.

Italy.

Unfortunately the visit to Harfleur to visit Bernadette's old friend turned out to be less than exciting.

A drafty stone manor an hour's ride from the nearest village was hardly Christian's idea of society. Worse, the vampire they'd come to see was an aging Norman crusader named Angelo, and he could not have made a bigger contrast to the affluent men of Paris. He wore long breeches, heavy boots, and a wool tunic. His hair hung down his back, and his face was so preternaturally pale, he could barely pass for human.

Worse, he looked Christian up and down in poorly hidden disgust.

To Christian's shock, Bernadette laughed like a girl. "Don't be fooled. He's not the dandy he appears to be."

"Mmmmmm?" Angelo grunted, sounding unconvinced.

"I've been training him. He's a lovely companion."

Christian did not enjoy being spoken about as if he weren't standing right there; nor did he appreciate being compared to a lap dog in training, but he said nothing.

However, within a few nights, Bernadette seemed to realize he was bored and miserable. Although what had she expected when there was nothing to do here and no one interesting to converse with? No one at all to admire him? She called the visit short, much to his relief.

But in their brief time with Angelo, two things of note occurred.

First, one night Christian was so bored he'd resorted to scanning the bookshelves in Angelo's study, mainly historical or philosophical texts. But then he noticed a large, leather-bound book on the table titled *The Makers and Their Children*. Something about the title pulled at him. There was a quill and a jar of ink beside it.

He was just reaching down for the book when Angelo walked into the study, mildly surprised to see him. "I was just going to work on that, to start an entry for you."

"For me?" A cold feeling began to settle in Christian's stomach, similar to what he'd felt in Paris, that something dark was coming.

Moving closer, Angelo nodded. "It's a record I'm keeping for all of us." He paged through until he found the account for Madame Bernadette Desmarais, with detailed information and an illustration of her face.

The cold feeling in Christian's stomach grew. "Why do you do this?" he asked.

"Keep the record?" Angelo seemed puzzled by the question. "It's good for us to have knowledge of one another. Anyone can come and read it, and I don't tattle anyone's secrets. If someone wants something removed, I remove it. This is just a record to show who we are and that we exist. It's important."

"Has anyone ever asked to be left out?"

"No . . . Why?"

Christian didn't know this man anywhere near well enough to ask him for a favor, but his stomach had turned to ice, and he felt something pitch-black looming above. "Please . . . leave my name out. Don't include a record of me."

Angelo frowned. "Why wouldn't you wish to—"

"I'll do anything you ask. If you ever need a favor of me, I swear I will serve you any way I can. Just leave me out of the book."

Angelo shook his head in confusion, but he said, "As you wish."

The cold feeling in Christian's stomach began to ease.

The other event of note occurred on their last night at the manor. He'd finished his packing, resenting that he'd had to do it himself. Angelo appeared to employ no servants and lived entirely alone. Christian went downstairs and headed toward Angelo's study, where he thought he might find Bernadette, but upon hearing both their voices inside, he paused to listen.

"What do you mean, he has no gift?" Angelo asked.

"That's not what I said," Bernadette answered. "It's just not like any I've ever known. He exudes no aura, no influence as we do, but he can plant suggestions in someone else's mind, and the result is astonishing. He can pick whatever emotion he wants the victim to feel. He's not limited to inducing a single emotion . . . as we are."

There was a moment of silence, and Angelo asked, "Has he ever tried it on you?"

"On me? Don't be ridiculous. He adores me."

"Mmmmmmmm?" Angelo grunted, once again sounding unconvinced.

"There's something else," Bernadette went on. "He's still young, but I've never seen telepathic ability develop as quickly as his. He can stand in a room full of people and read five minds at once. It's uncanny."

Their voices lowered, and then Christian heard steps coming toward him. He backed away quickly and pretended to just be coming down the stairs.

"There you are." Bernadette smiled. "Ready to go? Angelo will take us as far as Rouen in his carriage. From there we can arrange a hired coach."

Christian nodded and offered to carry her luggage, but her words from the study kept echoing in his mind.

*   *   *

The next visit proved a revelation to Christian, but it was also the point in his existence when everything began to change.

He enjoyed traveling from Rouen to Florence. Once they reached Italy, Bernadette had him busy reading the thoughts of every person they encountered, and to his amazement, the foreign words in their minds made perfect sense to him. Inside of a week, he was speaking fluent Italian.

However, they did not spend a single night in Florence. Bernadette took him straight through to a villa about thirty minutes outside the city, where he met two vampires who were expecting them, Demetrio and Cristina.

Almost immediately, Christian felt something in the world shift.

The villa was lovely, with gardens and an orchard, and the décor inside was tasteful and understated. The tables and chests were carved, polished wood in natural tones, and the few paintings on the walls were either portraits in rich, dark colors or still lifes of fruit and flowers. Somehow, he knew that each painting had been chosen with care.

Demetrio was slender, with dark curly hair, and he wore simple but well-tailored clothing and no wig. He'd been an artist during the Renaissance, but after being turned, he'd developed a fear of unknown places and spent almost all his time at home. He'd made a companion for himself, Cristina, and she was devoted to him. She wore simply cut gowns, which looked exquisite on her, and her wheat gold hair was piled on her head, with long strands wisping downward.

She grasped Christian's hand with a warm smile. "You are most welcome."

Her voice was sincere. Her expression was sincere, and moments later, once she'd stepped away, Demetrio took his hand and smiled with equal warmth. "Do you play chess?"

"I prefer a good discussion," Christian answered, as he'd never played chess but did not yet wish to admit it.

Bernadette laughed, and for the first time, the sound of her voice grated on him. "Christian prefers a good party. He likes being the center of attention."

"Truly?" Demetrio asked. "We do have some society here in Florence. Let us see what we can arrange."

But Christian was embarrassed by Bernadette's comment. He looked around, gazing through the dining room out over the terrace. These rooms felt real. This place felt real.

The calm, powerful aristocratic aura surrounding Demetrio felt natural and real.

Christian turned to look at Bernadette in her overly embroidered gown, tight at the waist, with its huge, oversized skirt billowing around her. He looked at her powdered face and rouged lips, and to his surprise, she seemed coarse and vulgar to him. When he thought of their apartments in Paris, with everything painted white and gold, the furnishings suddenly seemed cheap and false.

He didn't understand.

Until this moment, Bernadette had seemed the finest creature he'd ever known. He'd loved their apartment in Paris. Now both she and their previous home seemed . . . beneath him.

Looking into his eyes, Bernadette froze, as if she could see what he was thinking, and he glanced away.

"Perhaps you could teach me to play chess?" he said to Demetrio.

"It would be my pleasure," Demetrio answered. "Come this way."

But as Christian walked out of the room, he could feel Bernadette's anxious eyes follow him.

A week later, Demetrio arranged a gathering at the villa, and Christian was introduced to the society of Florence. Rather than a sit-down supper, Cristina had employed servants to walk around serving delicacies on trays. The guests were all mortal, and of course they did not know the truth about Demetrio and Cristina, and this method of dining made it easier for the four vampires to mingle without having to pretend to eat.

Christian drank wine as he read every mind around himself, reveling in the differences of their thoughts from those of his fellow Parisians. It wasn't that the Italians of Florence had radically different thoughts on politics, music, art, or poetry, but rather that their opinions were their own, as opposed to whatever would achieve the greatest reaction or make them look the most informed. In Paris, image was everything and looking the fool was the worst thing anyone could endure. Nothing was ever said without careful consideration first.

Here, in this villa, Christian heard a number of people just saying what they actually thought.

This didn't really affect him in his own right, as he had no real opinions on any of these topics. But on the whole, he was enjoying himself, and he was clearly admired by everyone in attendance, and that was all that mattered.

Unfortunately, Bernadette continually reappeared at his arm, and his feelings toward her continued to degrade. He'd begun to see her as more coarse and vulgar every night, and he had no idea what to do about it. He couldn't leave her. No matter how many bills he charged to her accounts, she always paid them, but she'd made a point of keeping the coins in his purse to a minimum. He was beginning to understand why. Without her patronage, he would soon be nothing again.

And he had no intention of going back.

However, a few hours into the night's gathering, something else took precedence over his internal struggles. He could feel the people around him becoming restless, even bored. Apparently, they all admired Demetrio a great deal . . . but he was not an entertaining host, and the gathering was becoming dull.

For once, Christian thought of someone besides himself. He was grateful to Demetrio for both his hospitality and his fine company and didn't wish his new friend to have a reputation for dull parties.

Christian set down his wineglass.

"Might I suggest a game?" he said, and everyone began to turn toward him. "I have a great confession," he said in a conspiratorial whisper that still carried. "My family line has a touch of the gypsy, and I can read minds."

Everyone laughed, and he could feel a spark of energy growing in the room.

"I can tell fortunes and spill secrets just by looking into your eyes," he went on, and the amused smiles gratified him.

"Prove it," a young woman named Isabella challenged him.

"Ah," he said. "She doubts me." He turned a full circle. "I shall ask a question, and when she thinks of the answer, I shall pluck it from her thoughts."

He had the full attention of everyone in the room by now, and some people were leaning toward him.

Looking into Isabella's eyes, he asked, "Where is the most beautiful place a man has spoken words of love to you?"

She blinked in surprise at the question, and he immediately saw the image of an orchard beside a vineyard, and her first cousin, Lorenzo, was on his knees, gripping her arms, swearing his undying love. He was so unhinged in the moment that he'd knelt on an overripe plum and had not noticed. Then he stood up, gripping her harder, and pushed his tongue into her mouth. She could not marry him, as he was the second son of a second son with no prospects, but he was handsome and exciting, and she did not push him away.

But now, for Christian, came the tricky part. He had

to do this just right. She was unmarried, and he wanted
to give her a thrill and maintain the high energy in the
room, but he had to do this without marring her reputation. Boring questions entertained no one, so he had
to ask the spicier ones, but if he upset her family, he'd
ruin himself.

He straightened. "Ah, I see a vineyard . . . No, you
are in an orchard near a vineyard, and there are blos-
soms blowing in the air."

She stopped smiling and turned slightly pale. Then
she forced herself to smile again.

"There is a handsome young man on his knees. His
hair is dark, and he is swearing his love for you so vio-
lently that he's knelt on a plum and ruined his breeches
and doesn't know it yet."

The people hanging on his every word all broke into
laughter, and Isabella tried to laugh, but she turned
even paler.

"Then you spurn him!" Christian exclaimed. "And
you walk away, back to your father's house, leaving the
poor young man unsatisfied."

Everyone laughed again, and Isabelle dropped to sit
on a low couch in relief, but she was watching him
warily now.

"Read me next," a man named Francesco called out.

Christian turned to see him, glancing inside his
thoughts. Apparently, Francesco was a well-known
rake with no reputation to lose. "You?" Christian said.
"I fear nothing in your mind will be suitable to share in
the company of ladies."

The laughter was louder this time, but Christian then asked him, "Did you ever have a mistress who left you first? Who broke your heart?"

Across the room, he could see Demetrio watching him with a slight smile. Bernadette was watching him with desperate eyes, but she attempted to look amused.

Christian kept up this entertainment for more than an hour and finally had to plead exhaustion even though his audience begged him to go on. Afterward, the conversations were all quite animated regarding his astonishingly close guesses.

However, he did notice another person watching him carefully through the entire hour. The Countess Catherine Passerini did not ask him to read her thoughts, nor did she laugh much. She just watched him. But something about her caught his attention. She was attracted to him, as most women were, but she was more guarded. Approaching fifty years old, she was a wealthy widow. Her hair was still pale blond, but it had lost much of its luster, and her face still held traces of loveliness, even though lines were beginning to form around her eyes and mouth.

She did not speak to Christian that night, but after the party was over and all the guests had gone back to Florence, for some reason, she lingered in his mind.

The gathering was considered a great success.

Five nights later, Christian found himself in Florence at a dinner party hosted by the Countess Catherine Passerini. Of course, Bernadette, Cristina, and Demetrio had been invited, but only Bernadette attended, and no one had really expected Demetrio to leave the villa. His eccentricities were widely accepted there.

Bernadette spent the evening with a brittle smile on her face, and Christian was grateful that he'd not been seated beside her at dinner.

Afterward, the young women in attendance begged him to read their fortunes, and he took them each, one by one, to sit by the fire, and he painted their futures for them, reading their minds and telling them what they wanted to hear.

The countess paid only the barest attention to these entertainments, but as Christian was preparing to leave that night, she approached him.

"Several people in attendance here had already sent their apologies," she said. "But when word spread that you'd been invited, their previous engagements all vanished." She smiled ever so slightly. "I think everyone was here to see you."

He offered a short bow. "I doubt that very much, and I thank you for the kind invitation."

Bernadette said little on the carriage ride back to the villa. Perhaps she sensed they were beyond words.

But after that, the invitations began flooding in. Christian was in great demand, and Bernadette made one last desperate effort.

"I think we've been here long enough," she said. "We are overstaying our welcome. I thought we might move on to visit some friends in Germany."

"Germany? No."

Her eyes narrowed. "Are you saying you wish to stay behind? Without me?"

Panic washed through him. He wasn't ready to leave Florence yet. But then something Angelo had said back in Harfleur rang in his ears: *Has he ever tried it on you?*

Carefully, he flashed a single impulse into her mind, hoping she would not hear the actual words, but only feel the emotional impulse as a mortal would. He'd never tried this on another telepath. *Stay a little longer. He will love you again. Just a little longer.*

"Could we stay through the rest of the month?" he asked aloud.

She turned away. "Yes, through the end of the month."

He kept his face still, but inside, he rejoiced. His gift worked on other vampires.

A week later, he was at a small card party hosted by the countess when she asked him to accompany her to a different drawing room to give his opinion on a new painting she'd acquired.

As soon as they were alone, she looked directly at him and said, "I think I understand the arrangement between you and Madame Desmarais." She paused. "I wondered if you might consider a change."

This offer was made so bluntly it caught him off guard, but at the same time, every muscle in his body tightened. She was asking him to become her own "escort."

He wanted it. He wanted it as badly as he'd first

wanted to stay with Bernadette. But there were complications now, and he feared the countess might expect more than he could give.

"There may be some difficulties," he said, deciding to match her candor. "I find you beautiful, but due to issues regarding myself, I cannot share your bed."

She didn't even blink. "I've no wish to share your bed. I was done with all of that two weeks into my marriage. But I am not such an easy mistress in other regards. I would expect your strict attendance whenever it was desired."

She wanted him at her side, and she was willing to bargain. He felt a sense of power.

"As long as you only expect my attendance at night," he said. "I do not like the sun, and I tend to live at night." This time he paused. "Also, one night a week I will need to go out by myself, alone . . . and I cannot ever share meals with you. I will gladly sit with you, but I will not eat. You may have noticed I do not eat in front of others."

"Yes, I had noticed." She tilted her head. "What are your other conditions?"

"Conditions? I have none. In all other things, I would gladly be your slave. I couldn't stop staring at you that first night at Demetrio's villa, but I couldn't think of a way to speak with you."

Her eyes widened, and he knew he'd surprised her. She was more than pleased. For a moment, she couldn't speak. "Then," she said finally, "we have arrangement."

*   *   *

The countess was the first, and he stayed with her for seven years.

Given the fact that Bernadette had already threatened to leave him, he'd found separating himself from her far more messy and distasteful than expected, but in the end, she moved on to Germany. Demetrio didn't hold this against Christian, as apparently he had left his own maker many decades ago.

He and Christian remained friends.

A year after Christian's move to Italy, revolution broke out in France, and many of his old friends there lost their heads. He remembered the feeling of darkness that had loomed over him. But he was safe in Italy, and all was well, and he tried to forget the past.

He played his part perfectly for the countess. He showered her with the same gratitude and unadorned masculine flattery that he had once given Bernadette.

But then he met a wealthy, aging Spanish widow who offered to take him to Barcelona, and after seven years in Florence, he was drawn by the promise of someplace new. A pattern developed, and he learned to look for the right type of woman, one who wanted him on her arm but would not object to him sleeping alone and during the daylight hours. Someone suitable always managed to find him just as he was tiring of the last one. After spending eight years in Spain, he went to Austria and then Switzerland and then Belgium and then England.

Occasionally, he was challenged by a rival—as

wealthy widows certainly attracted more attention than his—and he'd killed a few men in back-alley duels. But he never broke the first law. He never killed in order to feed.

Then in 1818, the world began to shift again.

He was living with a minor duchess on the south coast of England, when Demetrio wrote him a disturbing letter.

> *My friend,*
>
> *You have not been one of us a sufficient time to be part of councils or privy to issues we discuss among ourselves, but something unprecedented has happened of which I must make you aware.*
>
> *Angelo appears to have lost his reason and has broken the second law. He made himself a son at the turn of the century, and just this year has made another son, a Welsh lord named Julian Ashton, who is damaged. He has no telepathic ability at all and cannot follow the first law. We are hopeful that he will improve.*
>
> *But this has caused concern among us, and I will keep you informed. Let me know how you are when you have the time. You are often in my thoughts.*
>
> *Demetrio*

Almost immediately after reading the letter, that same icy feeling began to grow in Christian's stomach again. He tried to ignore it, to convince himself that nothing could touch him here on the coast of England.

Then, not quite a year later, he received a letter from Angelo—to whom he'd not spoken since 1788. He never learned how Angelo knew of his location, but the letter was a summons to Harfleur, along with a veiled threat and a reminder that a favor had come due. Christian immediately left for Harfleur.

What he found there filled him with disbelief and disgust. Angelo met him at a tavern in the village, as Christian did not want to go to the manor.

"I need your help," Angelo said without even a greeting. "Come into the forest with me."

What else could Christian do? He had promised a favor, anything that Angelo asked.

Not far into the forest, they came upon the sight of a shirtless vampire, with wild, filthy hair, drinking blood from the open stump of a headless woman.

He'd murdered her.

"Oh no," Angelo murmured.

Christian stood frozen, but Angelo ran into action, grabbing the crazed vampire and pinning him down, sitting on his chest. "Philip, stop!" he ordered.

"Kill him quickly," Christian said, finding his voice and running to help.

Angelo looked up. "I can't kill him. He is my son, my third son."

Reality came crashing down on Christian. Angelo had made another son, less than year after this Julian Ashton of whom Demetrio had written.

Christian looked down at the blood-smeared creature twisting and snarling on the ground beneath

Angelo. Even on the streets of Paris, he'd never seen anything so repulsive. What did Angelo expect him to do?

He walked over to look at the mangled woman. The sight made him feel ill. He didn't feel pity exactly. Just revulsion. It was all so vulgar.

"Shhhhhhhh," Angelo was saying, stroking Philip's cheek. "Be still now."

The sight of this seemed more macabre than the dead body. "Jesus Christ," Christian said. "This is madness, Angelo. Do you see this woman? He's torn her head off. You have to put him down."

"No!" Angelo shouted.

"This is wrong," Christian said, striding back. With the exception of the first law, he'd never paid much attention to them, but now he was beginning to see their importance. "And you know it. You've broken the third law, and this is the price. Is this why you lured me out here? To stop this slaughter? If so, we're too late. He's a danger to our secrecy, Angelo. Either you put him down or I will."

Angelo sat straight, but he did not get off Philip's chest. "I will not, and neither will you. You owe me, Christian."

Both of them fell silent, and the uncomfortable sensation of ice began growing in Christian's stomach.

"*I* make the demands here," Angelo said. "Or you will become a new chapter in my book . . . and I have many details to include."

"You swore you'd leave me out."

"And in return, you swore to do me a service when I asked. I am asking now."

Philip suddenly tried to pitch Angelo off again. But Angelo held him down.

"What do you want?" Christian asked raggedly.

"He cannot speak, so I have no idea how much he understands. Go inside and help him to find words. You're the only one who can implant suggestions. Just help him to find speech. After that, I can help him myself."

"Inside his mind?" Christian asked, incredulous. "No. I'm not going in there. Not for you. Not for anything."

"Then you leave me no choice."

Staring at Angelo, Christian suddenly wondered how this man had learned so many "details" about him, but then he knew: Bernadette. They were probably in close contact, and she'd told him anything he wanted to know.

Christian was trapped. For some reason he could not explain, he did not want to be included in Angelo's book.

Slowly, he sank to his knees. Feeling a dread he'd known before, he pushed his thoughts into Philip's.

Even after Christian returned to England, it took him nearly a year to recover from the madness and blood he'd seen in that feral vampire's mind. But he did recover and tried to go on with his life.

The thing was . . . he was growing weary of being

the perfect escort, the perfect host to draw entertaining company to lonely women. But he liked good living too much and didn't know how to else to achieve it.

Worse, Demetrio did not write often anymore, and the feeling of darkness looming over Christian did not go away.

Then in 1826, he was living on the west coast of Denmark with an aging heiress when the last letter arrived.

My friend,

I don't know how to tell you this, so I will simply write it out.

Angelo is dead. His first son, John McCrugger, is dead.

Your sweet Bernadette is dead.

Several others of us, whom you have never met, are now dead.

I have been hiding some events from you, but in recent years, many of us began to counsel Angelo to destroy his second son, Julian, and third son, Philip . . . but most pointedly, Julian, who shows no sign of developing his telepathy and will never be able to follow the first law. Our quiet counsel soon turned into a demand and then finally into threats of taking this matter upon ourselves. We fear Julian learned of our plans. He must have believed Angelo would eventually side with us.

Julian's presence cannot be felt, and he is coming from the darkness to take our heads. I do not know how he is finding us with such ease and haste.

But you must leave Europe as soon as possible. Take

a ship to America and flee until this madness is over.
Let me know when you arrive. Please do this for me.
Your friendship and kindness to me have meant a great
deal.

With my love,
Demetrio

Christian stared at the letter. Less than an hour later,
he booked passage on a ship heading south toward
France.

He crossed France on land and made it to Florence
as fast as he could, going straight through to the villa.
His own sense of loyalty, of protection, surprised him,
but he was not leaving Demetrio to some murdering
son of Angelo's.

When he reached the villa, however, it was quiet,
and he went in the back door, climbing the steps and
going through the dining room to the terrace. The feeling of darkness was pressing all around him now, and
he walked slowly toward the terrace upon seeing Cristina's dress and Demetrio's suit on the floor. Small piles
of blowing dust filled and surrounded the clothes, and
Christian sank to his knees. They were already gone.
Dead long before he'd reached this place.

But his sorrow lasted only a few moments, and then
some of Demetrio's last words passed through his mind.

Julian's presence cannot be felt, and he is coming from the
darkness to take our heads. I do not know how he is finding
us with such ease and haste.

Christian stood up. He had a fairly good idea of how Julian was finding everyone, and this house was listed in Angelo's book.

Christian ran.

He fled across Italy and France. Then he crossed the channel and moved up the west coast of England in order to book passage on a ship sailing to Boston. He knew that the elite of Europe normally sailed out of England, as Liverpool now offered several lines providing "comfortable" travel for those who could afford it. He had enough money with him for the ticket and probably for the price of a week in a decent hotel when he got to Boston . . . but after that, he had no idea what he was going to do. He knew no one in America, had no connections and no one to introduce him into society.

Sitting in the silence of his cabin that first night, he was afraid.

He never forgot the first time he saw Ivory Daniels.

For one thing . . . she was breaking into someone else's cabin. Not that theft was so unusual, but she was so young and fresh, wearing a flowing white gown, with her blond hair piled up on her head. She looked like an angel.

It was his second night on board, and he was heading down a passageway. He'd just started to turn a corner when he saw her and stopped.

Something about the tight stance of her body made him pause, and he pulled back slightly. Then she took a thin tool from her bag, glanced around furtively, and picked the lock.

She hadn't spotted him.

He waited a few moments and then made his way quietly to the cracked door. Peeking inside, he saw her rummaging through a travel chest, careful not to disturb much. She was reading letters and looking at photos, but she wasn't stealing anything.

More than curious now, he reached out to read her surface thoughts.

There must be more than this here. Were in the hell is that hired investigator's report? I'll have to cancel the séance tonight if I can't find more.

She was looking for a hired investigator's report? Christian knew a little of these men, who undertook the sordid business of spying for other people. Of course he'd never met one, but he'd heard the stories.

Suddenly the girl stopped as she reached the bottom of a suitcase, and she pulled out a large envelope. Christian could feel the relief in her mind as she read *For Madame Aurelie Dupuis* on the outside. After glancing toward the door, she pulled out the contents and began reading an account by one of these paid spies who had been following Madame Dupuis' husband.

Inside the girl's thoughts, Christian picked up that her own name was Ivory Daniels, and she was intent upon learning everything she could inside this cabin in a matter of minutes.

He also picked up that Madame Dupuis' husband was recently dead and his body was being transported for burial. His name was Jerome Dupuis, and he was an American—of French heritage—and he'd made a fortune trading cotton and tobacco.

Christian wanted to know more, a good deal more.

But laughter and footsteps sounded down the passage, and frustrated, he decided to turn around and head back for the open deck. His mind was racing, and he knew he'd just witnessed something important. He just wasn't sure what yet.

The first-class passengers were outside, sitting at tables, having afternoon tea, and Christian approached a servant carrying a tray.

"Pardon me," he said. "Could you please point out Madame Dupuis?"

"Of course, sir. That is her sitting near the rail."

Christian passed the man a coin and approached a woman about forty-five years old, wearing a striped silk gown and wide-brimmed hat. He went into charming mode with a bow.

"Madame, forgive my intrusion. Let me offer condolences to you in this sad time. I know we've not been introduced, but I am a colleague of Mademoiselle Ivory Daniels, and she has asked me to join her at the small . . . gathering tonight. I may be of assistance to her. But I wished to ask your permission first. Would you allow me to attend and take part?"

Her mind was an open book, and he saw she'd been given use of a dining cabin for a séance that evening. But more important, she was taken aback by the handsome man asking permission to join in. She found his face and eyes and hair startling, and she fought to keep her expression still.

In spite of this, he wasn't taking any chances and flashed into her mind, *Tell him yes. He will be a great help.*

"Of course you may join us, Monsieur . . . ?" She trailed off.

He smiled. "Christian Lefevre, at your service."

When he walked into the dining cabin that night, four people were already inside, and Ivory turned to look at him in surprise.

She was beautiful in her white gown, and there were glass lanterns glowing everywhere, flickering their light upon the walls. Before Ivory could say anything, Madame Dupuis stepped between them.

"Ah, Monsieur Lefevre, you are here." She turned to Ivory. "I am so glad you included your friend this evening. I already feel he will be a help to you."

Christian had to give Ivory credit for a decent confidence trickster. Her face didn't flicker as she rapidly assessed the situation. He flashed an emotional impulse. *Do nothing. Play along or you'll ruin this.*

She smiled. "Yes, of course. Shall we sit down?"

But he could feel her mind churning, anxious, wondering what was going on. She spoke French fluently, but her accent was strange—not British, but close. Then he realized it was American. He'd heard similar accents before.

A round table had been set up with chairs around it, and Christian sat down beside Ivory. He surface-read a few thoughts around the room and quickly sized up the other two people as Madame Dupuis' sister, Marguerite, and Marguerite's husband, François.

Christian absolutely could not wait to see what happened next.

"Everyone please join hands," Ivory said, though she was still nervous about Christian's presence and wondering about the wisdom of continuing. But she didn't want to quit, and then Christian picked up that she was being paid five hundred American dollars for this little show. No wonder she hadn't bothered stealing anything from Madame Dupuis' cabin. Why risk being arrested when you could be paid?

Both his interest and his excitement began to grow.

Ivory closed her eyes.

"Jerome Dupuis," she said, her strange accent sounding almost lyrical now. "Please hear me. Come to me. Speak to me."

She stopped talking and made a gently musical humming noise for a few moments. Then she sucked in a breath and opened her eyes. "I can see him. He is standing behind you, madame."

Madame Dupuis gasped. "Where?"

"Only I can see him, but he is a most impressive man, tall, with a Roman nose and thick hair. He's wearing a dark brown coat with a white cravat tied around his neck." She squinted, ever so slightly. "I see a small silver arrow pinned to his lapel."

Madame Dupuis began weeping. "Yes, I gave it to him the first year we were married. He wore it often."

The moment was a revelation to Christian. He could have done this without ever going inside the woman's cabin, but for Ivory to be this convincing astonished him. She'd looked at one photo of the man and had now proved to his wife that she could see him standing across the room.

Without waiting any longer, Christian reached inside Madame Dupuis' mind and saw the whole sordid story. She had accompanied Jerome on a business trip to England. But he'd begun spending long hours away from her and she had no idea of his whereabouts. Eventually, she began to fear he was having an affair, and she'd hired someone to follow him.

One night, Jerome had spotted the man following him and, with no idea who he was, had become frightened. In a moment of rushed distraction, he had stepped out in front of a speeding carriage and been killed. The investigator had not been able to prove an affair one way or another yet, and now Madame Dupuis was racked with guilt that if her husband was innocent, she had caused his death for no reason.

Apparently, she'd told Ivory none of this, and Ivory had simply offered to contact him on the other side. But clearly, Ivory had been able to learn bits and pieces of the story . . . enough to look for the report.

Although Christian could surface-read several minds at once, for a deeper read, he needed to focus, so he shifted into Ivory's mind. She'd read the full report and knew the findings were inconclusive, but now she had to assuage Madame Dupuis' guilt over the possibility that her husband had died an innocent man and somehow still allow the woman to save face and leave with her dignity.

Not an easy feat.

"He says . . . ," Ivory went on. "He says he forgives you for hiring the man to follow him. Does that mean anything to you?"

Madame Dupuis sobbed once. "Yes."

However, by now Marguerite's husband, François, was staring at Ivory with a more-than-wary expression on his face.

"He says to tell you that you were right," Ivory went on. "He had fallen from grace and been seduced by a woman who was far beneath you. He'd let himself be trapped, and he was struggling to escape from her. She threatened to tell you, and he was trying to find a way to tell you himself." Ivory paused and drew in a sobbing breath. "He begs your forgiveness and says you were the finest thing that ever came into his life. You were right to send someone after him, and you should never blame yourself."

Madame Dupuis was weeping into her hands now. She turned to the empty space behind her chair. "Of course I forgive you. Please forgive me."

A moment later, Ivory said, "He's gone now."

In the seconds that followed, the room erupted into mild chaos as Marguerite jumped to comfort her sister and Madame Dupuis kept thanking Ivory over and over.

Christian just watched in amazement. Ivory had

earned five hundred dollars for telling someone exactly what she'd needed to hear.

There was money to be made in this, with little to no legal risk. It had been many years since he'd feared being arrested, and he had no intention of ever sinking that low again. He needed to find a dependable source of income without endangering himself.

While no one was watching, he slipped out of the room.

Later that night, he spotted Ivory up on the open deck, looking out over the rail at the sea. She was sipping a glass of white wine.

He walked right up to her.

"That was impressive," he said. "And I'm not easily impressed."

She glared at him but kept her voice low. "I don't know who the hell you are or what you were doing in there, but you'd better stay out of my way."

Her manner surprised him. Women never spoke to him like this. She wasn't remotely affected by his face or his eyes. He didn't like it.

"Jerome wasn't having an affair," he said.

She blinked, less certain now. "What?"

"He was simply working around the clock to make new connections for tobacco sales. Their finances were not as secure as Madame believed. She will find this out shortly after landing in Boston, so it's a good thing she paid you in advance."

"And how do you know that?"

He'd read it in François' mind.

"It doesn't matter. You told her what she needed to hear. That is a talent." He smiled. "I have a few talents of my own, and I find myself . . . shall we say, short of funds. If you can set up another of these gatherings before the ship reaches Boston and let me take the lead, I promise you will not regret it."

Although her face was calm, he could read her thoughts. He was a complete stranger, and she had no interest in taking on a partner.

But she hadn't yet seen what he could do. She'd change her mind soon enough. He sent an impulse. *Do what he wants. You can get away from him later. For now, just do what he wants.*

"All right," she said. "But I don't have any other fish on the hook here."

In that moment, he saw in her mind that she often worked ships like this one, as people traveled for all sorts of various personal reasons, and away from home, they gave in more easily to the idea of a spiritualist.

He smiled again. "Just have Madame Dupuis tell any of her friends on board about you. You won't have to fish. They'll be knocking on your door."

The first séance in which he took the lead remained in his mind as one of his greatest triumphs—but only because of the expression on Ivory's face afterward. He'd found it a pity that she was not a vampire like himself, as he would have preferred for her to be reading his mind, seeing what he was doing throughout the entire event. As things stood, the best he could do was to send her emotional impulses, which hardly compared to telepathic communication.

But she'd found him a wonderful mystery to solve— one that looked complex on the outside but was really quite simple. Those were always his favorites.

The ladies who hired him and Ivory were three American sisters in their midfifties, simply known in their circles as "the Bertram sisters." The sheer size of them had put him off for a moment when he'd first been introduced—via Madame Dupuis—out on the open deck, but he'd recovered quickly and kissed all their hands. They were loud and large and dressed like peacocks, but they'd offered three hundred dollars for a séance. At first Christian had been a little disappointed with the fee, as he was hoping for more, but money was money, and from what he understood, three hundred dollars would go a long way in Boston.

The ladies all spoke French badly and with grating accents. After living in England, he spoke fluent English and assured them their own language would be fine. They insisted he call them by their first names: Martha, Clementine, and Amelia.

"But we don't want to tell you too much," Clementine said, giggling, which caused her large bosom to bounce up and down. "Not until our . . . gathering."

"No, no, my dear," Christian assured her. "Whoever I contact for you will tell me all. But I must know to whom you wish to speak. I must know whom to call."

"Oh yes, of course," Martha said.

"Our eldest sister, Charlotte, died last year," said Clementine, "and after our time of mourning ended, we all took a trip to England to try and lift our spirits."

"But on this journey back," Martha said, "something has gone mis—"

"Martha!" Amelia cut in. "Don't tell him more."

Ivory stood quietly by, just listening. But she'd been the one to earlier announce that he was taking the lead and that the ladies were in good hands.

"Until this evening, then," Christian said with a bow.

As he and Ivory walked away, she whispered, "What are you going to do? You've got nothing."

"Just arrive on time, hold my hand, and watch."

Sitting down that night, he wasn't surprised to see that Madame Dupuis was also taking part, so that made six of them around the table, with lanterns flickering all around. Christian couldn't help an unwanted sensation of glee, but he also couldn't wait to show Ivory what he could do.

You've got nothing, she'd said earlier.

She had no idea.

He decided to begin as she had. "Everyone please join hands."

"Oh, this is so exciting," said Clementine.

Christian closed his eyes. "I need you all to think of Charlotte, to use your minds to call her with me."

Instantly, images of Charlotte surfaced in all three of the sisters' thoughts.

"Charlotte Bertram," he said. "Hear me. Come to me. Speak to me."

Rather than hum as Ivory had, he simply left a few moments of silence, and then he called for Charlotte again while he busily read the sisters' minds.

He opened his eyes.

"She is here," he said, "standing beside the table."

"No. Really?" Martha said, looking where he was staring.

The images he was picking up were certainly not flattering. Charlotte had been an enormous woman with a bosom like a jutting shelf and apparently . . . a penchant for brightly colored wigs. But he did see the dress she was buried in.

"She is a woman of great stature," he said, "wearing a red velvet gown with a single string of pearls around her neck. She tells me the pearls were not her favorite, but that Clementine always said they made her look more distinguished."

Martha and Clementine gasped aloud. Amelia looked wary.

Their thoughts were all churning now, and he picked out a few bits and pieces before going for the throat. He knew why they were here and what they wanted, but he decided to build things up a bit first.

"Martha, Charlotte tells me that your father, David, is so thankful to you for staying at his bedside those days when he died of blood poisoning. He couldn't tell you then, but it meant a great deal to him."

Ivory's fingers tightened on his hand, but the three sisters fell silent.

Then Clementine said, "Ask Charlotte if she knows what's become of the big blue sea."

Christian turned back to the empty space where he'd first been staring. "Charlotte, where is the big blue sea?"

He paused a moment, just nodding, and the room was dead silent. "Clementine, she says that you were right to decide to sell the necklace and give the money to charity, but one of your sisters did not agree. She also says the maid who was blamed had nothing to do with its loss, and that is why you've been unable to locate it through searches of the girl's room. Does this mean anything to you?"

He heard several sharp intakes of breath, but he ignored them. Most of his energy was focused in Amelia's mind now. Charlotte had owned a sapphire necklace worth thousands, and she'd been unable to choose which sister should inherit, so she'd left it to all three. But the joint ownership had only caused strife and arguments on the trip to England, until finally Clementine had insisted that upon reaching Boston again, they would sell the necklace and give the money to a hospital for the poor. Both her sisters had consented.

Martha finished a gasp. No longer sounding excited or amused, she asked, "What does she mean the maid didn't take it? The captain's steward swore he saw her coming out of Clementine's cabin long past scheduled hours for cleaning."

"No," Christian said. "That maid was never in Clementine's room. Charlotte says the steward was well paid to tell you that. Upon closer questioning, he will probably admit it."

"By whom?" Martha asked. "Who paid him?"

Christian looked across the table. "Your sister Amelia. If you have her held here and send someone, you will find the big blue sea in a false-bottom compartment of her suitcase."

Amelia jumped to her feet as fast as a woman of her size could possibly jump. "That's an outrageous lie!"

He continued looking her directly in the eyes, and she sank back into her chair again.

"Clementine," he said. "Shall I send someone to look?"

Neither of the other sisters looked particularly happy at this outcome, but Clementine nodded. "Yes, send someone."

Turning, he saw Ivory staring at him with an expression he couldn't quite read, but in her mind he saw that she was certain the sapphire necklace would indeed be found at the bottom of that suitcase.

After that, Ivory was in his company every night. They drank and talked. She shared secrets of her trade, and they made plans for how they might use each other's skills in the same séance.

When he'd told her he could read minds, she'd believed him.

She'd had other partners before, never for very long, but although she didn't know Christian well yet, she knew the real thing when she saw it, and he was the real thing.

He'd never kept company like this with a young woman before, and the experience was quite different from flattering aging women. Ivory didn't seek flattery. She used her lovely face as a mask. That was all.

However, if truth be told, she was a bit rough around the edges for his taste. She had a temper, and she was a survivor like him, so occasionally she behaved in a manner he found . . . unladylike. But she valued him, and he needed her, and at first that was enough. He knew he'd found his calling. There would be no more catering to the egos of aging ladies for him.

If he and Ivory could make connections with an even wealthier circle, there was a great deal of money to be made.

A few days before reaching Boston, a spark of genius hit him, and he saw how this game might really be played.

He pictured how the séance would go if Ivory could read his mind. He could play the spiritualist, and she could play the conduit. If he could read minds, ask questions aloud, and then feed her the answers, what a stunning show that would make. The drama would be twofold, and no one would doubt them.

Also . . . in some ways, occasionally when he looked at Ivory, he couldn't help seeing something of himself, someone who was restless, someone who never stayed too long. But in this case, he needed her to stay.

He wanted her to stay for many years, lovely and fresh and his partner.

She was a born actress and a born confidence trickster. He'd never known anyone like her in all his existence.

That night, he asked her to his cabin. She was comfortable with him by now and came right on time, with a bottle of white wine in her hand.

"We're almost there," she said. "Maybe two more nights, and we'll make harbor. You give me a few weeks and let me try to get something big set up . . . for people with real money."

He took in her delicate profile. Her basic thoughts consisted of remembering one confidence game after another since she was about sixteen years old. He hadn't picked up any stray thoughts in her mind from before then.

"Don't you have questions about me?" he asked.

The sudden switch of topic caught her off guard, and she half turned, slightly cautious now. "What do you mean?"

"Why don't I eat? Why don't you ever see me in daylight? How is it possible that I can read minds?"

She grew tense. He didn't need to bother with her thoughts to see that.

"That's none of my business," she said. "You're good at what you do. That's all that matters."

Yes, for a while, he thought. *Until you want to move on to someone else.*

He was dead set on the idea of himself playing the spiritualist and her playing the conduit. What a show that would make.

"What if I told you I could make it so you could read minds, too?" he asked. "So that you could read my mind? I could pretend to ask our visiting spirit questions, you could read me, and I could pass you the answers to speak aloud. That would be impressive, no?"

She seemed to relax a little, maybe thinking he was joking and she'd taken his initial questions too seriously. "Yes, it would." She smiled at him. "But I don't think you can touch the top of my head and make it so I can read minds, too, Christian. You're one of a kind."

"I'm not," he said, letting his voice drop. "And I *can* make it so you can read minds. I can make it so you'll never age another day. But there's a price. You won't be able to eat food anymore, and you won't ever see the sun again. You'll need to hunt about once a week, and feed on blood from someone's wrist and then blur their memories so they won't remember. But I can do this for you if you'll let me."

He was well aware that he'd not been undead for a hundred years yet, and he'd be breaking the second law, but he didn't see a choice here. He just kept going over how perfect the show would be with the two of them involved, but they both needed to be telepathic . . . and he didn't want her to age another day.

There was only one answer. Of course she would agree. He was offering her a great gift.

But she started backing toward the door. "It's late. Maybe I should go back to my room."

He flashed a suggestion. *No, stay with him. Listen to him.*

To his shock, she fought the suggestion and kept on backing up. It was difficult for her. He could see that. But she was still moving. She turned around when she reached the door, grabbing for the handle, but he stepped forward and held the door shut.

Angry, she whirled back to face him. "Christian, let me out of here."

He'd never in his existence had to use physical strength to keep a woman in a room with him.

"Listen to me," he whispered. "I'm offering you a great gift. All you have to do is consent. I'll do everything else. I can make you just like me. You won't believe the power, Ivory. You'll feel like you've been blind your whole life and then suddenly you can see everything."

She shoved against his chest, hard, but she couldn't move his body, and he was still holding the door closed.

Confused, he read her surface thoughts and saw that she thought she'd trusted him too quickly, and that he was dangerous and mad, and if she got out of this room, she'd find a way to vanish somewhere on the ship where he'd never find her again.

Anger and fear rose inside him at the same time.

He didn't know how to deal with being refused.

Women didn't refuse him, and he'd never made such a glorious offer to anyone before. He tried to calm himself. She was fighting him only because she didn't understand. Afterward, she'd thank him, and the two of them would have a profitable future together.

Grabbing both her arms, he pulled her back toward the bed, and she went wild, fighting and scratching and screaming. He'd never dealt with anything like this, not even when he was mortal. But she wasn't strong, and he was. It took him only a few seconds to pin her to the bed with one hand over her mouth, and once she'd felt the strength in his arms, her anger vanished and her eyes stared up with open fear. They were begging him to stop.

He wished he could make her understand. She'd thank him afterward.

He knew how to do this. He remembered exactly what Bernadette had done. Without hesitating, he drove his teeth into Ivory's throat.

She was still screaming into his hand.

chapter nine

N o more!"

On the edge of his awareness, Christian heard someone's voice. The ship's cabin around him vanished, and he suddenly found himself in an over-furnished bedroom. But he could still feel Ivory's panicked breath on his palm.

Someone slid off the bed and started choking on the floor, repeating the phrase, "No more."

Then everything came rushing back.

His vision cleared, and he saw Eleisha on the floor in her shimmering evening gown with her face twisted in pain, and he remembered something about her having asked to read a few memories.

But he'd just relived years and years of his existence. The thought turned him cold. Had she seen all that?

"You forced her," Eleisha choked. "How could you do that?"

She had seen it. She knew everything, every dirty little secret of his life . . . that he'd slept in alleys, that he'd cut purses, that he'd sold his companionship, that he'd broken the second and the third laws.

He wasn't given to blind rage, but it swelled up inside him, and he dropped to the floor beside her, grabbing her by the throat. She'd tricked him, seduced him into dropping his guard, and then she'd laid his whole existence bare. She would despise him now, spurn him. She would tell the others.

How could he stop any of that from happening?

No one could ever know of his past. He didn't want to know some of it himself, and most of the time, he still believed himself to be Christian Lefevre, the fourth son of a minor nobleman from the south of France.

Still lost in a sense of betrayal and rage, he snarled into her pretty face and tightened his hand, watching with some satisfaction as the revulsion in her eyes turned to fear.

But then something unexpected happened.

Freeze!

The panicked mental command hit him like a club. Every muscle in his body went rigid, and he couldn't move at all. Somehow, Eleisha shoved his hand away from her throat and scrambled sideways. But she didn't scream or call for help. She just watched him.

Slowly, he started to gain control of his muscles again, and he stared back at her. How could he have been so stupid? How could he have taken her at face value as fragile and helpless? She could do things he could not. What else was she capable of?

Good God . . . she'd been using her gift on him just before he'd consented to the memory reading.

But while struggling to regain control of his body, he also regained some control of his emotions, and he noted that the shocked expression on her face was gone now, replaced with . . .

"Why did you turn her like that?" she whispered. "Were you so afraid of being alone in America? Of not being able to run the game by yourself?"

He couldn't believe it. Compassion and honest questions were shining from her face. She was genuinely asking him for a reason, and she was willing to listen to the answer. He could play on that. He could play on her pity and her guilt for having seen what she should not have seen. Perhaps nothing had changed after all.

"You were wrong to do that to me," he said, ignoring her questions. "I thought you were beginning to care for us, for me, and then you rape my mind like that?"

She flinched. He'd known she would.

"You've seen things I don't even want to see," he went on. "How can I forgive that?"

She moved closer, reaching out but not quite touching him. "Christian, I'm sorry. Please believe me. But I had to do it. You weren't telling me anything, and you make a joke out of everything, and I needed to see who . . . what you were before taking you home. I didn't mean to embarrass you."

That hurt, as if she was openly acknowledging he had something to be embarrassed about. He glanced away and then felt her hand on his arm.

"I'm sorry," she whispered again. "But you turned her because you were afraid, didn't you? Julian was killing your friends, and you were running, and you didn't know what else to do?"

He knew she needed to hear it, so he said, "I was terrified." Then he leaned back against the bed. "So do you still think I'm fit company for the others in your underground?"

"I think you'll do almost anything to get what you want, but so will a lot of people."

He turned his head and looked at her in surprise. He'd never met anyone like her.

"Do you still want us to stay here?" she asked. "Do you want me at this séance?"

He did. He suddenly wanted it more than anything. She knew almost everything about him, and she was still sitting on the floor talking to him, apologizing to him, begging his forgiveness, practically dying to absolve him of his own sins. He could not remember an exchange that had felt this *real* since the last time he'd spoken with Demetrio. Any remaining shred of anger faded away, and his determination to follow his original plan solidified.

He was keeping Eleisha.

"Yes, I want you there," he answered, climbing to his

feet, still working to get full control of his body again. He fell back into his practiced persona and smiled. "Well, this was quite a little drama, wasn't it? Is your throat all right?"

She nodded. "I don't blame you. It was a natural reaction."

"There's nothing natural about us, my dear."

He glanced at the clock, startled to see that several hours had passed. Yet he'd seen so many years of his own existence, as if living them all over again. How long since he'd given Bernadette a thought? He couldn't remember.

Turning back to the bed, he moved to the end and picked up a pair of slacks, a dress shirt, and a jacket he'd laid out earlier. "Take these for Wade," he said. "They should fit him."

She stood there a moment, just watching him, her expression awash with concern. "I really am sorry, Christian. I had to do it. I had to see."

He didn't answer. Instead he said, "Remember what I told you. When the show starts tonight, don't try to read anyone else. Just stay inside my head, and you'll be able to see everything that's happening. I want you to feel how this works."

Without looking at him, she took the clothes for Wade and walked toward the door. "We'll meet you downstairs."

He watched her slip out, but his thoughts were already turning over possibilities for what he was going to do next.

*   *   *

Eleisha's hand was shaking as she opened the bedroom door and slipped out into the hallway. Guilt and worry and confusion were all swirling around inside her head, making her dizzy. Christian was so proud, and she'd just embarrassed him. No, she'd more than embarrassed him. But he was also . . . *more* than she'd first realized. She wasn't exactly sure what that meant yet, but there was even more to him than met the eye.

When backed into a corner, he really would do anything to get what he wanted, and she'd best never forget that. But she reminded herself that Philip had once committed acts far worse, and she had no intention of giving up on Christian.

The memories she'd seen were still fresh in her mind, and she couldn't stop thinking about the differences in how Bernadette had taught him to hunt. They didn't put their victims to sleep, nor did they replace memories. Rather, they dazed their victims and then simply blurred the memories. Perhaps that was how Bernadette's maker had taught her. There was so much Eleisha didn't know about her own kind in the distant past.

But poor Ivory. No matter how desperate Christian had been in the moment, she'd been turned against her will—and so brutally. Eleisha had experienced the same horror herself long ago. As soon as she could, she would try to offer more open friendship to Ivory. They had one thing in common.

As she closed the door behind herself, she paused,

just glad to be alone. At least that emotional scene with Christian was behind her now. She could spend a few moments in the bliss of solitude.

But then she turned to head down the hallway, and she froze midstep.

Philip was standing ten feet away, leaning back against the wall, taking in the sight of her gown, hair, and makeup. His arms were crossed, and the muscles in his face were tight.

"I thought you were playing cards," she said weakly.

"You were gone so long I came looking for you. I knocked on this door, and no one answered," he said. "So I looked inside and saw you sitting on the bed with him. I knew what you were doing, so I waited out here."

He sounded so cold that she couldn't help feeling a fresh rush of guilt, as if she'd been doing something wrong.

"I was just . . . I was reading his memories."

"I know." His eyes moved down to her bare arms, and he motioned to the gown. "Why are you dressed like that?"

Normally, he'd be thrilled if she wore anything besides a broomstick skirt and a T-shirt. But again, for some reason, she felt the need to defend herself. "He said we had to look the part." She held up the clothing in her arms. "These are for Wade."

He looked at the clothes for a long moment and then nodded, but his expression was still cold, and she wasn't quite sure why.

*   *   *

Wade's jaw nearly dropped when Eleisha came into his guest room carrying some slacks, a shirt, and a sport coat.

The front side of the dress she wore left little enough to the imagination, but when she turned to drop the clothes on his bed, his eyes ran across her shoulder blades. The skirt of the gown fit snuggly to just above her tailbone, and her entire back was bare.

"That's a new look for you," he said.

Then he saw that Philip was standing in the open doorway, frowning. The tension flowing from his body was almost visible.

"What's wrong?" Wade asked.

"Nothing," Eleisha answered. "But Christian says we need to look the part tonight. Could you put these on?"

As Wade glanced down at the clothes, Philip asked, "Do you need me to help?"

The suggestion that he needed assistance to dress properly for the evening was a tad insulting, but Philip's tone had been sincere.

"No, I think I can manage to put on some slacks and a dress shirt," Wade answered, struggling to keep the sarcasm from his voice.

"All right."

Philip came inside and closed the door. Eleisha turned away so that Wade could change. "I'm sorry we have to rush you like this," she said, "but we're expected downstairs. Dinner must nearly be over by now."

Her words registered, but again, he found himself looking at her back. It was so pale, without a spot or blemish, and her shoulders were so tiny. He glanced at Philip, who didn't meet his eyes.

Oh well. The show must go on.

Wade changed his pants quickly. "I'm decent now," he joked, pulling his Blue Öyster Cult shirt over his head and reaching for the dress shirt. Christian's clothes fit him fairly well.

"Have you eaten anything?" Eleisha asked, turning toward him.

He motioned with one hand toward a side table. "Yeah, Simmons brought me a dinner tray, but he said that Christian had ordered it."

"How thoughtful," Philip said dryly.

What was wrong with him? Wade buttoned the shirt all the way to the top and reached for the jacket, but Philip came striding over. "No, don't button it all the way like that if you're not wearing a tie."

Wade sighed and let Philip adjust the shirt. Then Philip picked up the jacket, and Wade slipped both arms in. Philip straightened it and brushed at it with one hand.

"Just like having a valet," Wade said.

"You wish," Philip murmured.

"If you two are finished, we really should get down there," Eleisha said, opening the bedroom door. She sounded edgy.

Wade threw her a questioning glance, but she wouldn't meet his eyes either.

Instead, she led the way, and both men followed her one floor down, then through the overstuffed living room, and finally though an open archway into a room with a large round table sporting an ornate candelabra.

Vera, Christian, and Ivory were already there, sipping red wine from long-stemmed glasses. There was also a young man in a dark suit, but Wade didn't notice him much at first. He couldn't seem able to take his eyes off Ivory tonight, not even during the card game earlier. She had on a low-cut black evening gown that didn't cover any more skin than Eleisha's, but whereas Wade had found Eleisha's state of dress surprising, he had a different reaction to Ivory's. It made the blood pound in his ears.

She ran her gaze up and down his jacket, and she smiled slightly, raising her glass.

For the first few seconds, he didn't hear anything that was being said around him. Then he was aware of Vera leading him forward toward the man in the suit.

"Justin, darling, this is Wade Sheffield. Wade, this is Justin Michaels."

Wade was vaguely aware of shaking the young man's hand and saying something appropriate, but he had no idea what. He was too busy trying not to stare at Ivory.

Vera finished the introductions, and someone stuck a martini glass in his hand. He drank it for the sake of the alcohol even though he didn't really like martinis— and he'd never liked olives.

It was only when Christian finally called for everyone to sit down that Wade realized he had absolutely no idea who this Justin Michaels was or why he wanted Christian's help, and then it dawned on him that Christian probably hadn't been given any information either.

That was part of the game.

"Sit by me," Ivory said in Wade's ear, and he looked down to see her at his shoulder, the small diamond pendant around her neck reflecting candlelight. He just nodded and sat down.

In spite of the fact that she was in such close proximity, he managed to keep his mind clear, and the truth was that he couldn't wait to see what happened next.

Eleisha sat with Christian on one side and Philip on the other. She was still edgy from her earlier experience with Christian and confused by Philip's cold demeanor, but she was determined to get through this séance with good grace—and then go put something else on and give this dress back to Ivory.

After reading Christian's memories, she had a good understanding of how some of this worked. But she'd not yet seen Ivory take an active role as the "conduit."

Just as she settled in her chair, she felt Christian inside her mind.

Stay with me. Follow everything I do.

Reaching back, she tangled her thoughts with his, and she heard Ivory's mental voice so clearly.

I am here, too, Ivory projected.

Eleisha forgot everything else as she allowed herself to become focused on this experience of being connected to them both at the same time—but from inside Christian's mind.

What about Philip and Wade? she projected.

No. Christian answered. *That would be too many conflicting voices. You can explain it to them later. Just stay with me. Just observe.*

Then, without any warning, Christian was inside Justin Michaels' mind, reading his thoughts, digging deep.

Of course, the man's basic reasons for being here were all on the surface, easy to see, and within seconds, Eleisha knew everything. The story was ugly and sordid. But she was still getting accustomed to being inside Christian's mind as he read Justin. This method of telepathy was unsettling and exciting at the same time.

"Justin, who is it you are trying to reach?" Christian said aloud.

"My mother . . . Her name was Irene." He leaned forward in his chair, and his eyes were intense, almost hostile. Eleisha watched him carefully. He was short for a man, perhaps five feet six inches, with a stocky build. The suit he wore didn't flatter him. His neck was too thick, and she thought he might look better in more casual clothes.

"I don't need you to ask her anything." Justin bit off the words as if they hurt. "I just need you to tell her something for me, and then I want you to tell me *ex-*

actly how she answers. I'll know if you're really talking to her."

Justin didn't believe Christian could contact his dead mother. Eleisha could see that in his mind—via Christian's mind—but he was desperate. He was willing to try anything.

"Of course," Christian answered. "I'm only here to help with whatever you ask me to do." His voice was so compassionate that Eleisha couldn't help turning to look at him. From the sympathetic expression on his face, if she didn't know better, she would have believed he had no agenda here other than to help Justin.

Christian closed his eyes. "Irene Michaels, hear me. Come to me from the other side. Come and speak to your son through Ivory."

He was silent for a short while, and then he repeated the same phrases. But Eleisha barely heard him. She was seeing images of Irene in Justin's mind.

"She's here," Christian said, opening his eyes, "standing right beside you."

Justin didn't look in either direction or make a sound.

"She's a delicate woman with pale hair," Christian said, smiling now. "Her features are soft, and she's wearing peach lipstick and a gray wool suit." He squinted slightly. "There is a scar running through her left eyebrow." He paused and spoke directly to the empty space. "How did you get the scar, Irene?"

Staring straight ahead, as if lost in a trance, Ivory

answered, "When I was a girl, I tried to put a doll's dress on our family's cat."

Justin gasped and gripped the edge of the table. Thick sinews stood out on the backs of his hands. But Eleisha could see Irene so clearly in his thoughts, along with quick flashes of his memories regarding his mother. She had told him that story about the cat. The physical picture Christian painted was perfect, and he was feeding Ivory answers.

"What is your message, Justin?" he asked.

"Just tell her I'm sorry."

Christian looked to the empty space beside Justin's chair. "He says he is sorry."

Ivory continued staring straight ahead as she spoke. "You should not have put yourself through all this, Justin. You've been suffering needlessly, and I have nothing to forgive. You were in love, and you could not have understood that Amy was filled with poison."

Christian turned to Justin. "Does that mean anything to you?"

Justin sucked in a loud breath. His mouth twitched from pain, and Eleisha was almost overcome by an impulse to put a stop to this. She could see Christian feeding Ivory the exact words he wanted her to say.

But Eleisha and Ivory already both knew what Justin wanted. Through Christian, they could see it and feel it all, turning and churning through his mind.

Justin was from Texas, and his family had made a fortune in oil. He'd had been close to both his parents until he'd fallen obsessively in love with a young woman named Amy Sheriche. His mother was ill, diagnosed with breast cancer, and so he was surprised when she began tiring herself even more by expressing open reservations about the girl. Then, when Justin announced his engagement, his mother had expressed more than reservations. She'd told him to break it off, that Amy served only herself, that Amy didn't love him, and that she was a gold digger who'd do anything to get what she wanted. The scene had been awful, with Justin shouting back, ending with him walking out and refusing to see his mother again. Three weeks later, she died. When he got the call, he was stunned and blamed himself that he'd not even told her good-bye. But then . . .

"I'm so sorry for what you had to go through," Ivory spoke again, "for what you walked in on."

Justin's grip on the table tightened, and the hostility returned to his eyes. "What? What does she think I walked in on?"

Christian asked the question aloud.

"You saw Amy in bed with your father," Ivory answered. "You were right not to go to their wedding, but you have to forgive him now."

Justin sucked in another loud breath. But his eyes were desperate and far too bright. He leaned over the table toward Christian. "You're talking to her? You're really talking to her?"

"Yes."

Eleisha wasn't sure how much more of this she could take, and she could feel her hands trembling.

Christian gripped down harder on her fingers, and Philip glanced at her and frowned. At this point, neither he nor Wade had much of an idea what was happening.

Justin sobbed once, and he seemed to be trying to get ahold of himself. "Ask her if she really forgives me."

"Irene," Christian said, "Justin needs to know if you forgive him."

"There is nothing to forgive," Ivory said, still looking straight ahead, seeming lost in the trance. "From the time you were a boy, I always loved your temper. Your spirit. You had no way of knowing I would go so quickly, and you were still hurt by the things I said. But you *must* forgive your father and make peace with him. He is all you have left."

Eleisha could feel something easing inside of Justin. He'd desperately wanted to forgive his father, to forgive himself, and Christian had made certain he'd heard all the right things. Her hands stopped trembling, and she wondered that if amid this sham, amid the fact that Christian was doing this only for the money, maybe he had helped Justin after all.

"She's gone now," Christian said. "We're alone again."

Justin slumped forward, weeping silently, and Vera got up, hurrying to his side.

Eleisha disliked deception. But didn't she use it herself on a regular basis in order to feed? The most unfamiliar thought appeared unbidden in her mind, that this evening had been exciting, and she wondered what it would feel like to sit in Ivory's place and speak all the right words to someone who needed to hear them.

Christian hadn't felt such a thrill from a séance in more than a hundred years. The feel of Eleisha inside his thoughts, following the drama of the moment, seeing and feeling everything he controlled and manipulated . . . well, it brought more than simple pleasure.

She wasn't like Ivory. She wasn't a natural-born confidence trickster. She'd been mentally gasping through the entire experience, and she'd made him feel so alive.

He wished they had another client lined up tonight so he could do it all again. But he had a more important task, and it couldn't wait. He had to strike while the moment was right, and he knew how to play this. He knew what she'd respond to.

So while she was still sitting there, holding his hand, recovering from the shock, he carefully, quietly sent an emotional impulse into her mind.

What would it be like to sit in Ivory's chair? What would it be like to help others by speaking all the right words and telling them exactly what they need to hear? Wouldn't that be exciting? Satisfying?

Her eyes flickered for an instant, and he could see the impulse take hold.

But he also hadn't missed the way Wade had been casting glances all night at Ivory, and he was hoping to stir up a little discontent in Eleisha's trio, anything that might cause her to turn to him for help or advice.

Casually, he turned to Wade, summoned an impulse, and sent it.

You'd do anything for Ivory. Anything she asks.

Wade blinked, and Christian wanted to smile. He wasn't quite certain how he could use this yet, but he had a few ideas, and at least the impulse was in place.

chapter ten

By the time Vera was getting Justin into his coat and walking him toward the front door, Wade decided he wanted *out* of the small "séance" room, and he headed into the living room to stand by the fireplace—trying to ignore the large painted carousel tiger.

Without anyone saying a word, he had a pretty good idea of what had just happened around that table. Several times, he'd been tempted to start reading minds himself, but he was afraid of interfering and throwing Christian and Ivory off their game.

He hadn't known precisely what he expected, but he'd not expected the outcome to be so emotional. Christian and Ivory had made that young man cry.

To make matters worse, Wade wasn't even sure

they'd done anything wrong. They might have helped him.

But still, it just all seemed like such a lie.

He was no longer sure how he felt about bringing Christian back to the church and exposing Rose and Maxim to his company. And what about Ivory? He knew nothing about her besides the fact that she was beautiful and that she seemed to do whatever Christian wanted.

That wasn't much to go on.

The fire crackled and popped, and he glanced back into the sitting room to see Christian standing by the table, still holding Eleisha's hand and whispering what appeared to be comforting words into her ear. Philip was standing behind them staring daggers, and Wade almost wished he hadn't paid any attention to the news story about the "spiritualist" back at the church. He almost wished he'd just let this one go.

But then Ivory broke away from the group at the table, and she began walking toward him.

He watched her coming all the way across the living room, and she stopped beside him.

"Quite a show," he said.

"That was the third one in the third consecutive night," she said softly. "I'm tired."

Something in her voice sounded different now. This was the first time he felt she might really be trying to talk to him.

"Do you want to go upstairs and rest?" he asked. "Have some time to yourself?"

Her eyes flew to his face as if she was surprised by his concern. Then she glanced around the claustrophobic room. "What I really want is to get out of here for a few hours. I'm hungry, and I need to hunt. Anywhere. I don't care where we go."

He wasn't certain what she was asking him, so he stayed quiet another moment, and she said, "If I go upstairs and change my clothes, will you meet me in the garage? We can take a car and go out for a while. Don't tell anyone. They'll just think we've gone upstairs to our rooms. If you tell Eleisha, she might tell Christian, and he won't let . . ." She trailed off.

Every alarm in Wade's mind screamed that this was a bad idea. If he took a car from Vera's garage and took Ivory out hunting without telling anyone, there would be repercussions from without and from within.

For one, Julian was out there somewhere.

But he had his gun, and he knew how to avoid the shadows, and just looking down into Ivory's face, he knew he wasn't going to say no.

"I'll meet you in the garage," he said quietly, and he called out more loudly, "Eleisha, I'm going upstairs."

A half hour later, Philip was alone with Eleisha in their guest room, and he watched her struggle out of the silk evening gown as quickly as she could, as if she couldn't wait to get the thing off.

But he couldn't even bring himself to talk. He'd never felt quite like this before—or at least not to this degree. He didn't even know what he felt, and he hated it. It was the worst feeling he could imagine. It was worse than fear. It was worse than being alone for years on end.

It started when he'd opened the door to Christian's bedroom, expecting to find it empty, and he'd seen Eleisha in that dress, with her hair styled and her eyes painted, and she was holding Christian's hand, reading his memories.

It grew worse after the séance while he watched Christian whispering in her ear.

It was the worst feeling he'd ever suffered, and he wanted it to go away.

She laid the dress on the bed and looked over at him. The only thing she wore now was a small pair of panties . . . and the jeweled clip in her hair.

"Are you all right?" she asked. She looked almost sorry for him, and the last thing he wanted was her pity.

He couldn't answer her. He didn't know how. A part of him couldn't help feeling that somehow she'd done something wrong, but she hadn't.

In three strides, he reached the bed and grasped the back of her head. Her bones always felt so light in his hands that he was careful when he touched her, but now he jerked her forward against his chest.

"Philip!"

He barely heard her and brought his mouth down to hers, pushing his tongue between her teeth. Then he leaned forward, lowering her rapidly onto the bed and moving with her until she was pinned beneath him.

He took his mouth off hers long enough to say, "Turn on your gift."

But he was vaguely aware of her struggling beneath him, and over the roar in his ears, he heard her trying to speak.

"Not like this . . . You're too heavy. Philip, stop."

He froze.

She sounded frightened.

He slid off her partially, removing most of his weight, but he turned on his gift. He wanted her to want him back, not to be afraid of him.

"Shhhhhh," he said. "Turn on your gift."

He let his gift wash over her and through her, and slowly, she began to relax and brought her hand up to his chest. He was addicted to her touch. He was addicted to her gift.

His gift was an aura of attraction, but he'd never considered it as strong as hers. He didn't force his mouth onto hers again, but let her kiss him this time, softly, the way she always did. He closed his eyes, running his hands down her sides, over her hips.

They'd never done this when he was fully dressed and she was nearly naked before, but he didn't want to stop long enough to get his clothes off.

Then she turned her gift on to join with his, only she channeled it, altering it slightly, focusing it on how helpless she was without *him*.

On how much she needed him.

He couldn't stop himself from pressing his body harder against hers and pushing his tongue deeper into her mouth. He let himself get lost inside her gift, letting it combine with his own, meshing and churning and being absorbed into his own until a great release exploded inside his mind, flowing down through his body while he jerked and gasped.

He had to stop kissing her because his teeth were so tightly clenched, but he held on to the back of her neck with one hand, with his temple pressed up against her face as his body jerked several times.

When the sensation finally faded, they stayed locked together like that for a while.

And then . . . he didn't know what to say. He thought this would take the pain away, but the awful feeling inside him remained.

Although he wasn't given to apologies, unbidden, the first thing out of his mouth was "I'm sorry."

"It's all right."

"Say you want to be with me," he said, "at the church, at home, in our room, on our hunts. Say you want to be with me."

"I always want to be with you," she whispered in his ear, running her fingers up his back. "I don't know what's wrong, but you never need to worry about that."

When she spoke, he believed her.

"Philip, it's too early to go to bed," she said quietly. "Can I get some of my own clothes?"

Her own clothes?

"Yes." He jumped up off her and crossed the room, grabbing a pair of her jeans and her little red T-shirt. They smelled like her. He'd never complain about her lack of interest in clothes again. He held them out. "These are yours."

She reached up to remove the jeweled clip from her hair. Then she took the clothes from his hand and pulled the T-shirt over her head. She looked like herself again.

He suddenly felt better.

Wade decided on a white BMW in Vera's garage. As they pulled up to the front gates, Ivory gave him the code without blinking, and he punched it in.

Then they were on the road, heading downtown.

She looked different now, with her hair loose, wearing tan cargo pants, a tank top, and a light jacket. But she didn't seem any more accessible than before, and he had no idea what to say. He didn't know her. He didn't know anything about her, and he'd just abandoned his friends without a word to take her hunting.

This was semicrazy behavior, and he knew it. But he couldn't seem to stop himself.

"I don't know this city at all," she said suddenly. "Do you?"

"Yes," he said, nodding with his eyes on the road, grateful to fill the silence. "We lived here for a few months last year. Up on Queen Anne Hill."

"You did?" She sounded surprised. "All of you?"

"No, just me, Eleisha, and Philip. That was before we started the underground." This seemed to be a safe conversation, so he asked, "Where have you and Christian lived?"

"Wherever the hell he decides."

Her tone was bitter, and her voice sounded completely different from back at the mansion, less cultured . . . less serene, as if she were two different people, and he was just now meeting one of them.

Then she sighed. "I'm sorry. We've lived mainly in the southern states. You'd be surprised at the money in Louisiana. People pay big bucks down there to talk to ghosts. We've changed our names more times than I can count over the years, but Christian changes back when he can. He seems attached to his name."

What a strange existence she'd led, moving from place to place, staying at mansions like Vera's, and running fake séances with an undead partner.

For some reason, he blurted out, "You don't like Christian very much, do you?"

"He's a bastard."

Her honesty startled him. "Then why don't you leave him?"

"I can't."

He slowed the car enough to glance at her. "Why not?"

She suddenly looked uncomfortable, as if she'd said too much. "Look," she said, "I'm hungry and I'm tired, and I'm just babbling. Do you know how this works . . . the hunting? Is there someplace we can go?"

He already knew where they were going. "Yes. I'll take you to the Seattle Center."

From what he remembered, that place would be perfect. He and Philip had gone there a few times together just for fun. It was crowded and busy, but a surprising number of people, especially young people, ran around the grounds all by themselves, and there were several buildings where Ivory might leave someone unconscious and helpless but safe for a few minutes until her victim woke up.

After he'd given her their destination, they were both quiet until he turned off Mercer onto First Avenue and pulled into a parking garage. Although he knew the basics, he'd never actually gone hunting with Philip or Eleisha, and he realized he'd need to know a few things before they got started here.

"Ivory . . . ," he began, shutting off the car, "what's your gift? I haven't felt anything that I've been aware of."

To his surprise, she suddenly smiled. Her whole face lit up, and he found himself looking at her small white teeth. "I only use it when I'm hunting," she said. "Christian doesn't like it." Tilting her head to one side, she said, "Have you ever gambled? I don't mean playing poker for a few bucks with Philip. I mean *really* gambled, where you lived through that one breathless moment of knowing you either scored big or lost everything?"

Confused, he shook his head. "Not really. I don't follow sports, and I've never been to Vegas."

He waited for her to go on, to tell him more, but instead, she opened her door and climbed out of the car. "Once I peg someone, just come inside my head and stay with me. You'll see."

To his surprise, the prospect intrigued him. He'd

lived through a number of feedings—and sometimes killings—inside Eleisha's, Philip's, Rose's, and Maxim's memories. But he'd never actually participated like this before.

He followed Ivory without another word.

Mary had been standing guard outside the mansion, wondering if anything was ever going to happen again, when the garage door suddenly opened and a white BMW pulled out.

She sensed at least one vampire inside, and she wondered what was going on.

All she could do was follow, but at least someone had finally come out of the mansion. It was a good sign. Maybe they weren't going to completely hole up after all.

The car headed downtown.

Sailing rapidly through the air above, she followed it to a garage on First Street, just outside the Seattle Center.

Floating near the ceiling, she tried to blend in with the concrete and still manage to watch what was going on below. Wade and Ivory got out of the car, and Mary tensed. Should she keep following them?

So far, Julian had expressed little interest in Ivory, and he seemed more focused on Christian . . . but still, he'd probably want to know about this, to know Wade and Ivory were here alone.

Coming to a quick decision, Mary blinked out to go report to Julian.

*   *   *

Wade just kept following Ivory, but she didn't go far and headed only a few blocks south to the Pacific Science Center, which was a large building with too many nooks, crannies, and shadows for Wade's taste. Julian always came swinging from the shadows.

"Ivory," Wade said, "stay out in the open, under the lights."

She didn't even glance at him but started watching the people all around. There were few families out and about this late at night, and the crowds consisted mainly of teenage kids in groups. Wade suddenly reached out with his thoughts and entered Ivory's mind. She didn't block him or try to push him out.

Just stay with me, she flashed.

He could feel her doing surface scans as the teenagers walked past, and then he felt her pause as she spotted a kid about seventeen years old, off by himself, smoking a cigarette, looking toward the front doors of the science center. He wore a skullcap and faded canvas jacket.

She walked up to him. "You want to get in, don't you? See the last laser show?"

He looked down at her face in surprise, and through her, Wade could see the boy's thoughts. He was wondering what she wanted . . . why a pretty woman was even talking to him.

The boy shrugged. "Sure. No money for a ticket."

"We don't need money," she answered. "I can get us in."

Wade was still standing a few feet away from her, but an unexpected sensation began to wash through him, a kind of anticipation mixed with excitement. It kept growing until he could feel his other senses begin to dull.

"What do you mean?" the boy asked Ivory, his eyes slightly glazed now.

She smiled. "This way."

She headed in the other direction, around the back of the building. The boy began to follow, but so did Wade, and the boy stopped at the sight of him.

"It's okay," Ivory told the boy. "He's with me. Come on. I'll get us inside."

The feeling of anticipation kept growing as they walked up to a darkened door. There was no one else around back here, and Ivory looked to the boy. "I can pick this lock and get us in, but I don't know who might be on the other side of the door. So either we get in for free and have a good time or we end up getting hauled away by security."

The feeling building in Wade's mind and chest took on a new element: danger, a sense of all or nothing, and he couldn't believe the excitement, the adrenaline running through him. His heart was pounding, and more than anything, he wanted her to pick that lock. He wanted to see if they'd succeed or be arrested. He could barely stand the wait.

"Pick it," the boy urged, and Wade could feel the same all-or-nothing excitement in his mind.

Ivory smiled and produced a small metal tool seemingly out of thin air.

Within seconds, she had the door open, and she peeked inside. Wade suddenly knew there was no one waiting on the other side because he could feel her doing a mental sweep. For some reason, he felt a stab of disappointment. But she led them all inside, and then they were standing in a darkened hallway, with passages leading left and right.

"Over here," she whispered to the boy, and she crouched at the corner of the left passage. "I need to show you something before we go on."

Wade could feel the state of the boy's mind. He was so lost in the adrenaline of the moment that he'd have done anything she asked, and he crouched down beside her. Reaching out with one hand, she grasped his hand and whispered, "Will you let me do this or will you run?"

The all-or-nothing excitement intensified, and Wade just stood there, staring. Without putting the boy to sleep, Ivory bit down on his wrist . . . and he let her. She drank mouthfuls of his blood, and through her, Wade could taste them. He could feel the experience just as she did.

Memories of the boy's recent life began flowing through her mind . . . longing for an absent mother, living with a grandmother who didn't want him, applying for a job at a gas station, falling in love with a girl at school who didn't know his name.

The memories sobered Wade and made him sad.

But then Ivory pulled her teeth out, and he felt her blurring the boy's memories of the last fifteen minutes.

The boy lost everything from the first moment he'd approached the building.

Leaving him there on the floor, staring into space, Ivory stood and grasped the sleeve of Wade's jacket. "Come on," she said. "He'll come back to himself in a few minutes, and he won't remember anything. But he's safe here for now."

Wordlessly, Wade followed her back outside, and they hurried toward the parking garage. But his thoughts were churning over what he'd just felt . . . the entire experience.

"The rush of gambling?" he finally managed to get out. "That's your gift?"

"I've always been a gambler," she answered, walking faster. "I just made one wrong call, and I've been paying ever since."

Walking swiftly beside her, he realized he had to find out what she meant by that last comment—and he had to find out tonight.

Christian was sitting by the fire, listening to Vera ramble on. In spite of the fact that he'd brought in several interesting guests to visit, he was aware that he'd been neglecting her most shamefully the past two nights, and that simply wouldn't do.

She was his hostess and patron, and she was the one arranging for clients.

So after the séance ended, after Justin had gone home and the others had all gone upstairs, he felt a little alone time with Vera was in order so he could flatter her generosity, her kindness, and her beauty.

"Oh, Christian, stop," she said, smiling. "You don't need to go on like that."

But he did, and he knew it.

Vera yawned and stretched. "That poor young man tonight," she said. "His fiancé marrying his father." She shook her head. "I hope you were able to comfort his mother as well."

"I was."

But even as he spoke attentively to her, he couldn't stop thinking about how Philip had pulled Eleisha off by herself so quickly after the séance. What were they doing? Of what were they speaking? Something had to be done about Philip and soon.

"Vera, darling, would you mind if I go up and check on Ivory? I think three nights in a row has taken its toll on her. She seemed a bit done over."

"Oh, of course I don't mind," Vera said, sounding concerned. "Go and check on her. Let me know if she needs anything."

"You are a dear."

He made his way upstairs quickly, but then he stopped outside Eleisha's door, at a loss. What was he supposed to say exactly? Knock and ask her and Philip what they were doing in there? Perhaps he could invite them downstairs to play cards. At least that way he could keep Eleisha near himself and pass a few more impulses into her mind.

He'd just raised his hand to knock when a feeling hit him that there was something wrong up here in the guest wing.

He turned and looked down the wide hallway. It felt . . . empty.

Ivory, he flashed on instinct.

No one answered, and he felt nothing. Moving into action, he strode rapidly down to Wade's door and knocked. "Wade?"

No one answered, and he opened the door. The room was empty. He went to Ivory's next. It was empty.

Before taking any action, he decided he had to check one more place, and he headed back downstairs, toward the garage.

Once Wade was settled behind the wheel and Ivory was in the passenger seat, he put the keys into the ignition, but he didn't start the engine. Now that they were locked away in the car, he had a feeling that neither one of them was in a hurry to get back to the mansion.

"Thank you," she said, "for doing this. I haven't had . . . I feel like I haven't had real company in a long time. You're good company."

Everything she said was a mystery, and it pulled at his heart at the same time. She made no secret of the fact that she was miserable with Christian, but she wouldn't tell him why.

He had at least ten specific questions that he'd planned to ask her, but they all vanished from his mind.

"If you don't like working with him," he said, "just

leave. Come back to the church with me, even if he won't come himself."

"I can't."

"Sure you can."

She studied him through her slanted green eyes. "You wouldn't want me there, and you sure as hell don't want him there." Her voice trembled slightly. "You should take your friends and just get out of here, as far from us as you can."

"No."

She leaned her head back. "Wade, you don't understand. You don't know him."

"Then make me understand."

"I wouldn't know what to say."

"Don't say anything. Just think about him and let me inside your head."

She turned. "What?"

"I'm serious. Think back to when he turned you or whenever you want. I can see your memories. I can live them just like you did."

She didn't believe him. He could see it in her face. Apparently, he and Eleisha had stumbled upon this ability by accident, and none of the elders seemed to understand it. But he didn't tell Ivory that once he'd locked on to a memory, he could keep her moving down a chronological path for as long as he wanted, and in spite of a flash of guilt, he wasn't about to stop or turn back now.

"If I show you Christian," she said slowly, "if I show you what he's like beneath that smile, will you take your friends and run?"

"If I think it's necessary."

"You will."

They were both quiet for a moment, and then she said, "What do I do?"

He reached over and grasped her fingers gently. "Just think back."

As he tangled his thoughts into hers again, he thought he heard muffled screaming on the edge of his awareness.

The interior of the car vanished, and he latched on to the first memory that surfaced in her mind.

chapter eleven

•

TWO DAYS OUTSIDE OF BOSTON HARBOR, 1826
IVORY

I vory was screaming into Christian's hand.

She'd been fighting off men since she was fifteen, but this was different. For a slender man, the strength in his hands was unbelievable, and although panic hit her when he pinned her to the bed, what he did next went beyond her fears.

He drove his teeth into her throat, ripping at her skin and drinking her blood. The pain was blinding. She bucked wildly to pitch him off, but he didn't seem to notice.

I'm going to die, she thought, still screaming into his palm covering her mouth.

He drank and drank . . . and it seemed to go on forever. She could hear her heartbeat slowing almost to a stop in her ears, and he pulled his teeth out. A dull sense of relief came when at least the ripping and drinking ceased. Though her throat still hurt, she had only a few seconds left to live, and at least she wouldn't die in so much pain.

But he wasn't done yet.

Sitting up, he put his wrist into his mouth and tore it open down through the veins.

A horror she didn't think possible filled her when she saw the bloody wrist coming toward her mouth. Too weak to fight, she tried turning her head and saying, "No," but his wrist kept coming, and he pressed it between her teeth.

"Drink," he whispered in her ear. "You'll thank me later."

His blood began to run down her throat, and she didn't remember any more.

When she opened her eyes again, she was still lying on the bed in his cabin. She couldn't feel the pain in her throat now. She couldn't feel anything at all.

Christian was sitting in a chair reading a newspaper, but when she tried to move, he looked over at her. "Finally," he said, sounding annoyed. "I was beginning to think you'd never wake up."

A flash of hatred hit her as bits and pieces started coming back. She touched her throat, but it felt whole. "What did you do to me?"

"Made you immortal. You owe me."

Her hatred only grew as she glanced at the door. She

was getting out of here, away from him, and she'd find a way to keep him away from her if she had to hire a bodyguard. She didn't want to think about the things he'd done to her on this bed . . . and about how she hadn't been able to stop him.

But then, as he stared at her, she felt something touch the edges of her mind, and his eyes narrowed, almost as if he knew what she was thinking.

"Maybe I shouldn't have used the word 'immortal,'" he said. "The sun will kill you, and you'll starve unless I teach you how to hunt, how to feed, how to develop your own power. You'll die without me."

He continued staring at her, and an unwanted sensation began to make her tremble.

Fear.

Fear like she'd like never known—not even when he'd pinned her to the bed—began welling up inside her, and somehow, she knew with absolute certainty that she would die an agonizing death without him. She had to stay with him to remain safe.

The thought made her ill, but she was terrified to leave him.

He smiled.

"Good," he said. "You must be hungry. Time for your first lesson."

After they'd both changed their clothes, he took her up on deck, toward the aft of the ship, where the lighting was limited. All her instincts kept screaming at her to run, but the continually welling fear never left her . . . that without him something far worse would happen.

"You won't be able to hunt on your own at first," he said quietly. "I'll have to lend you my gift until yours is strong enough."

She had no idea what he was saying, but she was far too numb to ask.

The people they walked past felt different to her now. She could almost smell the warmth coming off their skin. She could sense the blood pounding in the veins of their throats.

She was hungry, and Christian seemed to know what to do.

Following him to the very back of the ship, she stopped at the sight of a middle-aged couple, both with British accents, having what appeared to be a polite argument.

"You always say 'just a few hands,' and then you sneak into the cabin at three o'clock in the morning," the woman said. "I wish just once you'd come to bed with me at a halfway decent hour."

"Oh, come on, old girl," the man said, his tone more lighthearted than his expression. "There's little enough to do on this ship, and you know I've not lost more than a few pounds. Don't begrudge me what few amusements I have."

Christian saw Ivory watching them.

"Him," she said suddenly, not even knowing what was about to happen. "He likes to gamble."

Raising his eyebrows, Christian waited until the

woman finally huffed and walked away. Then he looked directly at the man. "I'm bringing him over," he whispered. "Lure him to the shadows of the wall, and then I'll show you what to do."

But Ivory moved forward on her own, intercepting the man, as if she already knew what to do. She smiled.

"Sorry, but I overheard some of that," she said. "Are you still looking for amusement?"

His eyes widened, and he seemed more than surprised by her pretty face and the muslin gown she wore. She looked nothing like a prostitute.

"I need some amusement, too," she went on, "and your wife could change her mind at any minute and come back." She motioned to a darkened passage just behind them. "Shall we risk it?"

The most satisfying sensation suddenly began building inside her, flowing outward, drifting toward the man. It wafted through him. The excitement of the moment, the prospect of either quick, heated sex with a lovely young woman or a divorce if his wife came back and caught them seemed to fill the air and make it crackle.

He breathed quickly and grasped her hand, pulling her into the passage.

Christian had the good sense to hang back, but to her shock she heard his voice in her head. *Feed from his wrist. Don't kill him.*

"Wait," Ivory whispered once she had the man hidden in the shadows. "Let me do this."

She took his hand and brought it to her mouth, kissing it softly. The aura of all or nothing inside her increased, and his eyes began to glaze over. Without thinking, she bit down on his wrist and began drinking his blood.

The act wasn't revolting. It didn't even seem wrong. His blood tasted good.

Then Christian was beside her, kneeling down, and she felt him inside her head again. *Take just enough. Keep track of his heartbeat.*

Memories from the man's mind began flowing into her . . . many polite arguments with his wife . . . hiding his gambling losses . . . drinking brandy alone out of fear she'd find out just how much he'd lost.

Stop now.

She stopped, pulling her teeth out.

Reach inside my head with your thoughts.

She did, and she could feel Christian inside the man's mind, blurring his memories, letting him remember everything up to the moment his wife walked away, and then nothing until he woke up here in the darkened hall with his wrist bleeding.

Ivory trembled with an unwanted feeling of accomplishment. She knew on some level that she'd just done far better at this than was expected for a first attempt. She could feel it in Christian's thoughts.

"Come," Christian said, but his voice was cold, almost disgusted.

His tone surprised her. She thought she'd done so well. When she stood up and followed him, in spite of herself, she couldn't help asking, "What's wrong?"

Walking down the deck, he said, "That is your gift? To titillate some man to the point of almost hoping his wife will catch you?"

"It worked, didn't it?"

"It's coarse and vulgar." He stopped walking and looked down at her. "But then again, you are coarse and vulgar. You'll need a great deal of work to be ready for what I have in mind."

Ivory couldn't believe how much his words hurt. She'd never cared a whit what anyone thought of her. But no one had ever called her vulgar before. Could it be true? He kept his eyes on her face a little longer, and the terrible fear of being without him swelled up again.

"A great deal of work," he repeated, "and you'll do whatever I say, won't you?"

"Yes," she whispered. "I'll do whatever you say."

The evening they landed in Boston Harbor, Christian arranged for lavish rooms at the Concord Hotel, and she wondered how long their money would hold out if he planned to continue this style of living. Her instincts had always warned her to make the money last as long as possible, as she never knew when she might be able to set up the next game.

But almost immediately upon entering their rooms, he hurried to change his clothes into his best suit.

"What are you doing?" she asked.

"Madame Dupuis and two of the Bertram sisters have invited me to a late supper. I'll get them to intro-duce me to others of their circle. We have to start somewhere, but we'll need to move up the social ladder quickly if we want patrons with real money . . . enough to pay for the show I have in mind."

"Oh." She looked to her luggage. "Let me find an evening gown."

"You?" he said, sounding scornful. "Hardly. Those women might have paid you for a little entertainment on a ship, but you're not even close to ready for dining in society."

She stared at him. No one had ever made her feel as small as he did.

But the sickening fear of being without him rose again.

"You'll stay in this room and wait until I return," he said. "Do you understand?"

Hating herself, she answered, "I understand."

He got back late that night, and she'd never seen him so agitated. Nearly rushing through the door, he barked, "Get packed. We're leaving."

"What? Why?"

Hadn't he just been off to dinner to try to get them a few new marks set up?

"Hurry," he said, still distracted as he grabbed his own bag.

Her head felt clearer than it had since the night he'd changed her, and she felt more like her old self.

"Christian," she said, "what have you done?"

He stopped with his hand in midair and glanced at her.

"Something I shouldn't have, but I didn't have a choice."

She waited. Although he was in quite a state, at least he was speaking to her as a partner now.

"Madame Dupuis offered to give us an introduction to her second cousin in Georgia," he said, "a Camille du Blois . . . apparently the cream of Atlanta society. It's perfect, Ivory. When we arrive, we can present ourselves however we wish, as longtime professionals. Then we'll show them what we can do, and the bookings will start flowing in."

He stopped.

"And?" she asked.

"We have to arrive in style . . . to look the part. That means the right clothes, the right carriage, and the right hotels."

Something in his voice made her feel cold. "What have you done?" she repeated. "Did you kill someone?"

"Kill someone? No." He shook his head abruptly. "But I went home with Clementine Bertram, and I used my gift to get her to open her family safe and give me five thousand dollars."

Ivory gasped. She still had no idea what he meant when he spoke of "his gift," but pulling a five-thousand-dollar confidence game was serious.

"I blurred her memory, but once she finds the money gone, she still might make a connection. I've never done anything like that before, and I don't think she'll make an accusation." He paused. "I just hope the money's enough. I'm not accustomed to . . . paying for things." As she wondered what that meant, he rambled on. "It's so much easier to simply have the bills sent on without ever seeing them."

That was the first time Ivory realized that she knew nothing about him. How old was he? What kind of an existence had he been living where he didn't pay his own bills?

But then he seemed to notice how closely she was watching him, and he straightened. The fear of being without him swelled up in her throat again, making her want to choke.

"Just get packed," he ordered.

The carriage journey to Atlanta seemed endless. Being trapped alone in a small space with Christian was bad enough, but as they moved inland, she couldn't help the panic of leaving the coast behind.

Running games on the ships had been good to her for a long time, and she felt as if she'd just been cut off from everything she knew. Christian had something else in mind for his vision of the game. She didn't know exactly what yet, but she knew he'd be playing for much higher stakes—and that he viewed her as a necessary tool.

All night, as the wheels rolled onward, he kept at her about her diction, her accent, and her posture, forcing her to practice a detached smile and to say things like, "How lovely to meet you."

There were only a few phrases he really wanted her to have down, but he made her practice them over and over again. Some nights, she'd get a break from this tedium when he fell into a black mood and would stare out the window into the darkness, murmuring things like, "How could I have fallen into this?"

One night, as they were about halfway through North Carolina, she surprised him by asking, "How did you fall into this? What chased you out of Europe?"

He turned from the window and looked at her through angry eyes. "A great, mad vampire wielding a sword, that's what."

As he spoke, she felt the fear rising inside her again.

"Have I told you that there were once a number of us existing in Europe?" he went on. "Leading our happy little lives until one us of lost his reason and started killing the others, coming from the darkness with a sword and slicing off our heads."

He suddenly seemed to be enjoying this, and Ivory sat frozen. She wanted him to stop. She would have done anything—even practice her diction—to make him stop.

"His name is Julian, and he has no idea you exist," Christian said softly. "But if you ever try to leave me, I'll find out where you are, and I'll tell him."

The sickening fear inside Ivory kept growing, and she sat there, still frozen, until he finally turned to stare back out the window.

She didn't try to incite conversation again.

Christian booked them another lavish hotel in Atlanta. Then he hired a tailor and a dressmaker.

Within a week, Ivory was decked in a burgundy silk gown finer than anything she'd ever worn. The tiny slippers and the diamond earrings he'd purchased should have made her glow with pleasure, but they didn't. They just felt like a costume he'd designed.

He ordered her to sit in front of him at a dressing table while he did her hair himself.

Although she'd learned not to speak to him unless absolutely necessary, she couldn't help asking, "You know how to do a woman's hair?"

"Of course," he answered absently. "I used to do this all the time for . . ."

"For?"

He stopped talking, and she didn't press him.

But she had to admit that when he finished, she looked like a young lady fit for the finest houses of Georgian society.

"Just bring your velvet purse tonight," he said. "I'll have rest of our things sent."

She blinked, alarmed now. "Sent where?"

His nearly colorless eyes glinted, as if amused by her confusion. "To the estate of Camille du Blois, of course. Did I not tell you? I met with her this week. We've been invited to stay, and I decided I rather liked the idea of being her special guest. It lends us credence. She's arranged for our first séance two nights from now. If you do exactly as I say, more should follow. We'll be the toast of the town."

She stood up. "So soon? You said I wasn't ready. We

haven't even practiced. How are you going to play this?"

He leaned closer. "Just do as I've instructed. Speak only the phrases I've taught you when we're socializing. Watch your diction and your posture, and then when the show starts, just stay with me, inside my head, and speak the words I pass you." He smiled. "We'll dazzle them."

Two nights later, Ivory found herself sitting down at a large round table in the parlor of Camille du Blois.

Camille was an aging widow who seemed overly taken with Christian, but there were also three men present who appeared to be struggling not to stare at Ivory. She was well aware that she looked especially alluring tonight—in part thanks to Christian—and although she was beginning to wonder if Christian had ever run a confidence game in his life, he certainly had good instincts.

Distraction was eighty percent of success.

He seemed to already understand that, and the sheer physical presence of the two of them was proving quite a distraction. Before leaving the hotel to come here a few nights ago, he'd even pierced his ear and put in a gold ring.

"Touch of the gypsy," he'd said, smiling.

Now he was in command of the entire room—and the room was not short on powerful men.

"Colonel Gerard," Christian said, "before we begin,

can you tell me who it is you wish me to call from the other side? I only need a name."

In addition to Christian, Ivory, and Camille, there were three Southern officers sitting at the table, a lieutenant, a captain, and a colonel. Colonel Gerard sat between the other two, but his sharp gaze was moving between Christian and the candelabra on the table with some reticence in his eyes, as if he now regretted having requested this audience.

"It's all right, Colonel," Camille said gently. "Whatever you say here is in complete confidence."

Christian had gone to great lengths to make sure it was clear he'd been told absolutely nothing regarding the reason for tonight's séance.

"He's been dead a long time," Colonel Gerard began, shifting in his chair uncomfortably. "He served with me in my early career. His name was Anthony Leroy."

Christian nodded, but his face was unreadable. He looked detached, untouchable, and yet compassionate at the same time. Ivory could not help admiring his finesse. He'd been born to do this.

"Everyone please join hands," he said, and for a second, she wondered if the colonel would agree to join hands with two other men, but Christian added, "We must form a circle," and the officers obeyed him—quite a testament to his authority here.

Stay with me, Christian flashed. *Stay inside my head and see what I see. Then speak only the words I give you.*

Christian closed his eyes. "Anthony Leroy, hear me.

Come to me from the other side. Speak to me through Ivory."

Locked inside Christian's mind, Ivory could see a clear image of Anthony Leroy inside the colonel's thoughts.

Christian called for Leroy again, dragging out the anticipation, and then he opened his eyes. "He is with us in the room, standing beside the table."

Colonel Gerard started in surprise and looked to the blank space where Christian was gazing.

Christian smiled. "He's tall and lanky with brown hair in need of a cut." He squinted slightly. "He's missing the little finger of his left hand."

The colonel gasped, and both men with him turned slightly pale.

"He can see you, but he can hear only me," Christian said. "What would you like me to ask him?"

The colonel seemed at a loss now, as if he never truly believed matters would get this far. "Ask him . . . ask him if he cheated that night. He'll know what I mean."

"Did you cheat, Anthony?" Christian asked.

Instantly, Ivory felt him feeding her answers. She stared straight ahead as if in a trance. "I did, my friend. I was pulling cards from inside my sleeve, but you were not to blame. My being cashiered had nothing to do with what happened later."

She could even hear the pitch of Leroy's voice in Gerard's mind, and she managed to copy it effectively.

The colonel was trembling slightly now, his face white, and through Christian, Ivory could see the whole story. As a young man, Colonel Gerard had enjoyed the closest friendship of his life, and he'd been at ease with Anthony Leroy in a way he'd never known before. One night, they'd had far too much drink, and they were playing cards for money, along with three other young officers, and Leroy won so many hands that Gerard began to suspect him of cheating. On any other night, Gerard might have let it go, but he'd had a bad day, and he was drunk, and he called his friend out in front of witnesses. Cheating at cards was a serious offense in the military, and because of Gerard's outburst and accusation, a formal inquest was held. Leroy was found guilty. He was discharged in disgrace and sent home to Louisiana. Two months later, he shot himself in the head.

For almost thirty years, Gerard had suffered over this, wondering if he'd been so drunk that he'd accused his friend unfairly . . . wishing more than anything else that he could just take the whole night back.

Unfortunately, unlike with the Bertram sisters, no one in this room knew what had really happened that night. The only one who'd been there was the colonel, and he didn't know himself.

So Christian was working off the cuff, and he'd already decided to tell Gerard that Leroy had been cheating—thus easing him of one possible piece of guilt. But then Ivory felt his mind moving forward, and he began feeding her a story.

She kept her eyes straight ahead, still playing the conduit, and she copied the inflection of Leroy's voice. "But you don't know everything. I wasn't disappointed to be sent home. I was happy. I *wanted* to go home, to help my father with the plantation, to marry my girl . . . to live my life at home. But when I got back and Susanna found out I wasn't going to be a career officer, she broke with me. She never loved me, only the idea of what I'd be. But I loved her . . . and one night, I drank a bottle of brandy and put a gun to my head like a fool." Ivory paused. "It wasn't you, Gerard. You did me a favor getting me thrown out. It never had anything to do with you."

The colonel was staring at Ivory, and the muscles in his jaw were clenched. "Tell him I miss him."

"He misses you," Christian said to the empty space by the table.

"I miss you, too," Ivory answered Gerard directly. "Nobody ever listened to my stories the way you did."

"He's gone now," Christian said, turning his head from the empty spot. His voice was full of compassion. "Did you learn what you needed from him?"

The colonel nodded once, shortly. He seemed almost beyond speech, but he managed to say, "I'll have the money sent over tonight."

An hour later, Ivory sat in front of the mirror in her guest room, thinking over everything that had just happened downstairs.

Christian was right. Together, they were capable of quite a show.

With him asking the "ghost" questions and her giving the answers, it was impossible to doubt them, especially when he'd made a point of not even learning the dead person's name before sitting down at the table.

They'd been dazzling.

Astonishing.

So why wasn't she happy? She felt trapped and sick to her stomach.

The door opened, and Christian walked in, smiling. For once, the smile reached all the way up to his eerie clear eyes. "You were perfect," he said, "better than I could have imagined. Camille will have her friends on a waiting list inside of a week, and from now on, they'll be paying in advance."

But then he saw her face in the mirror, and he stopped halfway across the room, just watching her reflection.

The sickening fear began welling inside her, and she didn't think she could stand it tonight.

He finished crossing the room and reached over to pull a few pins from her hair. "I'll keep you safe," he said quietly, "and you'll do exactly as I say, won't you?"

Sometimes, if she agreed with him quickly, the worst of the fear faded a little.

"Yes, I'll do exactly as you say."

chapter twelve

Wade jerked away from Ivory's mind and gripped the steering wheel, gasping for air. The sickening fear he'd felt inside her was too much, and he hadn't been able to stay in the memory.

But she was choking beside him, her green eyes wild, and he fought to get control of himself so he could try to help her.

Coming out of this the first time was never easy.

"You're here," he managed to say. "You're with me in the car."

With both hands on the dashboard, she cried out, "Did you see that? All of it?"

For once, her defenses were completely down, and he couldn't help a stab of guilt for having put her through such memories, for making her relive them.

But the reality of what he'd just witnessed began to take hold.

"Oh, Ivory," he said. "Is that how you've spent the last two hundred years?" He shook his head in disbelief. "You're coming home with me. You have to get away from him."

She choked again, just one more time, and then whispered, "I can't."

With little else to do, Julian was stuck in his hotel room, just waiting for a report from Mary, waiting for something, anything, to happen.

The problem was that he had no idea what that might be, and he most feared that Eleisha and Philip would just take Christian, put him in the backseat of a rental car, and drive him home to Portland . . . which would leave Julian with the only option of attacking Christian at or around the church.

To date, he'd managed to create the illusion for Eleisha that the church was a safe zone. This belief had kept her going, kept her searching, even after he'd sliced the heads off a few vampires she'd so painstakingly located.

But he'd never attacked anyone near the church.

The last thing he wanted was for her to lose heart and give up. Losing someone she'd brought safely all the way home might be a final straw. He paced across the floor, wondering what he could do from here to make them leave the manor but not leave immediately for home.

The air beside the couch shimmered and Mary materialized.

The sight filled him with hope. "Has something happened?"

Her mouth was in a tight line, as if she was considering something. "Not the best," she said finally, "but something. Wade and Ivory left the mansion and drove to the Seattle Center by themselves. I don't know why. But they're both there now. Do you want to do anything?"

He put his fist to his mouth. That still left Eleisha and Philip guarding Christian, and everything Mary had reported so far left him with the impression that Ivory was one of the newer breed—and not much of a threat.

"Does Ivory seem important to Christian?" he asked.

Mary frowned. "They don't talk to each other, but I think he needs her for the séances."

"Did Wade have his cell phone?"

"I don't know, but I've never known him to leave it behind, especially not when they're away from Portland like this."

That was good enough. If he could pin Wade and Ivory down someplace, make them afraid to leave the center on their own, and frighten them enough, he might be able to get Wade to call for help. One way or another, that would leave Christian vulnerable.

He grabbed his sword. "Meet me there."

"They parked in a lot on First Avenue. I'd start around that area," she said.

Without answering, he headed for the door.

*   *   *

Christian finished climbing the stairs again, and he walked quickly toward Eleisha and Philip's room.

His inspection of the garage had resulted in finding a little white BMW missing. Although he was more than surprised by Ivory's actions, he couldn't have cared less where she'd gone.

In his vision of the future, he'd already replaced her with Eleisha, who would require so much less effort and energy to control. Indeed, although he chastised himself for not having paid enough attention to the control of Ivory these past few nights, this may not have worked out too badly. If he could convince Eleisha and Philip to join him in a search for Wade and Ivory, there might be opportunities to get Eleisha off by herself in the night, and this time, she would not be reading his memories or using any of her abilities.

He was going to use his.

While knocking on the guest-room door, he began going over the best way to sound convincingly accusatory . . . to sound like Wade had somehow taken advantage of his trust and "stolen" Ivory.

But when Eleisha answered and peered out at him, all such thoughts fled. She was wearing jeans and a red T-shirt. The jeweled clip in her hair was gone, and her hair was a mess, as if she'd been lying down or rolling on the pillows. What was left of her lip gloss was smeared on the right side of her face.

Inside, Philip was sitting on the bed.

Christian didn't like this.

He didn't like it all.

*   *   *

Although she'd just started to feel much better, as she peered out the half-open door, something in Christian's expression brought Eleisha crashing down again toward the idea that she was doing something wrong.

First Philip, and now him.

He was staring her mouth, and she reached up to touch it, realizing the remnants of her lip gloss had smeared. She wiped it away.

"What do you want?" Philip asked Christian, standing up.

That sounded rude, but Eleisha decided not to interfere or correct him.

Something in Christian's face shifted, and suddenly he looked angry. "Your friend has taken Ivory. They're both gone."

"What?" All traces of veiled hostility vanished from Philip's voice as he crossed the room in a few strides. "Wade's gone?"

"He wouldn't do that," Eleisha said. "He'd never leave without telling us."

"Well, they're not in the house, and a missing little BMW in the garage tells me something different," Christian said dryly.

Eleisha backed away and let him inside. What was going on? "Give me a minute."

Grabbing her cell phone from her bag, she hit the button to call Wade. His phone rang six times, and then she was sent to voice mail. It was a polite message from Wade himself, telling her to leave a message.

"Call me," she said. "Right now."

She lowered her phone and looked at Christian. "Wade would never 'take' anyone," she said. "Was Ivory hungry? Would she have asked him to take her hunting?"

"Ivory is perfectly capable of hunting by herself," he said.

"Not with Julian out there," she answered.

Philip was growing agitated. "We have to find him."

She agreed but wasn't sure where to start. He'd taken a car? What was he thinking?

"Maybe we should call Rose and have her send Seamus," she suggested. "He could track Ivory for us."

She thought Philip would jump at the idea, but his face was thoughtful as he strapped on his machete. "Not just yet. When we all decide to leave here . . . whatever we decide to do at that point, we're going to need Seamus at full strength. If Wade took Ivory hunting, I think I know where they went."

She blinked. "You do?"

"Back when we lived here, he always said the Seattle Center would be a good place to hunt. I never thought so, but he did."

Her mouth fell open slightly. "You talked about that?"

Philip nodded. "He liked to go there. I think that's where he'd take her . . . if they're hunting. I say we try, and if I'm wrong, we'll have to risk weakening Seamus."

Eleisha had no memory of Wade going to the Seattle

Center—as she had reasons for disliking the place—but Wade and Philip had sometimes gone out by themselves back then. It was certainly possible that Philip knew things she did not.

Christian had listened to this exchange without speaking, but he'd watched Philip strap on his blade and button his coat.

"I'm coming," he said, and his tone brooked no refusal. "I'll drive." He pointed to Philip's waist. "Just let me get my own."

Somehow, Eleisha wasn't surprised that he had his own sword.

As he sat in the car, with Ivory beside him, Wade's mind had gone into overdrive, turning over everything he'd seen in Ivory's memories.

"What's his gift? Fear?" he asked.

She shook her head. "No. I didn't figure it out for years. He plants emotional suggestions into people's thoughts, anything he wants them to feel."

"So he's made you terrified to leave him?" He turned to fully face her. "But if that's the case, if you do leave, get far enough away from him, won't the fear eventually go away?"

"I don't know," she whispered. "It hasn't been nearly as strong since you arrived. He's been ... distracted and hardly even noticed me. It's been a relief. A few nights ago, I never would have slipped away like this without telling him."

"Well then, that just proves my—"

His cell phone rang, and he swore under his breath before pulling it from his jacket pocket to see who was calling.

Eleisha.

"Don't answer it," Ivory said, "at least not yet. Christian just wants to know where I am."

He looked over at her and saw the pleading expression on her face.

Knowing full well that he should answer it, he shoved the phone back in his pocket and let the call go to voice mail. Eleisha and Philip would never leave the mansion and abandon Christian, so they were safe for now, and he was in the middle of something important as far as the mission was concerned. If he answered, he'd just spend the next ten minutes listening to Eleisha lecture him, and then he'd end up making his excuses, and he didn't want to break what little connection he'd made with Ivory. Was she beginning to trust him?

But then he thought about everything he'd seen in her mind, and he realized Eleisha and Philip were at the mansion with a vampire who could influence their drives and emotions. He needed to get back and get one of them off alone. This situation was shifting almost faster than he could keep up.

Hopefully, Ivory would keep talking to him. He started the car.

"I do think we need to get back," he said.

She seemed sad. "All right."

chapter thirteen

Eleisha sat in the backseat of the Mercedes, growing more and more unsettled the closer Christian got to the Seattle Center. Following Philip's instructions, he headed down the east side and took Fifth Avenue, turning into a large parking garage.

She hated this place.

The first night she'd met Philip, he'd stolen a car and forced her to come here with him. Closing her eyes briefly, she couldn't help seeing what he'd looked like back then, in his designer clothes, with his thick, red-brown hair hanging all the way down his back, his eyes devoid of almost anything besides boredom and hunger.

He used his gift to talk four teenagers into bringing him home. He'd murdered three of them and forced a situation where Eleisha had had to kill the last one. Then he'd tried to make her drink from his wrist, and she'd kneed him in the stomach hard enough to make him spit blood.

That whole night was one of the ugliest memories of her existence, and this place brought it all back.

She'd felt so off-kilter . . . so "not herself" since arriving here, and she didn't want to be reminded of what a savage killer Philip had once been. She didn't want to have to get out of the car and walk around in this place and see all the same places she'd seen that night.

But Christian pulled into an open space and shut off the ignition.

Philip turned in the passenger seat and looked back at her. "You ready?"

"Wait just a minute," she said. Maybe she wouldn't have to get out.

Focusing all her inner strength, she closed her eyes and reached out with her mind.

Wade? Wade, are you here? Please answer me.

She felt nothing. No one answered. They'd have to get out and go looking. She reached for the door handle.

"I'm ready." No matter what else was surfacing in her thoughts, she couldn't stand the idea of Wade out there trying to guard Ivory by himself—with just that gun for protection. "We have to find him."

Mary materialized back inside the First Avenue parking garage, and she got a surprise.

The white BMW was gone.

She wanted to curse, and she looked around wildly, hoping to see its taillights—or anything that might help her. But the car was gone. Quickly, she focused her senses and felt a jolt. Somewhere . . . not too far away, she sensed three distinct holes in the fabric of life.

Julian's rental car came rolling around the corner, and she blinked out, rematerializing in his passenger seat.

He started slightly, not having expected her to just appear like that.

"Game's changed," she blurted out. "Wade's car is gone, but I'm getting three clear signatures. Maybe the others came looking for him."

Julian's jaw twitched, and he pulled into an open spot. Then he got out of the car and looked around. "Get me an exact location."

She nodded in relief. Christian might be right here on the center's grounds. "I will. Maybe we can finish this tonight and you can send me back."

He'd been so distracted that her words seemed to catch him off guard. A flash of open surprise flickered across his face. It vanished just as quickly, and he said, "Yes, yes, of course."

His reaction made her nervous . . . no, more than nervous. Did he have any intention of keeping his promise?

What should she do?

In the moment, she didn't see any choice but to go on, and so she blinked out.

*   *   *

"The amusement park is well lit," Christian said, leading the way. "It should be a good place to get our bearings."

The Space Needle loomed above them.

In spite of his comment about staying in the light, Christian had reached a surprising revelation that after all these years, he wasn't afraid of Julian. This amusement park was not his home or anyplace that Julian had read about in Angelo's book.

They were on equal ground. He was armed. He was on guard and ready for an attack, and Julian probably knew it. In fact, if Christian got lucky, Julian might even try to take Philip out first. That was a pleasant thought. He pictured Philip's head flying across the bumper cars.

Only one thing disturbed him, and that was Eleisha's overly emotional concern about Wade. She seemed worried to an almost distasteful degree . . . about a mortal. He realized that if she was going to stay with him, he would have to isolate her completely, and that now appeared to mean getting rid of both Philip and Wade.

But he wasn't concerned.

Although the trappings of this situation were different from what he'd dealt with in the past, he'd easily dispatched any and all rivals before. The core of the matter was the same: two other men who had to go.

First, though, he wanted a little more time alone with Eleisha. He needed to set the groundwork to make her more dependent upon him. That way, once she really was isolated, she'd turn to him without thinking. She was such a different creature from Ivory, so anxious to please. He almost couldn't wait to make the change.

Her appearance displeased him at the moment, however. What was she thinking with that child-sized T-shirt and her hair hanging in a tangled mess down to the top of her jeans? Did she have any idea how unrefined she looked? He'd put a stop to that in a hurry once she was working with him.

As they walked among the carnival rides and canned music, Philip kept swiveling his head back and forth. He seemed so focused on finding Wade that Christian decided to make his move.

"Philip," he said, "Eleisha and I have a decent view for several blocks all around from here. This might go faster if you just leave us here and do a full sweep of the grounds by yourself."

Philip glanced back at him. "No."

The word was so adamant and so simple that Christian knew further argument would be fruitless. So instead, he summoned an impulse and sent the emotional suggestion into Philip's mind.

Eleisha will be safer from Julian here under the bright lights. You can move much faster on your own, and if you find Wade quickly, you can get her right back to the mansion.

Philip immediately stopped walking and turned around. "Eleisha, maybe I can find him faster on my own. You stay here under the lights."

Christian hid a moment of mild surprise. He hadn't expected it to be quite so easy. Philip's mind must be very open to suggestion. Manipulating Ivory took a good deal more effort.

"Are you sure?" Eleisha asked, grasping the sleeve of his coat. "I don't want you in the darkness all by yourself."

How distasteful. What a display. Christian wanted to pull her hand away and remind her to behave with some semblance of decorum.

"I'll be fine. You just stay right here," Philip answered. Then he jogged away, heading toward the monorail. Within seconds, he'd vanished from sight.

Once he was gone, Eleisha glanced at their surroundings, and Christian noticed something unusual in her eyes: revulsion. He was a master at reading faces.

"You don't like it here?" he asked.

"I hate it." She said this so bluntly that her own words seemed to surprise her, and she looked up at him apologetically. "I'm sorry, Christian. I know you're worried about Ivory. I promise we'll find her."

He smiled. There it was again, that eagerness to comfort him, to please him. He couldn't get enough of it.

He summoned an impulse and sent it.

You're safer here with Christian. Philip is too simple to outwit Julian, and Christian knows how to use his head. Just stay with him.

She blinked, and he could see her fighting the impulse, looking almost guilty at the feelings he'd inflicted. He'd get past her walls soon enough and start planting deeper impulses. But she had to begin depending more upon him first.

Turning his head, he gasped softly and pointed west. "Look. I think I can see Ivory's hair. Hurry."

He broke into a jog, and to his great satisfaction, she followed him without question.

Julian was moving east, away from the First Avenue parking garage toward the science center, when he heard a loud, "Psssssssst," coming from a shrubbery.

He stopped and peered through the budding leaves to see Mary hiding in the bushes.

"I haven't pinpointed Philip," she whispered, "but Eleisha and Christian are heading toward the Children's Theatre building. It's been closed for hours, so that whole area's a dead zone."

"Which way?"

"To your left. You can't miss it."

While he was relieved to have a location for Christian, part of this news frustrated him. Why did Eleisha always seem to end up as the single companion to his target? She was by far the most dangerous to him, and he didn't want to kill her yet. She was too useful in locating other elders.

He considered his options, which were limited.

"Is there anywhere to hide around the outside of that building?" he asked.

"Sure. I spotted a couple of deep doorways around the back, and I wasn't kidding. That place is deserted."

Well, that was something. Could he hit them both

with an onslaught of fear before even stepping into view? No, he was uncertain of Christian's telepathic abilities—or how well Christian could block another vampire's gift.

Better to fall back on tried-and-true methods. If he played this right, he could take Christian's head and not damage Eleisha too much. He'd just need to knock her unconscious first and then swing his blade for Christian's throat. As long as he moved hard and fast and didn't miss, he could end this tonight.

At least Philip wasn't there. That counted for something, too.

"All right," he told Mary, "this is what I want you to do."

Eleisha and Christian were just moving around a corner of the back of the Children's Theatre when she reached out to stop him. They were alone in the dark here, and there were nooks and shadows all along the back of this building. So far, she'd seen no sign of Ivory or Wade, and she wondered if maybe Christian had made a mistake.

"I don't see either of them," she said, "and we need to get back to the carnival. It's not safe for you here."

"For me?"

He sounded insulted, but he had no idea what they were up against. She steeled herself against worrying so much about his feelings.

"Yes. Philip and I both have . . . defenses."

"And what would those be?"

"He's good with a sword. Better than . . . forgive me, but better than you from what I saw in your memories. He's better than Julian, and Julian knows it." She could see that Christian didn't care at all for this conversation, but she didn't stop. "Philip's just had more training. His father started teaching him when he was about six years old, and after he was turned, he forgot his mortal life, but his body remembered things like how to ride a horse and use a sword."

Christian was silent for a few seconds and then asked, "And what about you?"

She hesitated. "Do you remember back in your room, when I made your body freeze?"

He glanced away, his mouth in a tight line, and she could see this topic wasn't any better.

"If you'd been ready, you could have stopped me," she rushed on, "shut me out. But Julian can't. He has no defenses against a telepathic attack. I can freeze him and hold him. I can send nightmares into his mind. I can drop him to his knees. But so far, he hasn't killed one of our core group, and we haven't managed to kill him. We've just . . . hurt him a few times."

She said this in a matter-of-fact voice. Eleisha took no pride in being able to hurt Julian. Regardless of how or why it had happened, he was her maker, and she'd never wanted to have to hurt him. He just hadn't given her a choice.

But Christian leaned closer, and his eyes glowed in

the darkness. She was suddenly startled by his handsome face and steel hair. He seemed interested in what she was saying now.

"You've faced Julian more than once?" he asked.

She nodded. "But when it happens, we have to move very fast. We have to keep him distracted or wounded until I can drive a command inside his head. We can't give him even a second to turn on his gift."

"What's his gift?"

"Fear. And I can't describe it to you. It's crippling. He may not be telepathic, but his gift is strong."

Christian seemed to be taking all this in carefully. His light eyes were still glowing when he said, "Eleisha, I can create fear, too. I can create blind rage or confusion or humiliation. I can send any emotion I want, and my gift is strong."

When he spoke, she felt the truth of his words inside her mind, and she nodded. "Yes, yours is good."

"And I may not have started training with a sword by the time I was six," he went on, "but if you freeze Julian, I'm certainly capable of taking off his head."

He said this with a smile, and she smiled back. Of course he was right. She'd been foolish to think she needed Philip to fight Julian. But beyond this, deeper inside herself, she thought it must be wrong to find a joke about Julian's death amusing. Why had she smiled?

"Now, I'm sure I saw something in this direction," Christian said. "Let's just look a bit longer."

A part of her heard his words and knew he must be right, but another part struggled against his suggestion. "Christian, there's no one back here at all. Why would Wade and Ivory come this—"

The air shimmered beside her and a flash of color made her look away from the back of the building.

"Ahhhhhhhhhhhhh!" someone screamed.

The girl ghost with magenta hair materialized, screaming and waving her arms, and without thinking, Eleisha stumbled backward into a dark doorway.

She saw the fist coming before it connected, but there was no time to form or focus a mental command. In the split second she had, she made one instinctive telepathic cry.

Philip!

Then a loud cracking sound echoed in her ears and everything went black.

Christian didn't flinch from the girl ghost, but alarm bells went off in his head the second Eleisha took a step back and he simultaneously heard the loud crack. Before she even fell, something glinted from the darkness, and he whirled just in time to see a blade sweeping less than an inch from his throat.

But it missed and kept moving into empty air.

His coat was open, and he jerked his blade from its sheath, managing a partial block as the blade in the air came back toward him instantly. But the weight of the sword and the strength behind it almost knocked him over. Somehow, he managed to stay on his feet and scramble backward, trying to regain his balance.

Eleisha was on the ground, as still as a stone, but

he'd only just glanced at her before a large, dark-haired vampire with a heavy bone structure came swinging out of the dark doorway.

Julian.

On little more than panicked instinct, Christian swung back. His blade was short and light—as he tended to depend upon speed—and Julian's sword was long and weighty, and it nearly knocked Christian's blade from his hand when he tried to block.

If Christian could just get an instant to stop swinging or blocking, he knew he could focus an impulse, but he remembered what Eleisha had told him about not giving Julian time to focus his gift.

It's crippling, she'd said.

So Christian kept swinging, but Julian had no trouble blocking, and his sword was longer. In a flash of clarity, Christian realized he was about to go down quickly, unless he tried something else.

He dropped and rolled, coming up six feet away, and as Julian rushed, Christian managed to send the first impulse that came to him.

Your arms are heavy.

It was a weak ploy in the heat of the moment, but at least it was something, and although Julian didn't slow down, his swing was slower, and Christian spotted the confusion on his face as Christian dodged more easily this time.

Your gift won't work. It's broken.

At that, he saw the confusion increase, and then he

felt the first wave of fear coming at him, but he fought for control.

No, it won't work. It's broken. You've lost it.

Julian roared and swung hard, aiming directly at Christian's head. Christian didn't even try to block that time but just ducked, feeling the sword rush past the top of his hair. Real fear mixed with Julian's gift hit him now.

He needed a moment to think of something, some deeper impulse to stop Julian, but the onslaught didn't let up.

Then he heard the sounds of footsteps coming toward them, and he glanced left just long enough to see Philip running along the ground at full speed, machete in hand.

He'll kill you, Christian sent to Julian. *You know he will. Your gift is broken.*

He glanced back to see Philip nearly flying over a sidewalk, but while glancing, Christian was also instinctively moving to defend himself from another blow, and when he looked back . . . Julian was gone.

The dark air where he'd been standing was empty.

Philip skidded to a stop, looking around wildly. "Where is he? Where did he go?"

"I . . . I . . ." For once in his life, Christian was speechless. He didn't know where Julian had gone. He knew only that he'd been inches from losing his head.

But then Philip spotted Eleisha on the ground, and his expression changed. He went white. "Eleisha!"

Crossing the distance in four strides, he dropped down beside her and pulled her up into one of his arms. "Eleisha."

Her right eye sported a dark bruise, and her body just hung limply over Philip's arm.

"It's all right," Christian managed to say. "He just hit her."

Philip's amber eyes flashed up to Christian's face, shining with open anger now . . . with an accusation. "What are you doing back here? You said you'd keep her under the lights!"

After the ordeal he'd just been through, Christian was in no mood to accept any blame for this from Philip.

Feeling spiteful, he summoned an impulse and sent it.

This is your fault, not his. You're supposed to be protecting them both, and you left them alone. Now look what's happened to her. You're not fit to have anything to do with someone like her.

With substantial satisfaction, he watched Philip's expression shift to guilt and suffering. Good God, he was easy to infiltrate.

But then Philip glanced around as if uncertain what to do. Still holding Eleisha with one arm, he dropped his machete, reached into his coat pocket, and pulled out a cell phone.

As Wade pulled into the garage at Vera's mansion, he saw Ivory suddenly stiffen in the passenger seat.

"What's wrong?" he asked.

"The Mercedes . . . the one Christian likes. It's gone."

Wade braked the BMW and followed her gaze. When he saw the empty parking spot, he wasn't sure what to feel. For a few seconds, he was completely numb.

"No . . . they'd never take Christian out of the mansion to come look for us," he said. "Eleisha wouldn't do it. Maybe Vera just had Simmons take her out for—"

His cell phone rang.

Pulling it from his pocket quickly, he looked at the caller ID.

Philip.

This time, he answered instantly. "Philip?"

"Where are you?" Philip's voice sounded strained and angry at the same time.

"At the mansion. Where are you?"

"Seattle Center. Julian attacked. Eleisha's down. You stay right there."

The line went dead.

"Philip!"

Wade just sat there, staring at his phone.

chapter fourteen

Christian drove back to the mansion amid tense silence.

Philip had carried Eleisha to the car and then climbed into the backseat, holding her against his chest. Christian found the whole display far too emotional for any semblance of good taste—and yet he'd wanted to kill Philip at the same time.

As yet, Eleisha's eyelids hadn't even fluttered.

However, Christian couldn't stop reliving the memory of Julian coming at him with that sword over and over. It was branded onto his mind. After all these decades of hiding from a phantom, he'd finally seen Julian . . . He knew what Julian looked like.

By the time he pulled into the garage and parked the Mercedes, he'd reached a decision.

Eleisha moaned, and he half turned to look into the backseat.

"Eleisha," Philip said, still holding her.

She opened her eyes and squinted in pain, looking up. "Philip . . . what happened?"

"It's all right. We're back at the mansion."

She gripped the lapel of his coat. "I knew you'd come."

That bothered Christian more than anything she'd said or done to date, and he tried not to frown. But then she struggled to sit up, looking frightened. "Where's Christian? Is he all right?"

At least he was her second thought upon waking.

"I'm right here," he said. "I told you I could hold my own."

Her head rolled toward him in relief. "Oh . . . yes, you did." Then her expression twisted into guilt. "I'm so sorry, Christian. I shouldn't have stepped back into that doorway."

He basked in her gushing apology, but before she could say anything else, Philip opened the car door and climbed out, still carrying her.

"I think I can walk," she said.

Philip ignored her and headed for the stairs, leaving Christian to get out and follow awkwardly. He seethed in humiliation and fantasized about the sight of Philip's headless body lying on the floor. But the next chain of events had to be set up carefully. At this point, he needed to kill three birds with one stone.

*　　*　　*

Wade was nearly sick with relief when Philip carried Eleisha into the vast, overstuffed living room and set her down on a couch. Christian followed a moment later, and although Eleisha was sporting a dark bruise around her right eye, everyone seemed to be in one piece.

However, Philip wouldn't even look at him, and Wade had a bad feeling that tonight's drama had just begun.

Christian stopped walking when he saw Ivory. He looked down at her cargo pants. "What are you wearing?"

She didn't answer, and he took a step closer. Wade tensed, as he wasn't about to let Christian bully Ivory even one more night. But he also realized that neither Eleisha nor Philip had a clue about the true nature of that relationship, and he had to be careful until they did.

Thankfully, Simmons walked into the room and addressed Christian directly. "Good evening, sir. Can I get you anything? Would you like me to have drinks brought in?"

Christian fell instantly into his lord-of-the-manor persona. "No, thank you, Simmons. Where is Mrs. Olivier?"

"Napping upstairs, sir."

Christian nodded. "Very good. You may go."

Simmons bowed and left.

For some reason, this brief but overly civilized exchange seemed to bring down the temperature in the room, and Wade walked over to check Eleisha's eye. "I'm sorry," he said. "Ivory needed to go hunting. I should have told you we were leaving, but I never thought . . . I never thought you'd come looking."

She still seemed dazed and just blinked at him.

"She called you," Philip said quietly. He still wouldn't look at Wade. "And you didn't answer your phone."

Oh, she had. Wade had forgotten about that, and the reminder made him feel even worse. What was wrong with him?

"Philip—," he began.

"Don't!" Philip snapped, and his vehemence surprised Wade. Had something else happened out there? Something worse than Julian attacking Eleisha?

"Bickering amongst ourselves is pointless," Christian said. "From what I saw tonight, I believe we all have the same problem."

Eleisha's eyes cleared a little, and she wrapped her arms around her knees with a questioning expression.

Christian spoke directly to her. "Julian. If we simply take out Julian, the same threat to all of us is removed."

Philip stood up and turned around. "How?"

Christian shrugged. "How did he find us so quickly?"

"That ghost you saw," Eleisha said softly. "The girl."

"She's loyal to him?"

Eleisha blinked again. "I don't know. Seamus seems to think Julian's somehow forcing her."

"Seamus? Your Highlander? He's spoken to her?"

He pushed his hair back and left his hand on his head for a few seconds. Then his eyes shifted back and forth. "Can he sense the girl . . . the same way he senses a vampire?"

Eleisha nodded. "I think so."

"Get him here."

For some reason she couldn't explain, Eleisha wanted to conduct her next task alone.

Although she was committed to their mission—devoted to their mission—a part of her was beginning to wish they'd never come here. She didn't feel like herself. Philip wasn't acting like himself, and Wade, who'd always been their rock, was taking unnecessary risks and couldn't seem to explain why.

She walked through the dining room, opened a set of large glass doors, and went outside alone onto the back patio, feeling the night air on her face and holding her cell phone tightly.

Then she lifted it and hit the button to call the landline at the church—located in Wade's office. It rang four times, and to her surprise, Maxim's voice sounded on the other end.

"Hello, Wade Sheffield speaking."

It was an almost perfect imitation of Wade answering the phone, and she realized that since this was all Maxim had heard or seen of someone answering a telephone, he must think it was the proper response.

"Maxim? It's Eleisha."

"Leisha? You coming home?"

Just the sound of his voice filled her with longing. She wanted to leave this claustrophobic mansion behind and go home.

"Soon," she said. "Are you all right? Is everything there okay?"

"I am here."

"Yes, I know. How are Rose and Tiny Tuesday and Mr. Boo?"

"Good. Boo wants Wade to come home."

"He does?" The thought of that tattered old pit bull missing Wade only made her more homesick. "Maxim, can I speak to Rose?"

"Yes, you know how to speak to Rose."

Eleisha paused, confused, and then realized she hadn't worded the question correctly. "Would you go and find Rose and ask her to come to the phone and speak to me?"

"Oh. Yes."

The line went quiet for a little while, and then Rose came on. "Eleisha, are you all right?"

"Yes, we're all right, but we need a bit of help." She hated to ask this so soon. "Can you send Seamus back?"

As soon as Eleisha left the living room to go and make her phone call, Wade began searching for any reason to drag Philip off alone—that wouldn't look suspicious—but nothing plausible came to him.

Ivory excused herself on the pretense of *wanting* to go and change her clothes. Christian had nodded his approval, but it seemed neither Christian nor

Philip was about to leave this room until Eleisha came back.

Standing up, Wade went over to a little side table and found a deck of cards. Then he went back to a couch near where Philip was pacing, and he sat down again. "Come play a few hands."

Philip looked down at him as if he'd grown two heads and then opened his mouth to speak. Wade could only imagine what was about to come out.

Shut up and play along, he said to Philip telepathically. *I have to tell you something.*

To Philip's credit, the anger faded from his eyes, and he sat down while Wade shuffled. Christian glanced over from the fireplace, but he didn't say anything.

Wade started to deal, and when he reached into Philip's mind again, Philip had dropped any mental blocks and left himself wide open for conversation. Good.

Christian's not what he seems, Wade projected.

I could have told you that, Philip answered, picking up his hand and looking at the cards.

No, listen to me! He's dangerous. He turned Ivory against her will, and he's kept her a prisoner for almost two hundred years. His gift is unusual, and he can send impulses in the form of emotions to manipulate people. Be on guard for any feelings or drives that don't feel like your own.

Could he be doing this . . . sending impulses to Eleisha? Philip asked.

I don't know. Maybe.

A muscle along the side of Philip's face twitched as he reorganized his cards. *If I kill him, Eleisha won't for-*

give me, he projected. *You know what she was like with Simone, and you saw her with Maxim. She only sees the good until she's proven wrong.*

Well, that was certainly true. Wade pretended to drop his cards, and he fussed about, trying to pick them up. Even if he told her everything he knew, she'd still want to believe Christian could be helped, saved, and brought into a community.

I do have one idea, Philip went on, *but if Christian truly has a plan to kill Julian, we should follow through on that, and then—*

Eleisha walked back into the living room. She looked to Christian. "Rose is sending Seamus."

As Eleisha spoke this message to Christian, the bone around her right eye was pounding, making it hard for her to keep from squinting. But in spite of the pain, she could still sense tension in the living room, as if a great deal was going on beneath the surface, and she had no idea what.

Wade and Philip seemed engaged in a card game, which was certainly out of place at the moment. Christian was standing well away from them by the fireplace in what appeared to be self-imposed isolation, and Ivory was missing.

"Where's Ivory?" she asked.

"She went upstairs to change her clothes and do her hair," Christian said, glancing in disapproval at Eleisha's T-shirt. "In a setting like this, appearances mean everything."

Once again, Eleisha felt diminished and "wrong" somehow. But she'd just hated wearing that evening gown and wished she had the courage to tell him.

Philip stood up and walked toward her. "You look fine," he said. "Except for that eye."

She smiled, keeping her gaze on him. He kept her grounded.

But then unbidden, ugly thoughts began rising inside her that Philip said such things only because he didn't know any better. He was too simple to ever function in polite society, and Christian was much more aware, much more adept at this, and she should have remained properly dressed for an evening in the mansion.

The thoughts startled her, and she tried to push them away. Even if she had kept that dress on, it would be ruined by now anyway, since she'd recently been lying unconscious on the wet ground. But that was hardly Christian's point. He'd simply been commenting on her ability to maintain a ruse, and he knew best here.

The air beside her shimmered, and Seamus materialized. He looked better than she'd expected, and his colors were bright. That was a good sign. They might need him here for a little while. But as soon as he saw her black eye, he frowned.

"What happened?"

"Julian," she answered.

"He hit you?" Seamus asked angrily. "Was Mary involved?"

Eleisha held up one hand to stop him from talking. "Wait. I . . . we need you to try something, and it won't be easy." His transparent eyebrows lifted, but instead of explaining anything, she pointed to Christian. "Just listen to him now."

Although she'd fully agreed that Christian should be the one to put this to Seamus, as it had been his idea, unfortunately, Christian assumed the same tone and posture he used while speaking to Simmons, and Seamus was no one's paid servant.

"How well do you know this Mary?" Christian asked.

Seamus looked him up and down, and Eleisha could already see this was probably not going to go well. "Why?" he asked.

"Eleisha told me you think Julian has something he's holding over her, some way to force her to do his bidding," Christian said. "What makes you think that?"

Seamus glanced down at Eleisha, and she nodded.

"I don't know . . . ," Seamus began, only now he was speaking directly to Eleisha. "She loved that vampire Julian killed in Oxford. I know she loved him, and I don't think she'd go on serving Julian after that unless he had some hold on her."

This was all news to Eleisha, but she didn't remember that night in Oxford very well . . . as again, Julian had punched her in the face before the whole scene exploded.

"Is that all?" Christian said. "You must know more than that."

Eleisha could see Seamus' expression closing up, and she flashed into Christian's mind, *Stop talking to him like he's a servant.*

She knew it was bad manners to send telepathy without asking permission, but this situation was serious, and he was handling it wrong. Christian glanced at her, but his tone changed.

"Forgive me," he said to Seamus. "It has been a most unsettling night, and I am not myself. But I would like to speak with this Mary and see if perhaps we can assist her. If we can do anything to help her get away from Julian, she might be willing help us kill him."

Seamus' transparent mouth fell halfway open.

"It's worth a try," Eleisha said quickly. "Can you find her and get her to talk to Christian?"

"To Christian?" he asked.

"Yes." She nodded. "Under the right conditions, he can be very . . . convincing."

No one argued with her.

Seamus just stood there, apparently in deep but somewhat anxious thought. Then he looked at Eleisha again and said, "I'll try."

Seamus had a feeling he wouldn't need to go far to find Mary, but he was still uncertain about this entire venture.

However . . . although he didn't trust Christian, this was the second time Julian had left bruises on Eleisha's face, and if Christian truly had an idea to both free

Mary and rid the world of Julian, then Seamus wasn't going to refuse to help.

He just needed to make sure Mary was protected in the process.

Materializing outside in the ornately bricked courtyard, he sensed outward into the night and felt something just on the other side of the main gate. Blinking out, he rematerialized a few feet behind Mary, pausing a moment to look at her slender back and mesh T-shirt.

"Mary," he said.

She whirled. Apparently, she'd not been sensing for him or she would have felt him appear.

"Don't leave!" he said instantly. "Please."

He could see she was poised, ready to vanish, but for some reason, she stayed, just watching him.

"What do you want?" she asked. "We shouldn't be talking to each other."

"I . . ." Then he was at a loss. How could he put this to her? "Is Julian forcing you to help him?" he asked. "Is that why you're doing this?"

"Forcing? No, not . . . really." Her voice hardened. "Seamus, what do you want?"

He steeled himself. "I want you to talk to Christian."

"What?"

"He thinks he can help you. He says that if you'll help us, he'll find a way to help you." Seamus floated closer to her. "I won't let him take advantage of you. I won't let him use you. But if he can get you free of Julian . . ."

Mary started to shake her head, and her face was sad now. "No, I can't get free until . . ." She trailed off and then looked at him sharply. "Wait, Christian is supposed to be some expert on ghosts, right? I mean, he's running a scam, but even to fake it, he's probably had to learn a lot about ghosts, right?"

Seamus had no idea where this was heading, but he nodded. "I suppose he would."

She paused for a few moments, and then she floated closer. "Okay. I'll talk to him."

Almost the instant Seamus vanished, Christian excused himself to go up to his room, claiming he needed a few moments to himself.

But he was hoping that Seamus would zero in on him and bring the girl up here—as he wanted to talk to her alone. He had no idea if this venture would bear any fruit at all, but he strongly suspected it might, and he wanted full control of a polite interrogation.

Eleisha's instincts down in the living room had been good, but he wanted no interference here.

If there was one thing Christian did well, it was talking to women.

The air shimmered by the bed, and both ghosts suddenly appeared. Seamus looked enormous beside the girl, dressed in his breeches, with his blue and yellow plaid across one shoulder.

The girl was a different story. Christian had seen only a glimpse of her at the Seattle Center, but now he took a good look and pegged her immediately. The cropped magenta hair and nose stud spoke volumes. She would be prickly and easily offended. But underneath, she craved attention and approval.

He smiled at her. "Thank you for coming." Then he glanced at Seamus. "Thank you as well. You may go now."

"No," Seamus answered.

The tall, transparent ghost didn't move an inch, and Christian realized—to his annoyance—that Seamus had no intention of leaving. Well, there was nothing to be done about that. Christian couldn't make him leave, so he might as well proceed.

He smiled at Mary again. "Our Seamus here seems to think you are much too nice a girl to be working for Julian unless you were being forced."

Mary blinked in surprise. "He does?"

Seamus started slightly, but Christian just kept talking. "Is that true? Is Julian forcing you, or has he promised something you want?"

Her face flickered at his second phrase, and he knew he had her. Christian had been connecting emotions to facial expressions for hundreds of years. He didn't need to be able to read this girl's thoughts. Her face was an open book.

"He's promised you something?" Christian said. "Something important."

She looked wary now, but her eyes were locked into his, and he was sure he could see a hint of hope beneath their surface. "Yeah . . . ," she began. "He pulled me out of the gray plane himself, so he's the only one who can send me back. I want to go back, and he promised that if I helped him just once more, he'd send me."

"Oh, Mary," Seamus interrupted. "No. Why do you want to go back?"

" 'Cause Jasper's there. He must be. Seamus, I can't leave him all alone."

Christian just listened. Maybe having the Highlander here wasn't such a bad thing. The girl talked to him more openly. But who was Jasper? Then he remembered Seamus having mentioned something about a vampire the girl had loved . . . a vampire Julian had beheaded.

Christian knew what she wanted.

"I can send you back," he said quietly. Both ghosts fell silent and stared at him. "I'd be glad to send to you back if that's really what you want."

Mary floated a little closer. "You know how?"

"Of course. You both know I'm no expert in speaking to real ghosts, but I daresay I'm more educated than Julian on the matter. I've had to be. It's my trade." He tilted his head. "Mary, how did Julian learn to call you over in the first place?"

Her eyes were growing excited now. "He read books. I know one in particular helped him a lot 'cause he keeps it out on the table—"

"*Geister Aufforden*, by Gottbert Drechsler," Christian suggested casually.

She gasped. "Yes. You've read it?"

"Of course I've read it, my dear. As I told you, this is

my trade. I may not have been the one to call you over, but I can certainly send you back."

Seamus was still silent, but Christian guessed that had more to do with Mary's actual request than with any doubts he might harbor regarding Christian's abilities.

"Are you certain that Julian means to keep his promise?" Christian went on. "You trust completely that as soon as you help him finish things up here, he'll hold up his end of the bargain?"

She didn't answer, but he could see from her face that she didn't.

"Let me pose another offer," he said. "If you help *us* to . . . shall we say, 'finish things here,' I can promise that we'll free you of Julian forever, and I'll send you back to the gray plane myself." He paused for effect. "You may not know me, but I think you do know Eleisha, and she'd never let me break a promise."

Mary's eyes flooded with hope. "No, she wouldn't, would she. Eleisha would never . . ." She glanced up at Seamus, who still didn't look happy, and then back to Christian. "What is it you want me to do?"

His heart soared. That had been easier than he'd expected, but then again, he was a master at telling people exactly what they needed to hear. But now he needed a few things from her.

"We'll chat about that soon enough," he said. "First, I need to know a bit more about what we're up against. For one, why did Julian knock Eleisha unconscious instead of taking her head when he could have?"

"Oh, he doesn't want to kill Eleisha yet, not unless he has to. He wants her to keep finding more vampires like you."

That made sense. "What about Wade?"

"No, probably not—again, unless he had to. Wade's the one doing the searches, and Eleisha's the one you guys all seem to trust. Julian needs both of them. But I think he'd cut Philip's head off in a heartbeat now."

That got Christian's full attention. "Really?"

"Yeah, these hunts would be a whole lot easier without Philip in the mix."

Goodness. This meeting was turning out to be far more of a treasure trove than he could have imagined.

"All right," Christian said. "I want you to wait until dusk tomorrow night. Then I want you to go to Julian, and this is what I want you to tell him . . ."

chapter fifteen

The following night, ten minutes after waking up on Philip's chest, Eleisha found herself alone in their guest room, as he'd gotten dressed quickly and gone downstairs to help Wade set up their trap.

The plan struck her as complex and simple at the same time, but much of it depended on Mary. Eleisha still had no idea how Christian had managed to win her over to their side, but the remainder of the previous night had been short and rushed and absorbed by the rapid formation of this plan—and everyone had been concerned about different aspects.

Eleisha was most worried about Vera being kept far away from Julian, and frankly, she wasn't keen on Ivory getting anywhere near Julian either, as Ivory appeared to have no real defenses. Christian backed her up in both these concerns.

But this then created an unfortunate role for Wade in tonight's events, which he'd opposed vehemently. But after a somewhat heated argument with Christian, in the end, Wade finally agreed to play guard dog to both women in an upstairs room.

Eleisha, Philip, and Christian would handle the fight downstairs . . . by using Christian as bait.

But far worse than the prospect of a battle with Julian, Eleisha was left with the unfortunate task of deciding what to wear. They were going to have a short stint of playing the socialite spiritualists for Vera before the main event was set in motion, and then more important, later tonight she'd need to fool Julian into thinking she was Ivory—at least from the back and under dim lighting.

For both these reasons, looking the part was important, and except for her sleeveless linen blouse, she had nothing in her suitcase but jeans, T-shirts, and broomstick skirts. Maybe she could wear the blouse with a skirt.

A knock sounded on the door, and Christian said, "Eleisha, it's me," from the other side.

Hesitantly, she opened the door and peered out.

He was a holding a light pink evening gown and a cosmetics bag. "We need to hurry," he said without his usual polite greeting. "I've asked Vera to meet me up here in a few minutes. You're certain you can put her to sleep for several hours?"

"Yes."

But before she could say anything else, he pushed past her inside the room, dropping the gown on the bed. "Get the dress on. There's no séance scheduled for tonight, and she thinks we're all going out for drinks at the Belmont."

"That's what you told her?"

He shrugged. "She'll want to do whatever we are doing tonight, but I needed a reason to give Simmons and the maids a night off. I arranged symphony tickets for all of them, and I told Simmons that Vera would be going out with us. He'll be gone for hours. Now, you get changed and let me take a crack at hiding that black eye." He turned around and started pulling small bottles from the cosmetics bag.

Eleisha stared at his back. Once again, she was placed in the position of changing clothes with him in the room. But there seemed no way she could object or refuse without offending him . . . or looking like some prudish female mortal who didn't understand the seriousness of the situation.

So while his back was turned, she dressed quickly, finding this gown preferable to the one from the previous night. It was sleeveless, but the top section covered more. It had an empire waist and zipped up the back to between her shoulder blades.

"Better," she said. "I can move in this."

He turned and smiled. "I'm not completely oblivious. I know what we're up against tonight. Come here, and let me see what I can do with that eye."

Some of the bruising had faded, but she still looked like she'd walked into a door. Christian seemed different tonight, more matter-of-fact, and his manner put her at ease. She sat down at the dressing table and turned her face up to him without hesitation. He applied some makeup to a sponge and then started dabbing it over her eye.

Without any warning, his easygoing manner vanished.

"Eleisha," he said, his voice sounding intense. "You know . . . I mean, you've realized by now that although I believe Julian has to be removed, once this is over, I'm not going back to Portland with you. I'm not going to live in some church."

Suddenly she was aware of his close proximity, how his fingers were touching the skin on her face, blending the makeup. She wanted to pull away but didn't. An unwanted feeling began growing inside her that she didn't want to live in the church either. She wanted the excitement of sitting in Ivory's chair and playing the conduit to Christian's spiritualist. The pull toward that life was so enticing.

"Yes," she struggled to say. "I know you won't come back with us. It's all right. That life isn't your life."

He touched her shoulder with his other hand. "I knew you'd understand. But I hate the thought of losing you now that we've just become friends. Ivory and I have been alone for so long."

The desire to stay with him, to travel and play the conduit at his side, grew stronger, and she fought to push it away. She thought of Philip and Wade and Rose . . . and Maxim. They were the crux of her home. They were her foundation.

She sat frozen while he brushed her hair quickly, twisted part of it, put it up on top of her head, and held it there with surprisingly few pins.

Light footsteps sounded outside, followed by a knock. "Christian, darling, are you in here?"

"Yes, Vera." He went to open the door and Eleisha stood up.

Smile, he flashed into her mind, and it sounded like an order.

She smiled.

Vera swept into the room, wearing a gold and black caftan and enormous silver hoops in her ears. "Oh, Eleisha, how sweet you look. Not all women can wear pink and pull it off like that." She pressed her palms together cheerfully. "Christian said you wanted me to show you a few of the upper-hall paintings before we go out tonight?"

Christian hadn't said a word about any paintings, but Eleisha had an idea what he was up to, and her smiled widened. She honestly liked Vera. Who wouldn't like Vera? She was warm and funny, and for all her wealth, she still enjoyed the little things in life.

"This way, my dear," Vera said.

Eleisha left the guest room and followed her down the hallway to another set of stairs leading up. Christian came behind. When they emerged into a wide upper hallway, Eleisha could see a number of huge portraits hanging on the walls. She felt quite dwarfed by the sheer size of their frames. But the portraits themselves were interesting, and one of them depicted a man in a tweed suit leaning back against a 1920s black Ford.

"Oh, I like this one," she said, stepping closer.

"Yes, that's my great uncle Charles," Vera said. "He died before I was even born, but Mother said he loved that car."

"Are all these people your relatives?" Eleisha asked, genuinely interested, but then Christian caught her eye and shook his head. They were not up here to discuss paintings.

Eleisha moved around Vera so that Christian could step up behind, and then she reached out and touched Vera's arm. "You seem so tired. I think you should sleep . . . sleep for hours."

Eleisha had never questioned her own ability to do this. Even though Christian seemed to find it a useful skill, he'd never developed it himself. She was almost positive he could do it if he tried, but he tended to just daze his victim's mind while feeding, as that was how Bernadette had taught him.

Vera collapsed like a rag doll, and Christian caught her, picking her up as if she weighed nothing. He must be a good deal stronger than he looked.

"This way," he said. "I know a room up here without a window. It should serve well." He glanced back toward the stairwell. "Wade and Ivory should be on their way up by now."

*   *   *

Upon waking that night, Julian strode to the glass sliding door of his hotel room and looked out over the view of Seattle. He was still shaken over how quickly everything had gone wrong the night before.

For one, he hadn't expected to find himself engaged in an open sword fight on the grounds of the Seattle Center. His method for killing his own kind was normally fast and silent. He just stepped out and swung before anyone knew he was there.

Julian's first act of putting Eleisha down had gone well.

But Christian had somehow managed to avoid Julian's first swing. Then he'd pulled his own sword, and the whole world sped up to a hundred and twenty miles an hour. What really troubled Julian were the strange fears and feelings that had come over him in the middle of the fight, that his arms were too heavy to swing . . . and that his gift wouldn't work.

Christian's blade was small and his skills were adequate at best. Julian had been sure things would end quickly, and in his favor, until for no reason, he'd begun to doubt himself, and then Philip had come flying up the path.

He'd had no choice but to run.

Worse, Mary had reported that they'd all holed up in the mansion again, and after his attack, there was no telling when they might come out again. He wasn't certain what to do at this point.

The air shimmered and Mary materialized. He could

tell by the animated expression on her face that something had happened.

"What is it?" he asked.

"When they all woke up, Eleisha told Christian it wasn't safe here anymore, and that he and Ivory had to go home to the church with her . . . tonight. Christian said no, and they had a big fight, and then Eleisha told him she was leaving. He called her bluff. She and Wade and Philip took off about twenty minutes ago. They're already on Interstate 5, heading back to Portland. Christian and Ivory are alone."

He stared at her. "Eleisha just left them?"

That didn't sound right, but Mary was good at assessing situations quickly. She always had been.

"I don't think Christian ever had any intention of going home with them," she went on, "and Philip can't stand him. It just all got to be too much. But you need to hurry. Christian isn't stupid, and he's already told Vera that they're leaving soon, too. He may not want to go back to the church in Portland, but he's not staying here either. So if you want to kill them, you'd better do it tonight."

Relief washed through Julian. Both his targets were anxious and distracted . . . and alone at the mansion.

He grabbed his sword and his coat. "Meet me outside the front gate."

Wade made his way up a staircase he hadn't seen before, with Ivory right beside him. Tonight she was back in her slinky red evening gown, but if all had gone according to plan, Vera would already be asleep, and there would be no need to continue this ruse.

Still, he'd put on the slacks and sport coat—per Christian's instructions—and he had his gun in the back of his pants.

Emerging into a wide hallway, he felt somewhat overwhelmed by the sheer size of the portraits on the walls. Several of the frames were thicker than his thigh.

"Over here," Eleisha called, and he looked ahead to see her waving them onward.

He paused at the sight of her. She wore a simply cut, light pink evening gown that created a different effect from the one she'd worn last night. This one made her look more like a little girl playing dress up. He hoped she wouldn't try to read his thoughts as that image struck him.

"This way," she said. "Do you have an extra clip loaded?"

The little-girl illusion vanished.

"Yes," he answered.

She led them inside a small storage room, full of easels and frames and blank canvas. The place was dusty, as if no one, not even Simmons, had been inside for years. Vera was sleeping peacefully on a pile of blankets, and Christian was kneeling beside her.

Wade still didn't like this plan, and he would much prefer to just lock Ivory and Vera inside this room and go back downstairs to help Eleisha and Philip.

"I know," Eleisha said to him softly, perhaps reading his face. "If everything goes well, he won't get past us . . . but if he does, I need you in here. Just empty a clip into his face and chest, and then empty another one. That should give you time to get them both out of here."

He nodded curtly. On some level he knew she was right.

"I'm not helpless," Ivory said suddenly, surprising everyone. Her tone was different from anything Wade had heard her use before—almost offended. "If Julian is so open to a telepathic attack, I can certainly daze him."

Christian frowned and stood up. But Eleisha hurried to Ivory's side. "Of course you can. But we need as few people as possible downstairs to pull this off. You stay and help Wade guard Vera."

As condescending as that sounded, Ivory seemed grateful and nodded.

"You'd both better get down there," Wade said to Eleisha and Christian. "Philip wanted some input on the staging, and I don't know how much time we have left."

His words had a rapid effect, and both Eleisha and Christian headed out of the room, down the hallway.

Wade tried to smile at Ivory. "Just you and me now."

"I don't mind that," she answered, pulling a blanket over Vera's legs.

He closed the door, shutting all three of them inside.

Julian parked his rental car in the trees about a half mile from the mansion, and then he walked to the front gates.

Mary materialized beside him.

"Okay," she began. "The setup isn't too bad. Both vamps are in the dining room at the back of the house, and the patio doors are wide open. You can walk right up and look inside without being seen. They've got the lighting low inside, and they're using candles. You should be able to step in and take Christian's head. Once his psychic energy releases and hits the girl, taking her out should be easy."

Not too bad? This sounded ideal. Perfect.

He'd not had a setup this easy since Italy.

Perhaps his luck was finally turning for the better.

After checking his sword at his belt, he walked a short ways down the fence and jumped up to grip the top, climbing over easily and landing in the courtyard on the other side. Then he made his way toward the back of the house.

chapter sixteen

Down on the main floor in the dining room, Christian could not have been more pleased with the setup that he, Eleisha, and Philip had mutually arranged. It would serve his purpose well.

The trap was set, and everyone was neatly in place.

Philip was hiding just around the corner, outside the dining room, sword in hand, ready to swoop in.

Eleisha was standing up against a tall table with a glass of red wine, her back to the open patio doors. Christian stood close to her, but just kitty-corner, so that anyone looking in from either side of the patio would see his profile. His sword was placed out of sight, but within an easy distance, leaned up against a wine cabinet.

He was also sipping from a glass, while he and Eleisha pretended to converse in low tones. They didn't wish to speak too loudly and risk Julian recognizing her voice. They simply wished to resemble two vampires speaking in private—perhaps making plans for an impending journey.

The lights were low and candles burned around the dining room, creating soft illumination. Eleisha looked lovely to him tonight, and he'd done a good job of covering the bruises over her eye. She'd been so agreeable, so concerned for his safety, while they'd been planning the specifics of this trap. Just the sight of her standing there pulled at him, and he could not wait until this unpleasant but necessary event was over and she belonged to him, and they'd be free to engage in real evenings of talking softly to each other over glasses of wine. He enjoyed such evenings, and unlike Ivory, Eleisha liked to please him.

But first he had to complete his own plans for tonight.

So long as Mary got Julian to the patio, Christian knew he could handle the rest.

Everything was in place now, and he decided it was time to set the first phase in motion.

Still pretending to chat softly with Eleisha, he focused his thoughts and sent Ivory a telepathic message, not an emotional impulse, but a crystal-clear chain of words.

Kill Wade right now, and I'll let you go. I'll give you your complete freedom and the Wells Fargo savings account. You know I've never lied to you when it comes to business. Kill him, and I promise you'll be free with enough money to go anywhere you want.

After so many decades of playing the same role over and over at Christian's bidding, Ivory couldn't seem to help enjoying this unusual situation. She was hiding out in a room with a kindhearted, handsome mortal—with a gun down the back of his slacks—helping him guard an eccentric aging woman who was snoring on a pile of blankets.

Had someone told her four or five nights ago that this was how her week would end, she'd have laughed in the person's face.

But here she was.

And there he was.

Maybe it was just because he was such a sharp contrast to Christian, but she couldn't remember ever having liked anyone as much as she liked Wade. In her mortal years, "nice" hadn't held any attraction for her when it came to men, but right now, his unfailing kindness was a light in the darkness. He was always so nice.

How had she never appreciated that before?

In addition to enjoying his company over the past few nights, she'd also been reveling in the glorious experience of living almost without the sickening fear in her stomach. The barest traces of it remained, but her mind was clearer now than it had been since the night Christian turned her.

For so long, she'd existed in terror of what would happen to her without Christian . . . and now that fear was almost gone. She could think again. She was herself again. Her thoughts kept turning to the future.

Every time Wade talked about the church, the street where he lived in Portland, and the mission that he and Eleisha had undertaken, she found herself having fantasies about living there and helping them, and never wearing an evening gown or looking into Christian's cold eyes again.

But, of course, she knew she'd never be free. She had no idea what Christian's game was here, and asking him would be pointless. If she even suggested leaving with Wade or if she tried to break free, Christian would hit her with everything he had. If she ran, he'd find her, and he'd make her sorry.

She'd never get away from him. He was too strong.

Wade crouched down beside Vera. "Do you think she's warm enough?"

He was facing away from her, but she smiled at the back of his head. "I think so. I've got her legs covered."

Then . . . a voice rammed into her mind, and from somewhere downstairs, Christian spoke directly into her thoughts.

Kill Wade right now, and I'll let you go. I'll give you your complete freedom and the Wells Fargo savings account. You know I've never lied to you when it comes to business. Kill him, and I promise you'll be free with enough money to go anywhere you want.

Julian kept his shoulder up against the house, and he stayed in the shadows as he approached the patio.

Cautiously, he stepped just close enough to see around one open door and look inside.

As Mary had reported, a large dining room spread out before him, and two people were just inside, standing at a tall table, sipping glasses of red wine. They spoke to each other in low voices. Christian's profile was in clear view, but Julian could see the woman only from the back. He remembered Mary's offhand description of Ivory:

Skinny, blond, low-cut dress, blah, blah, blah.

From what he could see of this woman, she was slender and blond, wearing a long light pink gown. More important, he sensed no life coming from her. He smelled no blood pounding beneath the surface of her skin.

He was looking at a pair of vampires.

Sliding his oiled sword out silently, he tensed and readied himself to take them both in two swift movements. But he'd have to step past Ivory to strike Christian first.

Eleisha was having a little trouble pretending to carry on a polite conversation with Christian. For one, she kept expecting to see the glint of a sword at any second, and that was distracting enough. But even worse, the unwanted, pain-inducing thoughts of how much she wanted to join Christian kept passing through her mind, no matter how hard she tried to push them away.

Philip was standing just around the corner, ready to

attack, and she tried to focus on him, but that only made it harder to keep poised for Julian's swing.

Fighting to clear her mind, she took another tiny sip of wine and tried to think of some other pleasantry she might say softly to Christian and give him something to chat about for a few moments.

But just as she looked up at him, she saw him turn his head slightly to the left, and somehow she knew . . . she knew it had begun.

He shoved her and then started to whirl to the right. A flashing, glinting blade swept through air and missed his throat by inches. Eleisha grabbed the table to try to hold herself up. Forgetting Christian and Philip and everything else, she focused all her mental strength on the tall, dark form moving beside her as he pulled back for another swing.

Freeze!

She drove the command into Julian's mind with everything inside her, and his body went rigid as his eyes went wide.

She hadn't seen him clearly in some time, as he always managed to put her down quickly before a battle, but she knew every line of his face, from his near-black eyes to his thick jaw. She'd known him since she was twelve years old. He was her maker. He was her enemy.

The last thing she wanted to do was take part in his death, but he'd left her with no choice.

Knowing the command to freeze wouldn't last, she

locked onto his mind to hold him there long enough for Philip or Christian to take his head. She'd promised to do her part here, and she would.

She needed to daze him, to make him forget where he was, so she started firing images into his mind, memories of heads he'd taken and of the moment he'd struck . . . first his own maker, Angelo, whom he'd killed outside of the manor in Harfleur . . . then Maxim's maker, Adalrik, whom he'd killed in a library near Shrewsbury, England.

This is your legacy, she whispered into his thoughts, *nothing but the death of your own kind.*

She took no satisfaction from the pain twisting across his face as he saw the ugly images she showed him, from making him watch his own crimes over and over.

But this all happened in the span of a few blinks, and even while holding there in those split seconds, she was aware of Christian grabbing his sword by the cabinet, and then she was aware of Philip rushing around the corner of the dining room with his machete in his hand.

She held Julian fast, knowing that as awful as this was, she had to hold him, and it would all be over in a matter of a few more seconds. She thought Philip would reach him first.

But then Christian blurred past her, sword in hand, and he started to draw his arm back to take a swing. But somehow, as his right elbow came backward, it slammed hard into her head, right between her eyes.

She lost her hold on Julian, and everything went black.

Christian didn't bother watching Eleisha fall, as he knew he'd knocked her out cold, and he also knew that later, he could convince her it had been an accident.

But the sight of her hitting the floor did give Philip pause in his rush as he ran into the room.

"Eleisha!"

Christian focused all his energy on watching Julian break free of Eleisha's control and come back to himself. Julian leaped to one side, gripping his sword, and in that instant, Christian summoned and sent an impulse.

Kill Philip first. He's much more dangerous, and you'll die if you don't kill him first. But your gift is broken, so you can't use it. Remember that it won't work.

chapter seventeen

Wade was crouched beside Vera, watching her sleep, trying not to think of what Eleisha and Philip were about to face downstairs, still questioning his own agreement to stand guard up here. Christian had just been so convincing.

He reached out to pull Vera's blanket up a little higher, and he heard Ivory coming up behind him. "I wonder how long she'll stay out," he said. "We'll have a hell of a time explaining this to her if she wakes up."

But instead of answering him, Ivory reached under his sport coat and pulled the gun from the back of his slacks. The movement was so swift and unexpected that by the time he'd jumped to his feet and whirled, she was halfway across the room, pointing the barrel at his head.

"Ivory?" he asked, incredulous, not even sure what else to say. What was happening?

She looked so strange standing there, her blond hair glowing, her red dress reflecting an overhead light . . . but she held his gun like she knew how to use it.

"Wh-what . . . ?" he stammered. "What are you doing?"

The skin on her face had a wild sheen to it, and her eyes were too bright. She looked manic, and he couldn't even begin to talk her down until he knew what was wrong. In desperation, he tried reading her thoughts, but she blocked him.

"Don't!" she said, holding the gun straighter, and in that instant, he realized she was capable of pulling the trigger. She was going to kill him. He could see it.

Of all the ways he'd thought to die, this wasn't among them: shot with his own gun by a person he was beginning to care for.

"I have to!" she cried, sounding almost hysterical. "He said . . . he said if I did he'd let me go. He'd set me free. You saw inside me! You saw everything. You know I have to get free even if . . . even if it means . . ."

She kept the gun pointed at his head.

But her words were churning in his mind. She'd been promised that if she killed him, Christian would set her free? That made Christian capable of premeditated murder, and he was downstairs right now with Eleisha and Philip.

And Wade was about to die.

"You don't have to do this," he said, his mind racing for any way to make her lower the gun. "You can get away from him on your own. Just come back to the church with me. I promise we'll protect you. We won't let him near you."

"No." She shook her head. "You can't promise that." But she took a step back, and her eyes were shifting back and forth. "I've felt so different the past few nights, almost like myself again . . . like I can think again."

"That's because he hasn't been focused on you!" Wade nearly shouted. "I think he's been focused on us instead. Don't you see? As long as you're with him, he can keep you under control, keep you terrified to leave him, but if you get away from him, everything really will be okay, and you won't be afraid anymore."

She was watching him now, listening to him.

"Maybe I could get away," she whispered, almost to herself, "but I'd have to disappear." There was a small pile of broken easels beside her, and she dropped down into a crouch. Her eyes were less wild, but the sheen on her skin was worse. "Wade," she said, sounding like she was in pain. "Come and take the gun from me."

As she lowered it, he rushed over, wanting to take it from her but wanting to help her at the same time. Why would Christian want him dead this badly?

"Here," he said, crouching beside her. "I'm right here."

He reached out for the gun, but she dropped it so that it bounced off the floor. The motion confused him, and then she grabbed the leg of a broken easel and swung hard, catching him across the temple. He fell to the side, more shocked than injured, but he could hear the sound of running feet.

Touching the side of his head, he tried to struggle up. "Ivory?"

His gun lay beside him, but the door was open and Ivory was gone. Jumping up to his feet, trying to ignore the pain in his head, he ran for the door and looked down the hallway. It was empty. She was gone.

He remembered her whispering to herself, *I'd have to disappear.*

Somehow, he knew she'd get herself out of this house . . . and just run. He'd gotten through to her, but not in the way he'd hoped. She'd broken free of Christian, but she wanted to disappear.

"Ivory," he said softly, and the sadness welling up inside him was surprising. He barely knew her. But the thought of never seeing her again hurt.

Turning back into the room, he watched Vera sleeping soundly. Although he hated the idea of leaving her up here alone, he knew he couldn't stay with her. His friends needed him.

Striding back, he grabbed the gun, and after closing the door behind himself to try to hide Vera, he made a run for the stairs.

Even though Julian didn't need to breathe, he wanted to gasp for air. Eleisha had just had him under her control again. He could still feel her fingers in his mind, forcing him to watch himself over and over as he killed his own maker.

He dreaded nothing more than having Eleisha inside his mind, filling him with horror, controlling his body, making him her puppet. He wanted to choke. But then, somehow, he'd been released, and he stumbled across the dining room floor just in time to see Philip running in and looking down toward the floor.

How could they even be here? Mary said they were on their way to Portland.

"Eleisha!" Philip cried.

Something important had just happened, but Julian wasn't sure what. He had time for only a single glance down to see Eleisha lying on the floor before an urge hit him, and he knew exactly what he had to do.

Christian was not a danger. He would die easily, but with Eleisha down, Philip was the greatest danger in the room. He had to die first. Julian had to kill him.

Philip recovered almost instantly from the shock of seeing Eleisha on the floor, and he tossed his machete from his left hand to his right—as he was good with either hand, but slightly better with the right. Julian needed an advantage, and he started to call upon his gift, to send a wind of fear shooting around the room, engulfing and crippling everyone but him.

But then he remembered that he couldn't do this. His gift was broken, and it didn't work.

Snarling, he charged.

The urge was stronger now. He had to take Philip's head.

*   *   *

With Julian swinging like a mad crusader, Christian was free to focus on Philip. This was all going well so far. He'd managed to keep Julian from using his gift, as he himself had no desire to be crippled by an aura of fear.

By now Wade was certainly dead, and Philip was about to join him.

Christian stood by the table, focusing all the strength of his gift on Philip, and he started sending impulses.

You're weak.

You've forgotten how to use the sword.

You can't keep your balance.

Philip stumbled and missed his first swing. His eyes were lost and confused as he brought the machete back up without an ounce of finesse or power. He somehow managed to block Julian's swing, but he no longer seemed to know what he was doing.

Christian smiled.

The sound of clanking steel carried through Eleisha's ears and into her consciousness. She moaned softly.

What had happened?

The last thing she remembered was Christian's elbow coming toward her face.

Opening her eyes, she used both arms to try to push herself up, but the floor beneath her looked blurry . . . It was the dining room floor.

Everything came rushing back. She'd been holding Julian telepathically. Where was he? The sound of clanking echoed in her ears again, and she looked up.

The first things she saw were Christian's legs. Her gaze moved upward. He was standing just a few feet away from her, beside the table, and he was smiling.

Then she looked beyond him, and she wanted to gasp, but no sound came from her mouth. Julian was swinging a sword at Philip near the open doorway leading out from the dining room into the house. But there was something wrong with Philip, and he seemed barely able to block Julian, much less take a swing. He was nothing like the graceful fighter she knew. He was clumsy and stumbling . . . and confused.

Eleisha blinked hard, fighting to clear her head.

Why was Christian just standing there and watching? Why wasn't he helping? Why was he smiling? He looked so pleased that her stomach tightened. She had to help Philip. Trying to gather herself, she began calling on her strength to send a command into Julian's mind, anything to stop him.

Then Julian made a roundhouse swing with the point of his blade and slashed Philip across the chest, cutting through his clothes and flesh. Dark blood sprayed outward and began running down Philip's chest.

The command forming in Eleisha's mind vanished.

"No!" she screamed.

At the sound of Eleisha's cry, Julian froze. Then he whirled around. She was awake, up on all fours, staring at Philip in horror.

Julian still felt lost, even dazed with rage. He could

see that she was in shock from the sight of Philip stumbling backward, bleeding, struggling to keep on his feet.

But he knew her shock would fade any second, and she'd send a command to freeze his body again, imprison his mind in a telepathic attack, and trap him in his own nightmares. He couldn't go through that, not now, not ever . . . and his gift was broken.

As much as he wanted her to continue in her mission, after what she'd done to him only a few moments ago, he couldn't risk the chance of her entering his mind.

Gripping the hilt of his sword, he ignored Philip and started toward her.

Christian's delight at the sight of Philip's blood was short-lived.

Almost instantly, he heard Eleisha screaming, "No!" and he looked down to see her fully awake, staring at the scene. At first, he merely found this unfortunate.

But then Julian whirled around, and Christian saw his eyes.

Gripping the hilt of his sword, Julian strode across the dining room straight for Eleisha, and Christian had only seconds to act. He was a master of reading faces, and he was certain Eleisha was about to lose her head.

That would ruin everything.

With no time to summon an impulse and send it into Julian's mind, Christian rushed forward and wrapped his foot around Julian's ankle.

Julian had been so focused on Eleisha that he tripped and stumbled, leaning down. Without another thought, Christian jerked his sword up high and arced it back downward at Julian's throat.

The blade was sharp, and as it connected, it sliced through the back of Julian's neck, continued through, and severed his head. The heavy body in the black coat landed with a thud right before his head bounced once with a wet sound, and rolled across the dining room floor.

Eleisha's face twisted into an emotion he couldn't read, and she seemed beyond speech. Black blood poured from the stump of Julian's neck, spreading outward, moving between her fingers, spreading toward her knees. She let out a cry that reminded Christian of a rabbit being strangled.

But her shock was even greater now than when she'd watched as Philip's chest was sliced open, and Christian knew he had to act quickly—and kill Philip before she came back to herself.

Then he could tell her anything he wanted and use his gift to reinforce his story.

Philip was weaving slightly and still bleeding. But his eyes were starting to clear, and Christian knew he'd have to put a stop to that.

Gripping the hilt of his sword, he summoned an impulse to daze Philip again, and he was just ready to send it when Wade came running into the dining room, holding an automatic pistol with both hands and pointing it straight at Christian.

"Don't move!" he ordered, and then he stunned Christian further by saying, "And if I feel anything, anything I wouldn't normally feel, start coming into my head, I'll put a bullet between your eyes."

Philip was standing straight now, taking in the sight of Julian's headless body and Eleisha on the floor kneeling in his blood . . . the sight of Wade and the gun.

Wade glanced at his friend's bleeding chest and said, "Christian tried to kill me. He told Ivory to do it."

Philip's head was clearing rapidly, and he was on guard now, just watching Christian.

But Julian's body was lying on the floor, his severed head a few feet away, and Philip was still waiting for the psychic explosion that always happened when a vampire died, when the vampire's telepathic energy burst out, striking any other telepath in the vicinity.

But it never came.

With revulsion, Philip remembered what had happened during the fight with Julian, how he'd believed himself weak . . . how he'd forgotten how to use his sword. Then Wade's last few sentences echoed in his ears.

"Wade," he said slowly, "if you see me doing anything I wouldn't normally do, shoot him anyway."

The course of events was beginning to take shape now, and he realized Christian had gone to great lengths to get rid of both him and Wade. Why?

"What is it you want?" he said.

Christian's face was tight, as if he was uncertain

what to do next. He didn't answer but glanced down once at Eleisha.

Eleisha.

He wanted her.

Wade must have seen the glance, too, because he moved in, holding the gun higher. "Back up," he ordered. "I know this won't kill you, but it hurts, and I swear it'll put you down."

"Where's Ivory?" Philip asked him. He was taking everyone except Christian and leaving this house right now.

"Gone," Wade answered, and his voice wavered slightly. "She's already run off on her own."

"Gone?" Christian mouthed in disbelief.

Philip was still bleeding and his chest hurt, but he refused to let it show. Eleisha seemed to have lost herself, and she was just kneeling there in Julian's blood, staring at his dead body. He knew she wasn't mourning him. She'd known full well what the endgame was for tonight. But still . . . it was hard to look at the dead body of one's maker. He'd been through that a long time ago, and he still remembered it.

He had to get her out of here.

A threat that might work against Christian had occurred to him the night before, and he decided to use it.

"We're leaving," he said coldly, "and you will never come near Eleisha again." He stepped forward with the machete gripped lightly in his hand.

But his manner seemed only to bring Christian back to himself, inciting him to fall back into his normal haughty tone. "Or what? You'll take my head? I don't think she'd approve of that."

"No," Philip answered, shaking his head. "I'll tell Vera you're a fake. I'll tell everyone she knows. I'll tell Randall Smith at the *Seattle Times*. I'll tell them exactly how you do it, and if I have to, I'll show them myself. I'll expose myself as telepathic, and I'll tell them you've never spoken to a single ghost, ever. Such a story takes on a life of its own. Even the rumor of such a thing would ruin you."

Christian stared at him.

Philip backed toward Eleisha, keeping his eyes on Christian. "We're leaving," he repeated. "Don't follow us."

With blood soaking through his shirt, he reached down to grasp Eleisha's arm.

"Come with me."

She let him pull her up without protest. But then she looked from his bleeding chest over to Christian.

As Christian locked eyes with Eleisha, he still couldn't believe what was happening. Reaching out with his mind, he called, *Ivory?*

But she was gone. He couldn't feel her anywhere.

Philip began leading Eleisha from the room, and Wade was backing away with the gun still aimed at Christian's head.

So now . . . Christian was about to lose Eleisha as well. After what she'd just seen and heard, he might have lost her already, but if he could just talk to her, if he could just get her alone, he knew he could make her understand. If he could just make her stay with him, he'd find a way to stop Philip from making good on his threat.

But he had to keep her with him. She was to be his new conduit, and he couldn't play the game without her.

If he gave up now, all was lost.

Focusing on the back of her head, he gathered an impulse and sent it.

You can't just leave him like this. No matter what's happened, you have to say good-bye. Talk to him. Just give him five minutes and talk to him alone.

She whirled around, pulling her arm from Philip's grip. Instead of looking at Christian with guilt and sympathy, her hazel eyes were blazing.

Freeze!

The mental command hit him full force, and every muscle in his body went rigid. In blind terror, he realized he couldn't move.

Fall! Backward.

As if of its own volition, his body fell back onto the floor. He heard light footsteps on the floor, and then he saw her leaning over him. He lay there, frozen.

"I won't let Philip take your head," she said quietly. "But if you follow us, if you ever come near us again, I'll have Wade put six bullets in your face."

She raised her head, and he thought perhaps she was taking one last look at Julian's body. Then he heard her light footsteps heading away again. Within a few moments, control began returning to his body, but he didn't try to follow her.

He was all alone now, and he knew it.

It was a strange feeling.

By the time Eleisha followed Wade down into Vera's long garage, he'd stowed his gun and he was half dragging Philip.

Eleisha knew Philip was losing too much blood, and they had to do something to help him quickly. But the same phrase kept turning over and over in her mind.

Julian's dead.

Julian's dead.

Julian's dead.

She didn't know what to feel.

"Grab the keys to the Mercedes," Wade ordered, half carrying Philip toward the car.

Eleisha ran to the pegs on the wall and grabbed the keys, but she had no idea what he was doing.

"Unlock it," he said.

She hit the button on the key chain and then watched him drag Philip into the backseat.

"You drive," he said.

Still confused, she ran around to the driver's door and climbed in. "Are we stealing one of Vera's cars?" she asked. "What if Christian calls the police?"

Philip was stretched out on the seat, turning white, and Eleisha realized she was babbling out of sheer panic. But Wade stripped off his sport coat and started rolling up his sleeve. "Just drive," he said. "I know the code for the front gate. Take us back to our hotel, and we'll leave this car there and switch to our rental."

Leaning over Philip, he put his wrist into Philip's mouth. "Bite down."

And then suddenly everything seemed to make sense. Wade was going to heal Philip, and she would drive them to their car, and they would all go home. Turning around, she put the keys into the ignition.

Wade gasped, and she knew Philip had bitten down.

But Wade was focused on his task, and she focused on hers. She was going to take them home.

Mary did exactly as Christian had instructed, and she waited outside until everything was over. He'd told her that he could handle the situation so long as she got Julian to the patio, and she'd believed him.

In her life and in her death, she'd never met anyone as confident as Christian.

She waited outside for what seemed like forever, wondering if she should materialize inside and find out if Julian was dead. She had no mixed feelings about this. He'd killed Jasper without a thought, and he deserved to die.

The thought of Jasper filled her with longing. She knew he'd be waiting for her on the gray plane and she'd finally get to see him again tonight. He wouldn't be alone anymore, and neither would she. She'd miss this world, with all its life and color, but she missed him more, and Christian had promised he'd send her back. Mary hadn't seen Seamus since last night, but she figured he'd had to go back to Portland for a short while. For some reason, that made her a little sad. He'd been nice to her, nicer than anyone besides Jasper. She probably wouldn't see him again and wished she could have at least said good-bye.

A creaking sound, like a garage door opening, reached her, and she looked toward the house. A few minutes later, the front gates opened, and a Mercedes pulled out of the courtyard and onto the road. Who was leaving? And why?

Confused, Mary reached out with her senses, and she felt two black holes in the fabric of life. Two of the vamps were leaving? She wanted to get close enough to see who it was, but she hesitated until she had a better idea of what was going on.

Blinking out, she cautiously rematerialized on the patio and peered inside. There was no movement in the dining room, but a familiar black coat and a sword lay on the floor. She floated in and kept looking down.

Julian.

His body was beginning to dry out and harden and turn to dust. He was dead.

Good.

She'd held up her end of the bargain. Now it was time for Christian to hold up his. But where was he? And who had just left in that car? Focusing her senses again, she felt a presence—or lack of a presence, in the living room. Blinking out, she blinked back in to see Christian sitting on a couch in the darkness. He looked odd, almost ill.

"Are you okay?" she asked.

He didn't jump in surprise or alarm but simply raised his weirdly clear eyes to her face. He didn't seem to recognize her—or even care that she was there. The first hint of anxiety began growing inside her.

"Where is everyone?" she asked, hoping to make him snap out of . . . whatever this was.

"Gone," he answered.

"Where?"

He seemed annoyed now. "It doesn't matter."

Something was very wrong here.

Almost frightened, she floated closer, pitching her voice to sound matter-of-fact. "Well . . . Julian's dead. I just saw his body in the dining room. So now you can send me back. I did what you asked. It's your turn."

She couldn't wait to see Jasper, to assure him she'd been trying her hardest to reach him again.

Christian didn't move. His eyes glowed in the darkness.

"My turn for what?" he asked.

Anxiety turned to fear. "Get up," she ordered. "You promised you'd send me to the gray plane if I helped you kill Julian. Julian's dead. So you send me back. Now!"

The expression on his cold, emotionless face shifted, and unfortunately, Mary had seen that look before . . . on her own face in a mirror back when she'd been alive. He was hurt and angry and alone, and he wanted to hurt someone else.

She knew that look all too well.

"You stupid girl," he spat, standing up. "Do you really believe I know anything about the spirit world? I'd never even seen a ghost until your Scottish friend showed up a few nights ago."

She went numb. "But the books . . . You said you'd read the books . . . You knew the—"

"The titles?" he sneered. "Of course I know those titles. I have to be able to talk the talk. But I'm a master of reading fools, of dazzling clueless mortals, not of dabbling in nonsense."

"Nonsense?" she choked, trying to get her head around what he was saying. "So . . . Julian's dead, and you can't send me back?"

"Afraid not, my dear. But I do thank you for the assistance tonight. It was appreciated."

"You bastard!"

Seamus had promised he wouldn't let Christian use her, and then he'd agreed that Eleisha would never let Christian go back on his word. But they weren't here.

She rushed at Christian, wanting to scream into his face, but he just stood there, watching her pain, enjoying the moment. He'd really wanted to hurt someone tonight.

And he had.

chapter eighteen

lmost four hours after they left the mansion, Wade watched the familiar street sign as Eleisha made the last turn toward the church.

He was weak from having fed Philip, but although Philip's chest wasn't completely healed, the wound had closed up, and he'd stopped bleeding. Wade was well aware they both looked like death warmed over, though, and Eleisha kept casting concerned glances at them in the rearview mirror.

"Philip's going to need more blood soon," she said. "I'll figure something out. But, Wade, as soon as we're home, I'll defrost a steak and you can tell me how to cook it. You need food."

He tried to smile at her in the mirror. He didn't blame her—or any of them—for focusing on tasks at hand and for avoiding any open discussion of what they'd just been through.

That Christian had planned several murders.

That Ivory was gone.

That Julian was dead.

Wade leaned back against the seat, and his thoughts seemed filled with a mix of the trivial and nontrivial. For the former, about halfway home he remembered they'd left all their luggage behind at Vera's. Everything. He'd lost his canvas jacket with the plastic buttons and his favorite Blue Öyster Cult T-shirt.

Eleisha was still wearing that pink evening gown—stained with Julian's black blood—but she'd lost some of her favorite clothes, too.

In light of everything else, he had no idea why this would bother him.

In less trivial matters, he thought about Vera, whom he'd left in an unnaturally induced sleep on the top level of the mansion in an art storage room. But he knew she'd be all right. Christian was no danger to her, and she'd eventually wake up confused but safe.

Far less trivially, he wondered where Ivory had gone, and then he closed his eyes, trying to stop wondering.

"We're here," Eleisha said, pulling up to the curb right in front of the church. "Philip, do you need help?"

"No," he answered sharply.

They all climbed out of the car, and Philip glanced at Eleisha's stained dress, but she still hurried to see if he needed help.

"I'm all right," he said, his voice softer this time.

She opened the gates, and the church loomed ahead of them. "Thank God," she whispered.

For some reason, Wade found this an overly ironic thing for her to say.

But just then, the church doors banged open and a slender figure jumped off the steps, nearly flying toward them. He stopped about two inches in front of Eleisha, his face alive with eagerness, like he wanted to grab her but didn't know how.

"Maxim," she choked, and then she gripped the sleeve of his shirt, briefly touching her forehead to his shoulder. "You look just like home to me."

"I am home," he said.

"Yes, you are," she whispered.

Right on his tail came a heavy trotting sound, and Mr. Boo came straight to Wade. Dropping to his knees, Wade reached out and scratched behind his tattered ear. "I can't believe I'm saying this, but I missed you."

Boo grunted.

The air shimmered and Seamus appeared. Without even a greeting, or noticing what a mess they looked, he blurted out, "You're here? Where's Mary? Did Christian send her back?"

Wade had no idea what he meant, but he said, "I don't know."

"You're home," a breathy voice called from the front doors. Then Rose was hurrying toward them, taking in the state of them all. "Eleisha, are you injured? What are you wearing? Oh, Philip, you're so pale. Wade, did you cut your wrist? Come inside."

She didn't ask why they were alone or why they'd brought no lost vampires back, and Wade felt a quick rush of gratitude. She simply ushered them all inside.

They were indeed home.

Wade glanced back once into the empty night, wondering where Ivory had run.

A week later, Eleisha knelt by a white rosebush in her garden, pulling weeds and still trying to process what had gone wrong—what she'd done wrong—up in Seattle.

Their mission had been a failure.

Or had it?

Christian had no place here, but he knew the laws and fed without killing, so they hadn't left some untrained vampire murdering mortals in order to go on existing. She felt no guilt about leaving him behind. Because of them, Ivory had managed to break away from him, and although they hadn't been able to convince her to come back here, at least she was free.

And Julian . . .

She knew that outcome was the only one possible, and if she had to do it over again, she'd still help kill him. Yet she couldn't close her eyes and see his headless body there on the floor without a flash of sadness.

But tonight she was dressed in a long cotton skirt and a gray T-shirt. Her feet were bare, and she was pulling weeds in her own garden.

That was something.

The back door opened, and she looked over to see

Wade coming toward her with Mr. Boo at his side. She couldn't help smiling at the sight of them, Wade with his long strides and Boo trotting on his shorter, stocky legs. She was glad Mr. Boo kept him company. She knew this time around Wade was the one who felt he'd lost something on the mission, and she knew he was still thinking about Ivory.

"I thought I'd find you out here," he said.

His wrist was bandaged, but he tended to heal quickly for a mortal.

"And how did you know that?" she asked, still smiling.

"Because this is where you spend most of your time after we get back from a mission."

"Is it?" Perhaps it was. "Do you need me for something?"

He shook his head. "No, but now that we've all had a little time at home, I wondered if something had occurred to you yet."

She raised one brow and just watched him.

"With Julian gone, everything has changed," he said. "Everything."

"What do you mean?"

"I mean that we can look for lost vampires with having to worry about protecting them now. We never have to look over our shoulders again. We're free."

Seamus was downstairs in the kitchen when the presence hit him with a jolt. Rushing to blink out, he rematerialized outside in the garden on the north side of the church.

She was standing there, looking up at the stained-glass windows, just as he'd seen her a few months back that night in the rain. She looked sorrow laden. He didn't think he'd ever seen anyone so forlorn.

"Mary," he said.

She turned toward him.

"Don't go!" he begged.

He'd questioned both Eleisha and Wade about what had become of Mary, but they hadn't known.

She just floated there, with her sad eyes, until he asked, "What happened? Why didn't he send you back?"

"He couldn't," she whispered. "He lied. He didn't even know how."

"Oh, Mary."

But his pity for her was mixed with a guilty belief that maybe Christian's ignorance wasn't such a bad thing.

"You don't belong there anyway," he said. "You belong here, in this world."

"Here?" she asked, incredulous. "Seamus, I have nowhere to go."

He shook his head. "You could stay here with us, help us look for lost vampires. You're not tied to Rose like I am. You can go hunting for a signature and keep looking as long as you like."

"Stay with you?" Her expression of incredulity only

increased. "Are you serious? You don't really think Elei-sha would agree to that, do you? I've been *helping* Julian. She's watched vampires die because of me."

Seamus frowned. "If that's what you think of Elei-sha, then you haven't been watching her close enough this past year. She knew Julian better than you, and she'd served him herself once. She'd never hold that against you."

Mary went still, but he thought he saw some of the desolation in her transparent eyes fade and a spark of hope ignite. "You really think that? You think she'd let me stay?"

"'Course she would. You'll be more use to her than I am." With his own sense of hope growing, he floated a few feet toward the church. "Come on inside with me."

She hesitated just a few seconds, and then she floated after him.

Wade was walking though the sanctuary, heading for his office, when a knock sounded on the front doors. He tensed.

It was nearly eleven. He hadn't ordered any pizza, and the only people who ever knocked on the door were deliverymen.

He was alone, and his gun was in the office. Even Boo was downstairs with Maxim. But the knock sounded again. Bracing himself, Wade walked down the long sanctuary floor, gripped a handle, and opened one of the doors.

His heart nearly stopped.

Ivory was standing on the other side.

She looked a little bedraggled, still in the red evening gown, which was a bit worse for wear, as if she'd been hiding too deeply to find money or go shopping for anything else. But he still wondered if he was imagining the sight of her until she spoke.

"Did you mean what you said back at the mansion? That you and Eleisha could keep Christian away from me?"

His mind went nearly blank, but he knew the right answer—and he wasn't lying. "Yes."

They both just stood there. Then she said, "I don't want to be alone anymore. Can I come in? Could I stay for a while?"

He didn't trust himself to speak, but he stepped back instantly and held the door wide open. Then he managed to say, "Stay as long as you like."

Epilogue

Two weeks later, Eleisha came in from the garden and walked into the sanctuary to find Rose curled up on one of the couches reading *Great Expectations* aloud to Maxim. Mr. Boo was lying at their feet—which probably meant Wade was in his office with Tiny Tuesday, as Boo tended to avoid the cat.

"All right," Rose said, "now you try reading this paragraph to me."

Rose had a new theory that if she could reteach Maxim to read at his previous level, some of his gift might begin coming back. Eleisha couldn't fault her logic . . . and marveled at her tenacity. Also, Maxim seemed eager to master the books, so neither Wade nor Eleisha had interfered.

They made a pretty picture, sitting there with Charles Dickens shared in their laps and a dog at their feet. Eleisha walked past quietly so as not to disturb them, and she moved behind the altar, opening the door to the hallway behind it.

Almost immediately, she heard Wade and Ivory arguing about desk placement in the office, and she tried not to smile. Ivory had quickly revealed herself as a woman who did not enjoy being idle. At the same time, she had zero interest in gardening or reteaching Maxim how to read.

No, she preferred Wade's job, and she'd made it clear that her place in the household would be in his office, researching news stories and checking up on possible leads. Since he had no intention of giving up his own position, they'd ended up jockeying for time on the computer, and then finally, last night, Wade had ordered her a desk and a notebook computer.

However, rather than feeling threatened, he was quite taken with the idea of the two of them sharing an office, even though she argued with him openly and sometimes called him names when she thought he was paying too much or too little attention to a story he'd read online.

But he seemed to enjoy her feisty nature, and she seemed to thrive on finally being able to express herself. After two hundred years of Ivory being pressed under Christian's thumb, Eleisha didn't blame her.

"If we put the new desk here," Ivory insisted on the

other side of the office door, "for at least part of the month, I'm going to have moonlight reflecting off my screen. It has to go over there."

"You can't put it there," Wade answered back. "We'd have to move Tuesday's bed."

"Well, I don't think Miss Princess Kitty would mind having her bed moved."

Smiling, Eleisha walked past the office, on down the hallway.

Wade was having the time of his life.

She reached the stairs and headed down into the apartment below. The sounds of gunfire echoed in her ears before she stepped into the living room. Philip, Seamus, and Mary were all watching *Predator* with Arnold Schwarzenegger on Philip's big flat-screen TV.

Only Seamus seemed less than thrilled with the choice of film.

"I just don't see why we can't watch an old John Wayne Western sometimes," he said.

"Yuck," Mary answered.

The corners of Philip's mouth twitched. Philip had never been comfortable with anyone besides Eleisha or Wade. He was decent to Rose, and he tolerated Maxim and Seamus, but to Eleisha's pleased surprise, he actually liked Mary. Like him, she was easily bored, and they had a similar taste in films.

Of the two newest additions, Mary was the most damaged, even though she had great potential to help the group. For now, it was good for her to just hang around with Philip and Seamus—and heal a bit.

Both Seamus and Mary appeared to be in cross-legged sitting positions, floating a few inches off the floor. Eleisha was not surprised when Mary suddenly turned her transparent head toward Seamus and said, "I'm just kidding. You pick the movie next time."

She was clearly grateful for her place here in the underground, and she gave the credit to him.

Philip's long body was stretched out on the couch, but his eyes flicked toward Eleisha as she walked into the room, and he motioned to the empty space on the couch beside him. She smiled but didn't sit down and just kept going, passing through into the kitchen.

There, she stopped and looked down at a porcelain teacup someone had left on the table. The kitchen counters were somewhat cluttered by herbs that Rose grew in various colored pots, along with Wade's Crock-Pot and microwave. The place looked just like anyone else's kitchen.

Her mind drifted back to the previous spring when she'd first become determined to make this empty, lonely church into a home . . . and she'd dubbed it the "underground."

Nothing since then had worked out the way she'd imagined, but in just a year, the church had gone from being empty to being filled with five vampires, one mortal, two ghosts, a small cat, and an old pit bull.

And there were more lost vampires out there who didn't even know they had nothing left to fear.

Julian was gone.

Eleisha walked back into the living room and went

to the couch, curling up against Philip's side. But she kept thinking on Wade's words out in the garden a few weeks before. They could look for vampires without fear now. They never had to look over their shoulders again.

"What are you thinking?" Philip asked.

"I'm thinking that . . . we're free."

ALSO AVAILABLE FROM

Barb Hendee

IN MEMORIES WE FEAR

The fourth book in the "exhilarating"*
vampire series

A series of killings in England point to a new—and
feral—vampire. Vampires Eleisha and Philip and
their human companion travel to London to make
contact with the terrified creature, to offer him sanctuary and stop the bloodshed. But the vampire they
find is not what they expected...

*SF Revu

"Gripping."
—Darque Reviews

Available wherever books are sold or at
penguin.com

facebook.com/acerocbooks

R0125

R0053

R0075

Want to connect with fellow science fiction and fantasy fans?

For news on all your favorite Ace and Roc authors, sneak peeks into the newest releases, book giveaways, and much more—

"Like" Ace and Roc Books on Facebook!

facebook.com/AceRocBooks

Penguin Group (USA) Online

What will you be reading tomorrow?

Tom Clancy, Patricia Cornwell, W.E.B. Griffin,
Nora Roberts, William Gibson, Catherine Coulter,
Stephen King, Dean Koontz, Ken Follett, Nick Hornby,
Khaled Hosseini, Kathryn Stockett, Clive Cussler,
John Sandford, Terry McMillan, Sue Monk Kidd,
Amy Tan, J. R. Ward, Laurell K. Hamilton,
Charlaine Harris, Christine Feehan...

You'll find them all at
penguin.com
facebook.com/PenguinGroupUSA
twitter.com/PenguinUSA

*Read excerpts and newsletters, find tour schedules
and reading group guides, and enter contests.*

Subscribe to Penguin Group (USA) newsletters
and get an exclusive inside look
at exciting new titles and the authors you love
long before everyone else does.

PENGUIN GROUP (USA)
us.penguingroup.com

S0151